W9-CUS-986

DISCARDED

FATAL TRUST

FATAL TRUST

DIANA MILLER

Montlake
Romance

The characters and events portrayed in this book are fictitious. Any similarity to real persons, living or dead, is coincidental and not intended by the author.

Text copyright © 2014 Diana Miller
All rights reserved.

No part of this book may be reproduced, or stored in a retrieval system, or transmitted in any form or by any means, electronic, mechanical, photocopying, recording, or otherwise, without express written permission of the publisher.

Published by Montlake Romance, Seattle

www.apub.com

ISBN-13: 9781477818565
ISBN-10: 1477818561

Cover design by Inkd Inc

Library of Congress Control Number: 2013919812

Printed in the United States of America

MAX WINDSOR'S FAMILY

MURIEL JOHNSON—Max's widowed (and childless) only sibling, she's lived her entire life in Lakeview, Minnesota.

JEREMY WINDSOR—the oldest son of Max's late son Edgar. He works in finance in New York City.

SETH WINDSOR—the youngest son of Max's late son Edgar. He lives in California, where he videotapes weddings and other celebrations to support wife Joanna and two small children. He aspires to be a director.

CECILIA WINDSOR—the daughter of Max's late son Allen, she's just finalized her third divorce.

DYLAN WINDSOR—the son of Max's late son Allen, he's a computer genius with addiction issues.

BEN GALLAGHER—the only child of Max's late daughter, Rebecca. He's an auto mechanic and the owner of Ben's Auto Repair in Lakeview, Minnesota.

CHAPTER 1

Rule Number 147: Never open a letter from a dead man.

Catherine Barrington clutched her black leather briefcase with one hand and hugged her black Coach purse against her hip with the other as she stepped into the work area of Ben's Auto Repair. Four pickups occupied the cement-block room, one with a shotgun strapped above the seat and another with a set of antlers and a carton's worth of cigarette butts scattered around the bed. The scent of oil, as overpowering as the Chanel No. 5 at her mother's charity functions, fueled her already blazing heartburn. A radio blared some country song about a cheating man, not one of her favorite subjects.

For so many reasons, this was the absolute last place she wanted to be.

Catherine's hand tightened around her briefcase handle, the hard edges biting into her palm. She should never have opened that damn letter. And once she had, she should have ignored it. Max Windsor was dead, for heaven's sake. What would he have done? Come back and haunted her?

Although if anyone could figure out a way to haunt her, it would be Max.

Sweat trickled down Catherine's neck and under the collar of her turquoise silk shirt. The sooner she got this over with, the better. She headed toward a pair of wounded Nikes and faded jeans protruding from beneath the pickup with the antlers, taking care to avoid any oil spots that might stain the soles of her turquoise-and-black Jimmy Choos. They were her favorites, and not solely because she'd bought them as an admittedly juvenile mini-rebellion against her mother.

About a foot from the Nikes, she stopped and cleared her throat.

No response.

"Mr. Gallagher?" A plump woman in a flowered polyester pantsuit had assured her that he was the only person back here.

Still no answer, although Catherine swore she'd spoken louder than the radio. Maybe too many hours listening to strident steel guitars and twangy vocals had damaged his hearing. "Mr. Gallagher?" she repeated, nearly shouting this time.

The jeans and Nikes slid from under the pickup, followed by a torso and head. "Mr. Gallagher is my father, and the world doesn't need another son of a bitch like him," the man said, shutting off a radio on the floor beside the pickup. "My name is Ben. You must be Grandfather's Philadelphia lawyer." He wiped his hands on his jeans and gave her a slow once-over.

Jerk. Catherine responded reflexively with a once-over identical to the one he'd given her. He was around her age and attractive in a NASCAR kind of way, with thick, sun-streaked brown hair, killer blue eyes in a ruggedly handsome face, a strong stubbled jaw softened by oil splotches, and jeans and a black T-shirt tight enough to showcase a tall, nicely muscled body. A lot of women would consider him hot, but then she'd never been a NASCAR fan.

He flashed her a toothpaste-commercial grin. "Sorry if I seemed rude, but feel free to look at me all you want."

"I was searching for some resemblance to Max," Catherine lied. Her already warm face heated a few more degrees at the realization she'd acted so unprofessionally. Her only excuse was she'd already had a hell of a day, and it was just getting started.

"There isn't any. I take after the son of a bitch."

"You must have gotten my message."

He nodded. "I didn't read the letter Grandfather made me promise to FedEx to you if he died of something other than old age, but I assume it said what mine did. That someone killed him for his money, and he wants the two of us to figure out who." He leaned against the hood of the pickup, crossing his arms. "Mine also said he knew you'd come because as a responsible attorney, you'd want to make sure his murderer didn't get a cent of his money."

Catherine's lips twitched. "Knowing Max, I assume his actual description of me was more like 'my anal-retentive attorney who's got a stick up her ass.'"

"I was rephrasing for politeness," Ben said, displaying that ad-worthy grin again.

"Don't bother. Max never did." Especially about her need to loosen up.

Memory tightened Catherine's chest, and she blinked suddenly moist eyes. "I'm very sorry about your grandfather's death."

Ben's grin faded. "So am I. Although he had eighty-seven mostly good years. And he's probably smiling from the hereafter that he died in his Ferrari. He loved that car."

"I'm sure he'd have preferred to have died from natural causes," Catherine said. "Max was right that his murderer isn't entitled to a share of his trust. What do the police think about his death?"

Ben snorted. "Our police actually *thinking*? Not happening. The sheriff's even worse. If something could be an accident, it was an accident. End of story. Why waste time investigating when you could be out fishing?"

"How do you know it wasn't an accident?" Catherine extracted a crumpled Kleenex from the front pocket of her purse and dabbed at her forehead, soaking up several drops of sweat before they could drip into her eyes.

"I don't," Ben said. "I feel obligated to check it out, though, considering Grandfather's letter. And that he changed his trust."

Catherine raised her hand, the damp Kleenex under her thumb. "I swear that new provision wasn't my fault. I tried to talk him out of it." A couple of months ago, Max had called to request a trust amendment stating that instead of a funeral, he wanted his entire family to spend two weeks together at his estate, Nevermore, after his death. As an added incentive, anyone who didn't sleep at the estate every single night—or who challenged the amendment in court—forfeited his or her share of the trust.

"I don't blame you," Ben said. "I learned long ago that no one could ever talk Grandfather out of anything."

"I know," Catherine said. "He said he hoped being forced to stay together would make his family members learn to appreciate each other and get along, although I had trouble believing that was his true motivation." From what she'd heard of his family dynamics, Catherine had actually assumed the enforced togetherness was Max's way of making them earn their inheritance.

"Since he made the change after the attempts on his life, I figure he did it to give us time to find his murderer, if necessary."

"Max's letter mentioned a poisoning and a shooting, but didn't give specifics," Catherine said. "Do you know about them?"

"Yeah." Ben waved at a younger man, also wearing jeans, T-shirt, and oil splotches, who'd walked into the repair area. "Shawn's back from break. Let's go to my office so we can discuss this in private."

Catherine followed Ben across the cement, still stepping carefully. "I thought it would be cooler here." Although Lakeview, Minnesota, was located on the shore of Lake Superior and less than thirty miles south of the Canadian border, the bank thermometer put the temperature at ninety-three, and it felt humid enough to soak a sponge.

"We get an occasional heat wave, and today's a near record high," Ben said. "But don't worry. It'll probably snow in the next couple of days."

"Snow in June?"

"It usually does. That's why we enjoy the heat." He opened a door, releasing a blast of blessedly frigid air. "I turned on the AC since I figured you'd miss your climate-controlled office."

"I appreciate it." Catherine stepped into a small office, inhaling cold air that smelled of chocolate and coffee, courtesy of a scrunched-up Snickers wrapper and a partially filled NAPA Auto Parts mug on the gray metal desk. The green blotter was barely visible under an ocean of papers and a half-dozen capless Bic pens.

Ben opened a mini-fridge. "Can I get you something to drink?"

"I'd love some water," Catherine said, sitting down on the folding chair nearest the window air conditioner. Add a possible June snowstorm to the list of reasons why she did not want to be here. She had way too much work she should be doing for demanding clients who were still alive, for one thing. Small towns also made her antsy and claustrophobic, and with just over three thousand people, Lakeview was definitely small. Most important, she wasn't qualified to investigate a murder. Being an avid mystery reader didn't make her Sherlock Holmes or even Nancy Drew, for God's sake.

Not that she necessarily believed Max had been murdered. After taking a long, cooling drink from the bottled water Ben handed her, Catherine pulled a legal pad out of her briefcase. She flipped through the pages until she reached her list of questions. "Did Max ever mention that someone was trying to kill him?"

Ben sat down on the other folding chair, propped his feet on the desk, and popped open a can of Coke. "Not to me."

His words supported Catherine's best-case scenario, that Max had amended his trust to torment his beneficiaries and sent her the letter to force her into his family reunion fiasco until she figured out that the murder accusation was a hoax. "If Max had truly believed it, wouldn't he have done something?" she asked, logically she thought. "Hired a P.I., assuming he shared your opinion of local law enforcement? Or a bodyguard?"

From Ben's laugh, he didn't appreciate her logic. "Grandfather ask for help? He's only doing it now since he's dead and can't handle this himself." He shifted his Nikes from the desk to the gray linoleum. "In case you're wondering why he picked me to investigate with you, it's because I'm the only one in the family who doesn't give a damn about his money. And because he knew he could trust me."

"You lived with Max when you were a kid, right?"

"For just over five years. Moved in when I was thirteen, after my mom died. My dad and I don't get along."

"Yet despite your close relationship, Max never mentioned the attempts on his life while he was still alive," Catherine said. "Isn't it likely no one was trying to kill him? That this is one last work of fiction by the master?"

"I wondered about that myself, although Grandfather was more into horror than mystery," Ben said, tapping his Coke can against his thigh. "But the previous attempts on his life really happened, even though I didn't know that's what they were at the time. I knew Grandfather's living room window had been shot out when he was there because it was reported in a couple of tabloids, which pissed the hell out of him. He didn't tell me then, but in my letter he said he'd invented the group the articles said had threatened him, so of course they couldn't have been the ones who'd shot through the window. And the shots hadn't missed by a mile, the way the articles said, but had nearly hit him."

"What about the poisoning?" Catherine asked.

"Grandfather got so sick at Easter dinner that we had to take him to the ER," Ben said. "He told us later that it had been his gallbladder acting up, but after he died, Dr. Watson confirmed to me that he'd been poisoned. Grandfather told Dr. Watson that he'd taken the poison himself to see what it was like so he'd write about it accurately."

"And his doctor believed him?"

Ben shrugged. "Grandfather said he made sure it was a nonfatal dose and did it at Easter dinner when the whole family would be around to call 911, which we did. Dr. Watson thought taking poison to make sure he wrote about it right was a little extreme, but since Grandfather didn't seem at all senile, he dropped it." Ben rolled his eyes. "As if Grandfather would ever use anything as clichéd as arsenic poisoning in one of his books. But don't mention that's the poison he got. We might be able to use that to trip up the murderer."

Catherine nodded, then moved on to the next question. "Was it possible to tell whether the Ferrari had been tampered with?"

"No one's checked," Ben said. "Like I said, the cops are convinced it was an accident. I didn't want to inspect what's left of the car myself and be accused of faking evidence since I'm a beneficiary. We can do it together, though I doubt I'll be able to tell anything."

"Even if the car's mechanically fine, someone could have forced Max off the road," Catherine said. "We should still look at it. Do I have time to check into the Lakeview Inn first? I'd like to change."

"We can't see the car until tonight, so you've got plenty of time," Ben said. "In my letter, Grandfather suggested you stay at Nevermore. That will give you more chances to get to know the family and figure out who's guilty."

Catherine gave him a wry look. "He mentioned that in mine, too. I doubt the guilty party will let anything slip around your grandfather's lawyer."

"True. But you'll learn a lot more staying at Nevermore than at the inn, as long as no one knows who you are." He tapped his soda against his thigh again. "In my letter, Grandfather said you should pretend to be my girlfriend."

Catherine's jaw dropped. "Your girlfriend?"

He smiled faintly. "To be honest, that was my first reaction, too. No offense, but I'm not real fond of lawyers. The more I thought about it, the more I realized he's right. It gives you an excuse to stay at Nevermore and spend time with me. Considering how close I was to Grandfather, it makes sense I'd have my girlfriend come out to comfort me."

"A girlfriend no one's ever heard of?"

"I've had quite a few girlfriends, and not just from around here. We'll pretend I met you last month at a wedding in Kentucky. Lexington, specifically." He took a long drink of Coke.

"A place I've never even driven past."

"I'm pretty sure none of my relatives has either," he said. "All you need to know is it's got the University of Kentucky, a lot of bars, and even more horses."

"I don't know how to ride. Or have a hint of a Southern accent."

Ben waved his Coke. "So you grew up someplace else. You can't be a lawyer, though, or anything like that. Everyone knows I've sworn off career women. They're too damn much trouble." He grimaced. "My ex-wife's one of those smart, ambitious, successful corporate types."

Catherine hid her surprise behind her water bottle. "How did you meet her?" she asked after swallowing.

"At a wedding." He shoved some papers out of the way, then set his Coke on the blotter. "What you're really wondering is why a woman like that would marry someone like me, right?"

"Of course not."

"Of course you are." A corner of his mouth quirked, crinkling an oil splotch. "It's because I'm unbelievable in bed."

Even assuming Ben's claim wasn't macho egotism, Catherine couldn't believe any sex would be good enough to motivate a successful woman to marry an arrogant, small-town mechanic, especially one who lived where it snowed in June. Then again, it had been a while since she'd had sex. She also knew firsthand why that book about smart women and stupid choices had been a bestseller.

"Well, my ex-husband taught me men are all too damn much trouble. I've sworn off the lot of them, which is another reason your plan won't work."

"You can still *pretend* to be crazy about me. Lawyers lie for a living, after all."

That too-familiar gibe sparked Catherine's temper, and she narrowed her eyes at him. "This is from an auto mechanic?"

"An *honest* auto mechanic."

"There's an oxymoron to end all oxymorons."

Ben's lips quirked again. "Guess I deserved that. Though you've got to watch it. If you go using words like 'oxymoron,' people will think you're too intellectual to be my type."

"You expect me to limit myself to one- and two-syllable words?" Catherine had no idea why she was even discussing this since it was not happening.

"Like a lawyer could manage that." Ben studied her for a moment, rubbing his chin, then nodded. "You can be a college dropout. That's why you came to Lexington from Illinois or Indiana or some other northern place, to go to the university."

"I dropped out of college."

"After one year, because it was too much work. Now you're a cocktail waitress."

"Which everyone knows is the easiest job on the planet."

"No, it's damn hard work, too," Ben said. "But you like it more than studying, and it's got fringe benefits." He leaned sideways and wrapped an arm around her shoulders. "Like meeting me when I stopped in for a drink after the wedding."

Catherine slipped out from under his arm and turned to face him. "Even if I were willing to go along with your plan, it has a fatal flaw."

"You don't drink?"

"Your grandfather probably mentioned my name and that I'm his lawyer."

"I doubt it. He was pretty secretive about his legal and financial affairs," Ben said. "The letter about the two-week requirement that I got after Grandfather died was signed by some guy at First Trust in Minneapolis, not you."

"Trey sent me things fairly frequently." Thomas J. Donaldson III—nicknamed Trey—was Max's full-time accountant and had an office at Nevermore.

"Trey's off the suspect list since he just gets a year's severance pay," Ben said. "But he's been Grandfather's best friend for so long he's almost family and will be around Nevermore. If he knows who you are, he might slip up and give us away. You'll have to change your name." He folded his hands on what looked like six-pack abs, rocking back in his chair. "What about Cat? Or better yet, Tiger." He smirked. "Sounds like major fantasy material to me."

Catherine responded with the withering look that was one of the few useful skills she'd picked up from her mother.

His smirk morphed into a chuckle. "Spoilsport."

"I don't suppose you'd consider hiring a private investigator."

"Grandfather's letter said he didn't want anyone besides you and me looking into this and maybe uncovering family secrets not related to the murder. I wouldn't feel right disrespecting his wishes." Ben righted his chair. "If you aren't willing to help me, I'll go it alone."

Max had made the same request in her letter. She'd hoped Ben would be willing to disregard it, but no such luck.

Catherine thought for a moment, chewing her bottom lip. She had other work, but nothing that couldn't wait, and Max had insisted she be paid her regular rate so her firm wouldn't be losing billable hours. It wasn't as if Ben were proposing she do something unethical, either. If Max *had* been murdered, she needed to make sure her current client First Trust, which had taken over as trustee when Max died, didn't distribute any of the trust to his murderer. In fact, when she'd told the trust officer now handling the trust about Max's letter, he'd requested she do what Max had asked.

She also owed it to Max to make sure his murderer was punished. He'd been a good client, and getting his business had jump-started her career. And most important, her Aunt Jessica would have wanted her to do it.

She was only giving it a couple of days, though, just long enough to satisfy her conscience that she'd respected Max's wishes and her brain that this whole thing wasn't a hoax. If she hadn't identified the killer by then, the trustee was hiring a P.I.

She released her lip, along with a resigned breath. "My middle name is Alexandra, so I could be Alex. Or Aly."

"How about Lexie?" Ben asked.

"Lexie from Lexington?"

"It's easy to remember."

Did it matter? "Fine. Lexie it is."

Ben got to his feet. "Now we might as well go meet the family."

"First let me make sure I've got the names and relationships right." Catherine paged backward in her legal pad until she reached the relevant notes. "Max's sister Muriel gets five percent of the trust. Since Max's children all predeceased him, the remainder goes one-third to Edgar's sons Seth and Jeremy, one-third to Allen's children Cecilia and Dylan, and one-third to Rebecca's son. Max said your mother was named after Daphne du Maurier's masterpiece."

"Yep. She's lucky she wasn't a boy, or she'd probably have ended up named Poe." He picked a key ring off the corner of his desk. "Let's go. Unless you're scared."

"Of meeting Max's family?" Catherine smiled faintly. "He did say some members . . . have issues."

"Talk about rephrasing for politeness. I meant scared of staying at Nevermore. It's haunted, you know."

Catherine stuffed her pen and legal pad into her briefcase, and then stood. "Your grandfather made a fortune writing books that probably terrify Stephen King. Max would never own a house that wasn't supposedly haunted. Luckily I don't believe in ghosts."

"Neither do I." Ben's keys jangled against the blotter. "You need to dress more like my girlfriend would. Do you have any clothes that don't look quite so lawyer-like, or should we pick something up at The Clothes Garden?"

Catherine suppressed a sigh. Looking like the girlfriend of a man with Ben's admittedly Neanderthal taste in women was at the top of her Never to Do list, but she'd signed on to this. "Give me a couple of minutes," she said. "Where's the restroom?"

Ben pointed her to it, and she was glad to find that the restroom was warm but clean and had decent lighting and a large mirror. Catherine set her jacket on the toilet lid and pulled her turquoise silk shirt out of her black skirt. A few rolls of the waistband and the skirt was four inches above her knees, not exactly a mini, but she was closing in on thirty-five, after all. She tied the hem of the shirt so it covered the rolled waistband, then checked the mirror. The shirt had a few wrinkles, but the sauna outside should steam those out before she reached her car. Then she undid enough buttons to expose the top of the black cotton-and-lace camisole she'd worn underneath. The cotton hadn't prevented her shirt from resembling a saturated silk towel, but at least it was proving good for something.

Finally, she took out the pins securing her French twist, releasing hair she paid a fortune to keep what used to be its natural golden hue. She finger-combed it, reapplied her lipstick, and then studied herself. She probably still didn't look the part, but she was not buying anything at The Clothes Garden. With a name like that, she'd bet every item sold there featured flowers or ruffles, and she detested flowers and ruffles. She'd been raised in a world of solid colors and clean, elegant lines, and old habits were hard to break. Besides, her ex-husband Neil's new wife Deidre was a ruffly, flowery person.

Catherine opened the restroom door just as a redhead in cutoffs so short they were likely illegal in several states flip-flopped up to Ben, stopping right where he had a prime view of her cleavage above her gold halter top. "Hey, Ben. I heard my car's ready."

"It's parked outside. Trudy's got the key."

"I know, but I wanted to thank you personally for fixing it. You're so talented." The woman rested her hand on Ben's arm. Her glittering gold nails had to be more than an inch long.

"It just needed a new muffler."

The woman moved closer to Ben. "If you hadn't figured it out, the muffler might have gone out totally while I was driving and made my car crash. I could have been killed." She stroked his arm. "Let me know how I can repay you for saving my life."

"Trudy has the bill."

She touched a nail to his lips. "I wasn't only talking about cash."

"I'll remember that, babe. Call if you've got any problems with the car."

"I'll do that. Keep in touch." She turned and wiggled her way out of the garage.

Rule Number 148: Never get involved with a man who calls any woman "babe." Catherine pressed her lips together. Two new rules in one day. Definitely a bad sign.

At least her involvement with Ben was as fictitious as one of Max's bestsellers. She stepped out of the restroom. "I assume she's just your type."

Ben tore his gaze from the door the woman had exited through and looked at Catherine. "Absolutely. Although I'll have to wait to take her up on her offer until my girlfriend from Lexington's gone."

"I've changed my mind about that plan. I'm not up to acting like a Playmate of the Month wannabe."

Ben raised his eyebrows. "You've got a problem with puppies, bubble baths, and world peace? Those are Miss June's favorite things."

Naturally he'd know. "I've got a problem pretending to be dumb enough to think a broken muffler could make a car crash. The apparent double-D requirement is also way beyond me."

"I didn't say you had to be dumb, just not intellectual." He winked. "As to the other, I'm willing to make allowances for blondes. Follow my truck."

– – –

Ben drove his pickup down Main Street, Catherine's rented Taurus trailing behind him, resisting the urge to floor it and try to lose her. Jesus, what had Grandfather gotten him into? From what little he'd said about his lawyer—and all he'd left unsaid—Ben had always pegged her as a clone of his ex-wife, Olivia. But now that he was expected to work with her, he'd hoped he'd read between the wrong lines.

No such luck. Catherine's entrance into the garage had confirmed that, the way she'd tiptoed as if stepping on a year-old spot of oil would ruin her expensive shoes. And when it came to shooting condescending looks, Catherine had Olivia beat.

He hadn't realized he'd given her a once-over when he'd been trying to figure out whether she could carry off the girlfriend role, but at least he'd apologized. Not that she'd believed he'd meant it. She probably assumed a small-town mechanic like him spent his free time parked in his La-Z-Boy recliner in a room with deer and moose heads covering nearly every inch of wall space, chugging beer and watching reruns of the Miss Hooters pageant—at least when he wasn't out killing yet another defenseless animal to add to his décor. Okay, so maybe he'd encouraged that impression, but her attitude had pissed him off.

On the other hand, he could use her help. Ben's gut twisted, and he gritted his teeth. This thing with Grandfather really sucked. Knowing his great-aunt or one of his cousins was responsible made it even harder to take.

He owed Grandfather more than he could ever repay. He could put up with Catherine Barrington and this charade for a little while.

CHAPTER 2

Photographs of Nevermore didn't do it justice. After driving eight hilly miles northwest from Lake Superior—the last two on a road cut through a thick forest of pines and birch trees—the massive house appeared, set on an island of grass in an ocean of trees. Built of rose-colored stone with enough gray overtones to eliminate any hint of warmth, it featured a black roof and trim, three circular towers, dozens of wrought-iron stakes, and several gargoyles.

Although it looked as if it had housed Nathaniel Hawthorne's contemporaries, Max had built Nevermore himself more than forty years ago. He'd claimed the place had cost him a fortune—especially the ghosts he swore he'd bought to haunt it.

After parking in the circular drive and popping the trunk, Catherine stepped out of her car. The relative silence, broken only by trees rustling and creaking in the slight breeze, provided an ominous sound track. She hugged herself against a chill that had little to do with a temperature at least ten degrees cooler than in Lakeview.

"It looks like something out of a gothic novel," she said. "It's spooky even during the day."

"You should see it at night when the spotlights are on," Ben said, referring to a half-dozen lights scattered around the front lawn. "Grandfather claimed he had them installed to illuminate the driveway for late arrivals, but the way the light's filtered, I guarantee his real motive was to make the place even eerier." He walked over to the open trunk of Catherine's car.

"What are you doing?" she asked.

"Getting your bags." He grabbed the handle of her suitcase.

"I can certainly carry my own bags."

"My girlfriend wouldn't."

Catherine stepped away from the trunk. If he wanted to play Mr. Macho, fine. Her suitcase was so heavy she'd paid a surcharge at the airport.

Ben pulled the bag out of the trunk without grunting, but immediately dropped it onto the ground and flexed and unflexed his fingers a couple of times. Then he reached back in for a stuffed garment bag. "How long are you planning on staying? Six months?"

"Don't tell me that's all you need for two weeks," Catherine said, her gaze on the navy gym bag slung over his shoulder.

"I left some things here earlier," he said. "If I need anything else, I can stop by my house, since I'll be going into Lakeview every day to work. But everyone else will mostly stick around Nevermore, so you don't have to worry about getting lonely."

"Whoopee."

Ben slipped the garment bag strap over his shoulder. "Your sarcasm is definitely warranted."

"What's sarcasm?"

He looked at her blankly. "What?"

"I asked what sarcasm is," Catherine said. "Don't bother answering, because I'm just practicing. I assumed it was like 'oxymoron,' something one of your girlfriends wouldn't understand."

"Actually, even though you don't understand it, you shouldn't care enough to ask the definition."

She almost smiled until his serious expression made her realize he wasn't kidding.

Ben closed the trunk, picked up her suitcase, and headed up the stone steps to the massive front door. Before he could lift the gargoyle door knocker, the door opened.

A nun in a black-and-white habit stepped out. She had Max's brown eyes and wore bright red lipstick.

Ben dropped the suitcase and hugged her around the gym and garment bags. "How are you holding up, Aunt Muriel?"

"With God's help, I'm coping."

Max's sister was a nun. Catherine hadn't known that. Given his lifestyle, it must have been a difficult relationship for both of them.

"This is Lexie," Ben said, wrapping an arm around Catherine's shoulders. "When she heard about Grandfather's death, she insisted on coming all the way from Kentucky to comfort me. My Aunt Muriel, *Lexie*." He squeezed her shoulder.

Catherine started. That's right, her name was supposed to be Lexie. She'd better begin thinking of herself that way or she was going to screw this up. "Please accept my sympathy on the loss of your brother," she told Muriel.

"My brother's in a far better place," Muriel said, fingering the cross she wore around her neck. "At least I'm praying he is."

"Let's go inside." Ben picked up the suitcase again and carried it into a foyer decorated with a Persian carpet, dark wood paneling, and a stuffed grizzly bear.

"The bear starred in *See All Evil*," Ben said, referring to one of Max's books that had been made into a Hollywood blockbuster featuring a grizzly on a rampage in Vail. "Although Grandfather waited until the bear died of old age to have him stuffed."

"That movie terrified me." Lexie stepped up to the bear and forced herself to touch the fur. The hairs on the back of her neck rose.

"Igor, take our things to my room," Ben said.

At Ben's words, Lexie turned her attention from the menacing-even-when-stuffed bear to a thirty-something man in full butler garb who was approaching them. Ben apparently assumed they'd be sharing a room.

"You and your friend are not sharing a room," Muriel said before Lexie could figure out a logical reason to object. "Think of your grandfather." She twisted her cross.

"Grandfather wouldn't give a damn."

"Ben, it's okay," Lexie said, resting her hand on his bare forearm. "I wouldn't feel comfortable sharing a room with you under these circumstances." She curled her hand slightly, fingernails poised to press her point if he disagreed.

Ben was silent for a moment, and then shrugged. "Having two rooms will give us more space. Put her next door to me, Igor."

The man strapped Ben's gym bag and Lexie's garment bag over the same shoulder, then picked up Lexie's suitcase as easily as if she'd filled it with a single down jacket, instead of jamming it with clothing, hair products, makeup, and four pairs of shoes.

"His name is Igor?" Lexie asked when he'd headed up the spiral staircase at the end of the foyer.

"I doubt it," Ben said. "Grandfather's butlers are always called Igor. This one's the seventh."

"Actually he's the eighth," Muriel corrected. "The seventh was the one who left for Disneyland."

"He got a job playing Goofy," Ben told Lexie. "I forgot him since he was only here a few weeks. Grandfather thought the name was appropriate for a butler at Nevermore, and with what he paid, he could probably have called them all Tinker Bell if he wanted." He shifted his gaze to Muriel. "We could let number eight use his real name now."

"Why bother? He seems perfectly happy being Igor." Muriel lifted the skirt of her habit. "Please excuse me while I retire to say some rosaries for my dear brother. Although the way he lived, I'm afraid he may not have made it to purgatory."

"Sharing a room is not part of our deal," Lexie murmured when Muriel was out of earshot.

"It would have looked suspicious if I hadn't tried," Ben said. "I knew Aunt Muriel would object."

"Max never mentioned that his sister's a nun."

"That's because she isn't one," Ben said. "She was married for more than fifty years, but when her husband died, she decided to join a convent. Unfortunately she couldn't find one willing to accept her."

"Because she'd been married?"

"That she's Lutheran and didn't think she should have to convert was a bigger impediment," he said dryly. "She also discovered she'd have to give up her little cigars, Jack Daniel's on the rocks, and satellite TV, and reconsidered. So she bought a habit and wears it when she's in the mood to be Catholic. She's got a house in Lakeview."

Ben put his hand on the small of Lexie's back. "Let's check out the living room."

"Am I going to encounter a couple of Munchkins in there?" Lexie asked. "Or maybe the White Rabbit?" Between Nevermore, a fake nun in devil-red lipstick, and a butler called Igor, she was starting to feel a little like Alice wandering around Wonderland.

"The next best thing." Ben directed her into an enormous living room with the same dark paneling as the foyer, an ornately carved wood fireplace, and a sleek black leather couch and matching chairs.

"As you'll notice, Grandfather liked nineteenth-century architecture and mahogany, but he wasn't a big fan of the furnishings," he said. "The parlor and dining room are the only rooms that look like they belong in this place."

Lexie wandered over to the fireplace. Each end of the mahogany mantel held a statue of a black bird. "I assume that's in honor of the raven from Poe's poem," she said, pointing.

Ben nodded. "Grandfather thought it appropriate since the bird inspired the name of this place," he said. "And the other one's the Maltese falcon. One of several used in the movie and touched by Humphrey Bogart himself."

"You're kidding." She moved closer to examine it, resisting the urge to pick it up. After all these years she doubted she'd smudge any historic fingerprints, but some things were too sacred to disturb. "That's one of my favorite movies."

"You like old movies? Even when they haven't been colorized?"

Speaking of things that were sacred . . . "Colorization should be illegal."

"One of the first things we agree on," Ben said. "Except just so you know, none of my girlfriends would ever like black-and-white movies."

She gave him an over-the-shoulder glance, but his half smile and love of old movies torpedoed her planned derogatory retort. "That's what a year of college does for you," she said instead.

"Other items in this room are also movie memorabilia, although nothing's from Oz or Wonderland." Ben walked over to a high table. "This brandy snifter and martini shaker are from a Thin Man movie. That ashtray is from *The Big Sleep*, and the candelabrum was in *Dracula*. And several pieces are from movies made from Grandfather's books."

DIANA MILLER

Lexie crossed the room to a low curved chest that looked Italian or Spanish, displaying a pair of silver candlesticks and a bloodred bowl she remembered had played a prominent role in *Deadly Light*. Just looking at this stuff was giving her goose bumps. "This is amazing."

"Ben. Aunt Muriel said you were here." An attractive brunette wearing a deep tan and a white sundress strode into the room. She gave Ben a hug. "I've missed you."

"Speaking of amazing, this is my cousin Cecilia from Phoenix," Ben said, his smile now full and holding genuine affection. "Cecilia, meet Lexie. I met her at a wedding last month. She heard about Grandfather's death and came all the way from Kentucky to comfort me."

Cecilia turned her smile on Lexie, extending a manicured hand. "I'm happy to meet you. Great shoes, by the way. Jimmy Choos?"

"I live near a fabulous consignment shop," Lexie said, since new Jimmy Choos probably weren't in most cocktail waitresses' budgets.

"I'm sorry about your divorce," Ben said.

"So am I." Cecilia waved her hand. "I thought the third one would be the charm, but obviously that doesn't work for marriages. Or maybe it's just me and marriages."

"There's nothing wrong with you," Ben said firmly. "You've chosen the wrong men for the wrong reasons."

"Well, at the rate I'm going, I'll pass Mother before I'm forty." Cecilia's expression held a combination of regret and resignation. "My mother's on husband number six," she told Lexie.

"She's the major reason you keep choosing the wrong men," Ben said. "Is anyone else here yet?"

Cecilia's expression became even more resigned and regretful. "Just Dylan. He's in his room sleeping off a hangover. As usual."

"Is he still gambling?" Ben asked.

"He lives to gamble." The classic features Cecilia had inherited from Max tightened. "Although he had to stop once he'd borrowed the maximum a Las Vegas loan shark would lend him. I'm hoping he was smart enough to find one without Mafia connections, since his lender could very well track him down here."

The grandfather clock in the corner sounded. Instead of the usual tune, Lexie recognized the desolate first measures of the *Carmina Burana*.

"It's already five," Ben said when the clock began chiming the hour. "Lexie and I'd better head upstairs. See you at sherry hour.

"Sherry hour is from six to seven every night, followed by dinner," he explained as he and Lexie walked toward the polished mahogany spiral staircase. Two devils brandishing pitchforks guarded the steps, one carved into each of the bottom newel posts. "We dress up, but if you didn't bring anything—"

"Max mentioned that in my letter, so I'm good," Lexie said. "He said sherry hour would provide an opportunity to check people out."

"He's right. Thank God no one sticks to sherry, since those gatherings call for something stronger."

They ascended the stairs, and then started down a long hallway. Ben stopped at the second door and flung it open. "You're staying here."

Lexie walked into a large room with an attached bath. The sapphire silk comforter and drapes and the black lacquer furniture coordinated with a sapphire, black, and white Oriental carpet. "This is beautiful. How many bedrooms are there?"

"Thirteen, of course," Ben said. "Ten on this floor. Grandfather's bedroom is on the third floor, along with two tower bedrooms."

"I assume the tower rooms are supposedly haunted."

"According to Grandfather, all the bedrooms are." Ben turned and headed to the door. "I'll stop by at six."

– – –

"You know, you'd be a lot happier if you loosened up," Max said. He was sitting in one of the leather chairs that faced Catherine's desk.

His comment had come out of the blue—they'd been discussing a proposed revision to his trust. But Max frequently switched topics without warning. He claimed it was because he liked to catch her off guard. Catherine suspected it was really because when it came to estate planning issues, he was easily bored.

She rested her palms on her mahogany desk. "I thought we'd agreed that you pay me to be anal retentive," she said levelly.

"When you're my attorney," Max said, waving his hand. "But that doesn't mean you should act like you've got a stick up your ass the rest of the time."

His words made Catherine smile. "Aunt Jessica always used to describe my mother that way."

Max's smile was tinged with sadness. "I know. I owe it to Jessica to make sure you don't turn into another uptight Elizabeth."

"As Aunt Jessica also used to say, one Elizabeth Barrington is more than enough for the world."

"I'm sure your mother would say the same thing about me," Max said.

"No, she wouldn't."

"Don't bother lying to be polite," Max said, his smile now genuine. "Your mother's opinion really doesn't bother me."

"I'm not lying," Catherine said. "She'd never say it because that wouldn't be polite. Of course, that doesn't mean she wouldn't think it."

"Actually, I owe your mother," Max said. "She's inspired my next book."

"Do you kill her off in some particularly gruesome way?"

"Of course not," Max said, looking offended. "I could never kill off Jessica's only sister, no matter how much she disapproves of me and I disapprove of her. I'm planning to write about a town where someone puts a drug in the water supply that turns everyone into stiff, uptight, unerringly proper people who never smile or have any fun but are always courteous. I'd call them something like Bluenose Zombies." His forehead creased. "Not that, of course. It doesn't have the right ring. But you get the idea. A whole town full of pompous, polite paragons. Can you imagine a more horrifying place to live? Or even visit?"

"The drug wouldn't affect everyone in town," Catherine pointed out. "Not everyone drinks tap water anymore." Experience had taught her that Max not only wouldn't get back on topic until he was ready but he expected her to join in the conversation. To be honest, it was more fun than discussing trust distribution issues anyway.

"Good point," Max said, stroking his white beard. "I'll have to come up with another distribution system."

"What do these people do once they're affected?" Catherine asked. "Storm Las Vegas and try to convert everyone there?"

"That could be interesting," Max said. "I haven't figured that out yet. Although I do know I'll need a hero. A guy who burps and scratches in public and eats with his fingers. He ends up saving the town. What do you think?"

"I think it sounds ridiculous," Catherine said. "And I think that if you write it, it will still end up being a bestseller."

"Which is another reason for you to loosen up," Max said. "Otherwise I could very well put you in the book. Actually, maybe I'll *make you the heroine, the woman the hero teaches to loosen up. Once she does, she ends up helping him save the town."*

Catherine rolled her eyes. "Too bad for you that you can't manipulate real life like you do the characters in your books."

Max grinned. "So you think."

Lexie ran a brush through her loose hair, frowning at her reflection in the bathroom mirror. That conversation had occurred years ago, but she could still remember it perfectly. And Max had been right about his ability to manipulate real life. Thanks to his manipulation from the grave, she was now pretending to be Ben's girlfriend while spying on his relatives, something she was not looking forward to. She'd even called First Trust, hoping that after hearing the plan's specifics, the trustee would find some reason to object to it. No such luck.

She surveyed herself in the bathroom mirror. She'd selected tonight's dress because although it was navy silk, the V-neckline in both front and back made it the least conservative of the three dresses she'd brought along. For her investigation to succeed, she had to convince Ben's family members she was his cocktail waitress girlfriend, and you only got one chance to make a first impression. Rule Number 9.

She was applying her lipstick when Ben knocked on her door. She checked her watch. Seven minutes after six.

She replaced the silver cover and set the lipstick tube on the bathroom vanity, then went to open her bedroom door.

Her breath caught in her throat. Talk about cleaning up well. The man standing outside was Ben, but not the auto mechanic/NASCAR driver Ben she'd been with less than an hour ago. She'd never expected he'd own a suit, let alone a perfectly tailored charcoal one, which he wore with a white shirt and a silk tie that matched his eyes. With his hair damp and every trace of stubble and oil gone, this Ben had her stomach fluttering.

Which annoyed her. "You're late," she said, even though she hadn't been ready on time either.

"Sorry." He offered her his arm. "Let's go, babe."

The fluttering stopped. She *really* wasn't looking forward to tonight.

– – –

Sherry hour was held in the parlor, a room furnished with the kind of elegantly uncomfortable Victorian-era furniture Lexie's mother favored. Aunt Muriel was already there, still wearing her habit and bright lipstick as she drank what appeared to be whiskey on the rocks.

"I'll introduce you to Trey," Ben said, leading Lexie to the stately silver-haired man standing next to the fireplace.

"Trey, I'd like you to meet my girlfriend, Lexie. Lexie, this is Grandfather's best friend, Trey."

Lexie held her breath, ready for Trey to recognize her and tell everyone her true identity. But he simply extended his hand, not exhibiting a hint of suspicion. "Delighted to meet you, Lexie," he said. "Where are you from?"

"Lexington, Kentucky, believe it or not," she said, relaxing. "Although I wasn't born there, so I can't blame my parents for the 'Lexie from Lexington' idiocy."

Trey smiled. "I can blame my parents for my nickname Trey. My name is actually Thomas J. Donaldson III. My grandfather was Tom and my father was Tommie, so my parents decided I needed something completely different. They came up with Trey, which is based on the Italian word for 'three.' They claimed it was because I was conceived in Rome, although I have no idea if that was true."

"It makes a good story," Lexie said.

Trey nodded. "And after spending so many years with Max, I know the story is the most important thing."

"Let's go get something to drink, Lexie," Ben said.

"It's been very nice meeting you, Trey," Lexie said.

"I told you he wouldn't suspect," Ben murmured as they walked over to the drink table.

A few minutes later Cecilia came in, wearing an elegant black sheath and accompanied by a man who resembled her so closely he had to be Dylan. With his dark hair in a ponytail and striking features, Dylan was movie star handsome, although his red-rimmed brown eyes somewhat ruined the effect. He headed directly to the drink cart.

"I'll have to keep an eye on Dylan," Cecilia said as she walked up to them. "He could very well get drunk enough to head to the nearest casino for a couple of days and lose his share of the trust."

"I thought he was out of money," Ben said.

"I'm sure he can borrow more now that he's in line to inherit a fortune."

Ben draped an arm around Lexie's shoulders, pulling her against his side. He smelled like pine soap, which surprised her. She'd expected some men's cologne with a virile name and an overdose of spice and musk. "Why don't you get me another drink, Lexie? She's a cocktail waitress," he told Cecilia.

Lexie gave him a tight smile. "I'm off duty."

"I promise I'll make it worth your while," Ben said, his voice lowered suggestively.

She was supposed to be crazy about him, so instead of telling him where to stick it, she raised her chin. "I came out here to give you emotional support. Not to wait on you."

"Good for you, Lexie," Cecilia said. "Ben always dates twits who do whatever he wants. He needs someone who'll stand up to him."

Ben sighed as if he'd been ordered to haul stones across the Sahara for a new pyramid rather than his own glass across the room for a refill. "With the two of you ganging up on me, I guess I'll get my own drink."

"Bring me a glass of cabernet while you're at it," Cecilia called after him.

"They got me."

The words came from the man who'd just stumbled into the parlor. His light brown hair was all wild wisps and spikes, one sleeve of his suit coat was torn, and his shirt had been pulled from his trousers.

And he was covered with blood.

"They came out of the trees," he wheezed out. "I couldn't stop them. I tried, but I couldn't."

"Help me." His voice was just above a whisper. "Please."

Then he collapsed in a bloody mess on the parlor floor.

CHAPTER 3

Lexie froze, her body tensing and her blood chilling. "Oh my God," she said. "We need to call 911."

"Don't bother," Ben said. He hadn't moved.

Actually, no one else in the room had moved either. Meanwhile the man lay motionless on the floor, dripping blood onto the carpet.

"Someone's out there, someone who attacked him," Lexie said, her voice edged with hysteria. "Probably more than one person. And without medical attention, he's going to bleed to death. You can't just let him die." What was wrong with these people?

"He's not going to die," Ben said. "*Death Dreams*, right?"

Lexie's body unclenched as the bloody man got to his feet, grinning. "I should have known you'd figure it out, Ben," he said. "I thought it was a fitting tribute to Grandfather. Let me clean up, and I'll be right back."

"The housekeeper won't be happy about the blood on the carpet," Cecilia said as Seth left the room.

"It's water soluble," he yelled over his shoulder.

"That was my cousin Seth making an entrance," Ben said. "He was playing a scene from one of Grandfather's books."

Lexie nodded. "*Death Dreams*. I read it."

"You're a fan of Grandfather's, Lexie?" Cecilia asked.

"Who isn't? Which Max Windsor book is your favorite?" Lexie asked, seizing on a topic that would hopefully distract everyone from the embarrassing fact that she alone hadn't realized Seth's arrival had been an act. Although to be fair, she also was the only one who didn't know Seth.

A few minutes later Seth returned, minus the fake blood and torn suit coat, although his hair was still wild. "That was the most fun I've had since I played Dracula at the Fresno playhouse. Which was actually the last role of my career."

"Do you miss acting?" Cecilia asked.

"Not much," Seth said. "I was never big-screen or even cable TV material. Not like my wife, who just needs the right vehicle. And I prefer directing." He frowned. "Although I haven't had a directing job since that kids' show tanked nearly a year ago."

"Why was it canceled?" Cecilia asked. "I never heard, and I thought it was doing well."

Seth's frown shifted into a grimace. "It was, until the asshole who played the giant rabbit solicited a prostitute who happened to be an undercover policewoman. And then Mr. Sombrero the Mexican mouse turned out to be an illegal alien from Guatemala. We could have replaced them, but the sponsors decided that wasn't the type of show they wanted their supposedly wholesome but overly sweetened, artificial-ingredient-filled breakfast cereal associated with, and pulled the plug."

"Lexie, this is my cousin Seth Windsor," Ben said. "Seth, my friend Lexie. She's from Kentucky."

"It's great to meet you, Lexie," Seth said, shaking her hand. "Sorry if I scared you."

"No problem," Lexie said. "Maybe you shouldn't have quit acting. You were very convincing."

"Thanks, but I think it was the blood," Seth said. "Use enough fake blood and even the worst actor becomes convincing. When did you meet Ben?"

"Six weeks ago," Ben said, answering for Lexie. "I was in Lexington for Bill Hansen's second wedding. Afterward I stopped at a bar for a drink, and Lexie waited on me."

"Did you know Ben was Max Windsor's grandson, Lexie?" Seth asked.

"Actually, I didn't realize it until he called upset because Max had died," Lexie said.

"Ben really didn't mention it before then?"

"You think I need Grandfather's fame to get women?" Ben asked. "You sound like Jeremy. Or maybe I should say you're confusing me with Jeremy."

"That's not what I'm implying at all," Seth said. "I'm surprised because I use my connection to Grandfather whenever I can. I can tell you're not originally from Kentucky, Lexie. How did you end up in Lexington, of all places?"

"I don't appreciate you giving my girlfriend the third degree," Ben said sharply.

"What third degree?" Seth asked. "I'm interested in people, and I know everyone else here."

At that moment a crash sounded in the parlor. Igor was standing at the doorway, holding a small gong and mallet. "Dinner is served," he said.

"And that ends another cheery sherry hour," Ben said, and then he murmured in Lexie's ear, "I think you'd better read up on Lexington."

– – –

Everyone had just finished the delicious first course of figs and mozzarella in a balsamic vinegar reduction when Seth pulled out a camera.

"Smile, everyone." He got to his feet and circled the mahogany table, snapping pictures.

"What are you doing, Seth?" Ben asked.

"Taking family photos."

"When did you turn into such a photographer?" Cecilia asked. "I didn't notice you taking any pictures at Easter."

"I started taking more photos when we had the boys," Seth said. "And Grandfather's death made me realize how important the rest of my family is. This could be the last time the entire family is in one place, since the only thing that's ever brought all of us together is Grandfather."

"You have a point," Ben said. "But could you wait until we're done eating? I'd like my soup."

Seth sat down at the table as Igor served the soup. Everyone ate the spicy gazpacho in silence for a couple of minutes before Seth spoke again. "Ben, I heard you're taking parts from Grandfather's Ferrari."

"I'm planning to use whatever I can salvage," Ben said.

"How much of the car is left?"

"Not a whole lot. Why?"

"I want to take some pictures of the car before you tear it apart," Seth said.

"For God's sake, why?"

"As a remembrance."

"A remembrance that Grandfather burned up in his car? That's morbid as hell," Ben said.

"Perhaps Seth wants to remind himself to drive carefully," Muriel said, twisting the enormous cross she wore on a long chain around her neck. "Or to show it to those boys of his when they're of driving age to remind them to drive carefully."

"Or perhaps he wants to sell it to a tabloid," Ben said, glaring at Seth. "Like he's done a couple of times in the past year."

Seth responded with a glare of his own. "I have not sold anything to a tabloid."

"Well, someone did, and you're the most likely suspect," Ben said. His voice hummed with anger. "Who else has your Hollywood gossip rag connections? And the first article was all about how Grandfather wouldn't help out his grandson, the poor struggling director, by requiring or even requesting that he be hired as an assistant on the movie version of his latest bestseller."

"That was common knowledge."

"If it was, it was because you leaked it," Ben said. "Grandfather sure as hell didn't. He was furious when it came out. And a couple of months ago you sold the story about the group who'd shot out Grandfather's living room window. The ones who'd been sending him threatening letters because they were upset about the bleeding Virgin Mary statue in his last book."

"I didn't know there'd been a shooting until I read an article about it," Seth said. "I wasn't here when it happened."

"But you've got friends still in Lakeview who were. Including Eddie Maxwell, who was your best friend in high school and just happened to have fixed the window for Grandfather."

"I haven't talked to Eddie in years," Seth said. "You not only have contacts here, you live here, Ben. How do we know that you didn't leak it?"

"Because I don't care about money and fame," Ben said. "You can't deny that you do. I've made sure that no one has photographed Grandfather's car, and you're not going to change that. Grandfather deserves his privacy even more now that he's dead."

"You don't own the car, Ben," Seth said. "I assume it's part of the trust, which means it belongs to all of us. So tell me where it is. You have no right to object if I take a few pictures of it."

Ben dropped his spoon into his bowl, splattering tomatoey

gazpacho onto the white damask tablecloth. "I can object to any damn thing I want to," he said, jumping to his feet. "Lexie, we're out of here." He grabbed her arm and pulled her out of her chair.

"Thanks for dinner. It was delicious," Lexie got out before Ben dragged her from the dining room, although she wasn't sure who she was thanking. The cook was in the kitchen, and the host of this two-week house party was dead.

"What was that about?" Lexie asked. "Is it such a big deal if Seth takes a photo of Max's car?"

"It is if he sells it to a tabloid," Ben said. "You must know how much Grandfather hated publicity. He was furious about both those earlier stories and was sure Seth was behind them."

"Furious enough to threaten to disinherit him?" Lexie asked, spotting a possible motive.

"No, but furious enough that I don't want Seth to disrespect Grandfather's memory by publicizing a photo of that car. Change into jeans and meet me in the hallway outside our rooms." He started up the stairs.

"Why?"

"I'll explain later. Meet me in five minutes."

Refusing would result in an argument, and Barringtons didn't argue—except in a courtroom, of course. Rule Number 17. More important, her law firm dictated that the client was always right. Ben wasn't her client, but the trustee would want her to keep the trust beneficiaries happy. Lexie went to dig out her jeans.

"It's hard for me to believe pants that cost nearly three hundred dollars can be considered jeans," Ben said when she returned to the hallway.

"How do you know how much these cost?" Lexie had been appalled by the price, but the jeans had been so flattering she couldn't resist. Besides, this wasn't like college when she'd owned a dozen pairs in assorted sizes, styles, and shades of denim. She actually owned only this one pair—if PMS had her too bloated to zip them, she didn't wear jeans.

"I read an article about outrageously expensive jeans that mentioned that brand. In *Playboy*."

"Which you only buy for the articles, of course."

He snorted. "You gotta be kidding. Let's go."

"Go where?"

"Trust me."

"Now you've got to be kidding," Lexie said as she followed him down the stairs. "Where?"

"We're checking out Grandfather's Ferrari."

The outside air had cooled enough that Lexie was glad she'd put on a long-sleeved shirt. The sky glowed dull orange, the sun already setting behind the pine- and birch-forested hills to the west.

She stopped beside Ben's pickup, but he continued walking until he reached a motorcycle. "We'll take this."

Lexie's stomach backflipped. "I am not riding on a motorcycle."

"Why not?" Ben asked, picking a helmet off the grass. "Lexie would love it."

"Only if Lexie has a death wish. A motorcycle is a hopeful organ transplant recipient's best friend."

"I'm not some wild teenage kid. I'm an excellent driver, and I only had one drink." Ben walked toward her, holding out the helmet. "It's perfectly safe."

"Don't you have to worry about deer and moose crossing the road around here?" Lexie asked, grasping the back of the pickup with both hands. "It's dangerous enough when a car hits those things."

"On a bike they're easier to dodge."

"I'll follow you in my car." She was gripping the pickup so tightly she could feel her racing heartbeat in her palms.

"I think you should ride with me, and the client is always right." He thrust the helmet at her.

"You're not my client." To hell with the trustee's wishes. Risking her life to keep a beneficiary happy went way beyond her job description.

Ben lowered the helmet and tapped it against his black-jeaned thigh. "You know, if I get upset enough, I'll bet I could find a reason to sue the trustee for mismanagement of the trust."

"Your grandfather was the trustee." The corporate trustee had taken over only after Max's death.

"He hasn't been for five days," Ben said. "Big as the trust is, I'm sure at least one investment decision or lack of decision has already resulted in financial loss. Corporate trustees are held to a high standard." He offered the helmet again.

Lexie was surprised he knew that, but the Internet provided all sorts of information. She doubted he'd win a lawsuit, but he could find one to bring. And corporate trustees truly hated being sued.

She released her death grip on the pickup and reached for the helmet. Her shaking hand had moved only a couple of inches before common sense reasserted itself. At least she hoped it was common sense. "You're not going to sue the trustee because I won't ride on a motorcycle," she said with more confidence than she felt. "You're just trying to manipulate me."

Ben looked at her for a moment, his lips pursed, and she held her breath. Then his expression turned sheepish. "Guilty. But we need to check out the car, and after the last few days, I need to ride. This would kill two birds with one stone. Please."

Lexie looked at his face, at the helmet, at his face again.

"Please," he repeated, his eyes fixed on hers, his voice low and compelling.

She could certainly understand why he was upset. He had just lost his grandfather. Sighing, she reached for the helmet. "As long as we're not the two birds you're planning on killing."

By the time she was helmeted and situated behind Ben on the motorcycle, Lexie was regretting her momentary weakness. She closed her eyes and wrapped her arms around him. Her heart hammered against his solid back, his warmth barely permeating her cold and stiff body.

Ben started the engine, then immediately shut it off. "I lied before," he said, his voice muffled by their helmets.

Lexie opened her eyes to see him looking at her from behind his visor. "I hope it wasn't when you said you were an excellent driver."

"About the *Playboys*." Although his helmet hid his mouth, she could hear his smile. "I don't think I've even seen one since high school. I actually knew about the jeans because my ex-wife had a couple of pairs."

He turned his head and restarted the engine. Lexie closed her eyes again, said a quick prayer, and hung on as he took off toward the road. Between a clenching stomach and a heart beating nearly hard enough to burst through her chest, she could barely breathe. Addendum to Rule Number 148: Avoid involvement with any man who calls women "babe" and/or rides a motorcycle.

Ben drove fast, although not so fast he had any trouble with the curves, and the motorcycle didn't wobble or swerve or do anything that made Lexie feel they were about to tip, flip, or rocket off the road. But Ben's relatively smooth driving didn't change that she was on a motor vehicle going fast, with no protection besides a helmet, and they called things "accidents" for a reason.

After what seemed forever, he slowed, and then drove off the road. Lexie opened her eyes to see that they were in a grove of pines. "Why are we stopping?" Not that she was complaining.

"Because we've reached the lot. Take off your helmet and come on."

She removed her helmet and shook out her sweaty hair. Fear combined with the motorcycle's vibrations had weakened her legs, and she stumbled a couple of times as she followed Ben out of the trees. She couldn't see Lakeview, but lights glimmered to the south, and she could hear Lake Superior's quiet lapping, so they must be near town.

They walked until they reached a chain-link fence about six feet high, enclosing a brick building and a couple dozen cars. Ben grabbed onto the top of the fence and pulled himself up.

"What are you doing?"

"I'm going over. I'll unlock the gate and let you in. Unless you want to scale the fence, too."

Lexie snagged his foot. "We are not breaking in."

Ben lowered himself back down beside her. "It's not like I plan to steal or damage anything. All I'm doing is checking out Grandfather's car, which I have a right to do."

"Why don't we come back during business hours?"

"Because I don't want anyone to know I suspect Grandfather's death wasn't an accident." Before Lexie had a chance to object, he was over the fence.

Since her only alternative was waiting outside the fence—and Ben had a point about secrecy—Lexie stepped through the gate once he opened it. Then she followed him across the gravel-paved lot, navigating through cars displaying rusty holes, cardboarded windows, duct-taped parts, and evidence of collisions past.

Three-quarters of the way in, Ben stopped. "This is it."

Directly in front of them were the charred remains of an automobile.

Max's Ferrari.

Lexie's eyes filled and her chest tightened as she stared at the car. The odor of burned metal clogged her nose and throat. "Max's death never seemed real before," she got out over a lump. "But seeing this, it's very real."

Ben took her hand and squeezed it. "We have to believe that wherever Grandfather is, he's enjoying it as much as he always enjoyed life."

She swiped at her overflowing eyes with the back of her free hand, smearing tears over her cheekbones. Max had been demanding and occasionally a pain, but she'd been genuinely fond of him. She'd miss him, miss his wit, his warmth, his concern about her. She'd even miss the lectures that resulted from that concern. And he'd been her last real connection to her aunt. "I hope he died right away. I hate to think of him suffering."

"The coroner said he probably died on impact, before the fire."

"Were there any remains?"

"A few bones. Enough of his jaw to match dental records and confirm it was Grandfather. Not that he'd have let anyone else drive his Ferrari."

Lexie closed her eyes for a moment, her fingers tightening around Ben's. It was hard to think of a vibrant person like Max reduced to blackened bone fragments. "He wanted to be cremated, but I don't think this was exactly what he had in mind."

"The only thing we can do for him now is figure out who killed him."

"Assuming anyone did."

Ben released her hand. "That's what we're here to find out." He slipped under the car.

Rosy dusk had darkened to an eerie gray, turning the other vehicles into shadowy forms. Lexie's pulse accelerated, and a shiver slithered across her shoulders and neck, then slid down her spine. "This place gives me the creeps," she said, hoping the sound of her voice would calm her. "Max should have used it in one of his books."

"He did, or at least a place like it," Ben answered from beneath the car. She could see the reflected light of his flashlight. "In *The Key*."

"His second book," Lexie said, nodding. "He wrote that so long ago I forgot about it." Maybe that was why her subconscious found this place spooky. "Didn't a woman die in a car lot?"

"The accountant pushed a car on top of her to keep her from disclosing that he was an embezzler," Ben said. "He later hid in a car wash and was electrocuted when he accidentally turned it on and it shorted out. That book was followed by *Water over the Bridge*, where the sleazy lawyer tried to drown the hero and instead fell into the water himself and was eaten by an alligator."

Lexie smiled faintly. "Max wrote both of those before he was successful enough to have to admit accountants and lawyers have their uses."

"True." The light flickered, and she heard Ben fiddling with something under the car. "Don't worry. If this car crushes anyone, it'll be me."

While he examined the car, Lexie stood hugging herself and looking around, alert for the slightest movement. After several minutes Ben emerged from beneath the car and flipped his flashlight off.

"Did you find anything?" she asked.

He shook his head, wiping his hands on his jeans. "Too much fire damage. *Damn*."

The flash of approaching car lights and roar of an engine indicated someone was pulling up to the fence.

Ben grabbed Lexie's hand and started sprinting. "Come on."

"Who is it?" she asked, running beside him.

"Be quiet." He pulled her behind the building.

She had no idea what was going on, but from Ben's reaction, it wasn't good. Over the heartbeat drumming in her ears, Lexie heard a metallic rattle, then the creak of the gate opening. Heavy footsteps crunched over gravel, coming nearer, stopping. A flashlight shone along the edge of the building.

She pressed her back against the bricks to make herself as flat as possible, trying not to breathe.

CHAPTER 4

The gravelly footsteps resumed, but this time they were moving away. A moment later Lexie heard the gate close, followed by a car door slamming and an engine turning over. She let out a relieved breath.

"We're lucky Al's in a hurry to finish his rounds tonight," Ben said. "Otherwise he would have checked this place out closer."

Lexie released her tight grip on Ben's hand, relief shifting to anger. "You made me sneak in here tonight when you knew there was a security guard?"

"I didn't expect anyone to show up this early," Ben said. "Al's actually a cop. This is the police impound lot. They're holding the Ferrari until the beneficiaries tell them what to do with it."

She forced herself to count to ten. Twice. Getting angry was a waste of what little energy she had left after today's events. "Great," she said, managing with monumental effort to keep her tone level. "I've been here less than a day and was already nearly arrested."

"We've still got time." Ben took her arm.

She dug in her heels. "Sorry, but I have no desire to see the inside of a Minnesota jail cell."

"I was kidding," he said. "This time we won't do anything remotely illegal. On the way back, I thought we'd stop and check out the curve Grandfather's car missed."

– – –

Even riding wasn't helping tonight, Ben acknowledged as he sped over the deserted blacktop. Usually there was nothing better than flying through a summer night, especially with a woman plastered against his back. Lexie might not be a double D, but she was more than adequate in that department, and the legs that were currently pressing into his hips were world-class. She was attractive enough that under normal circumstances, he'd be enjoying having at least a little trouble keeping his thoughts on his driving. But he still felt as lousy as he had when they'd left Nevermore.

Lexie's arms tightened, and Ben checked the speedometer, saw he'd accelerated, and slowed. He felt bad about the way he'd pushed her so hard to ride with him in the first place. He'd dismissed her objections because he'd assumed she was a snob like Olivia, thinking that riding a motorcycle was beneath her. He'd been so upset about everything that they'd nearly reached the impound lot before he'd realized Lexie's crushing grip meant she was scared. She wasn't hanging on quite so tightly now—as long as he didn't speed up—so hopefully she'd gotten over the worst of her fear.

The Ferrari had plummeted off a downhill curve three miles from Nevermore. Ben pulled onto the grassy shoulder and parked his bike. Then he and Lexie walked along the gradual uphill. The sun was down, but a half-moon provided some light.

"This doesn't look that dangerous," she said. "I assumed it was an S curve, or something a lot sharper." The curve in question was more an elongated C.

"The road plunges into a ravine, and the shoulder's so narrow that if you lose control, you don't have much recovery room." He pointed down the hill. "It's too dark to see, but it's a long way down, and there aren't many trees to stop you. The Ferrari hit the bottom, then flipped over and started on fire."

"How horrible."

The waver in Lexie's voice confirmed what Ben had recognized at the impound lot. He'd misjudged her about one thing—she wasn't here solely because of her job or the fees the trust would pay her law firm. She'd honestly cared about Grandfather.

"You've got that right," he said. "Let's sit for a few minutes." He plopped down on the grass at the edge of the ravine.

Lexie sat beside him, hugging her knees to her chest. "Could Max have had a heart attack or stroke?"

"It's possible, although he had his annual exam last month and was declared healthy as a horse," Ben said. "And I guarantee he wasn't drunk. He believed in drinking and writing, but drinking and driving was an absolute no. Especially in his precious Ferrari."

She rested her chin on her bent knees. "Was he upset about anything? Not that I can imagine Max committing suicide, but—"

"No way. He loved life too much." Ben stretched out his legs, bracing his hands behind him, and shifted to a subject easier to discuss. "Trey saw Grandfather earlier that day, and he was in a terrific mood. His latest book had just knocked Stephen King's off the top spot on the *New York Times*' hardcover bestseller list."

"Was he working on anything new?"

Ben looked up at the moon. A couple of stars had joined it. "He was always working on something new. He claimed this one was going to be his best ever."

"What's it about?"

"Don't know." He shifted his gaze from the sky to Lexie. "Grandfather considered talking about a work in progress bad luck."

"I thought he wouldn't tell me because he was afraid an attorney would rip him off. As if I could write a Max Windsor bestseller even with a hundred-page detailed outline." Lexie returned her attention to the curve. "If Max's death was a murder, then someone either forced him off the road or tampered with his car. Or possibly drugged him. Were you and Muriel the only beneficiaries in Lakeview when he was killed?"

"Far as I know, but someone else could have sneaked into town. Or paid to have it done."

Lexie raised her chin from her knees and looked at him, her eyes widening. "Hired someone to kill Max?" From her tone, she'd never considered that.

"Believe it or not, finding a hit man isn't too tough."

"You've tried?"

Memory curved his lips. "No, but Grandfather did. For a book."

"*Hitchhiking Through Hell.*"

"Give the lady a gold star," Ben said, raising one finger. "He wanted to make sure it was doable. According to him, it definitely was."

Lexie released her legs and stretched them out in front of her. They sat in silence for a couple of minutes, and then she let out an audible breath. "So assuming it was murder, what do we do next?"

Muscles Ben hadn't realized he'd been tensing relaxed. He really did need her help. "First I think we should get some sleep." He got to his feet, then offered her his hand. "We've both had long days. We'll come up with a plan tomorrow."

– – –

Lexie spent the ride back to Nevermore lost in thought. Max was dead, and it was unlikely his death had been accidental.

Seeing the car and curve and talking to Ben had made that clear. Maybe she wasn't a trained detective, but Max had asked her to investigate and had confidence in her abilities. She'd give it her best shot.

By the time the motorcycle entered the Nevermore grounds, it was dark and the spotlights were on. The rose house was now dull gray with a single illuminated window, the sky behind it pitch-black except for the half-moon and a couple of stars. Fog seemed to swirl around the porch and towers, although the night otherwise was clear. Maybe the money Max claimed to have spent buying ghosts to haunt Nevermore hadn't been wasted.

Ben pulled the motorcycle up beside his pickup and removed his helmet. "Admit it. You liked riding tonight."

To be honest, by their final trek Lexie *had* been enjoying herself, but no way was she admitting that to Ben. Her enjoyment just meant that the stresses of today had her brain too exhausted to recognize danger. She got off the bike. "I like that I got back here alive."

"Bull. At the end you were barely holding on to me. Next time you'll be begging me to go faster."

"There won't be a next time." She pulled off her helmet and set it on the grass, then combed her fingers through her damp, flattened hair as they started to the house.

"Hell," Ben said, stopping abruptly. He looked as if he'd mistaken a cup of Pennzoil for his morning coffee. "The perfect end to a lousy day."

Lexie followed Ben's gaze to a man walking toward them from a dark Mercedes, wheeling a suitcase bag behind him.

"How are you, Ben?" the man asked.

"Do you care?"

"I was being polite, a concept that's clearly beyond you." The man turned his attention to Lexie, extending his free hand and smiling warmly. "I'm Jeremy Windsor."

Jeremy was tall, dark, and classically handsome, his suit and tie clearly expensive. Exactly her type. A pity she'd sworn off men.

"I'm Ca—Lexie," she said, returning his smile as she shook his hand.

Ben draped an arm around her shoulders. "Lexie came from Kentucky to comfort me."

And an even greater pity she was pretending to be involved with Ben.

"Where in Kentucky?" Jeremy asked.

"Lexington. I did a year at the University of Kentucky and stuck around. Now I'm a cocktail waitress and an aspiring novelist. I'm sorry about your grandfather's death."

"Thank you. Did you ever meet him?"

She shook her head. "I only met Ben a little over a month ago, and this is my first trip here."

"That's too bad, since I'm sure Grandfather would have been happy to help with your book. He always liked beautiful blondes."

Ben's arm tightened around her shoulders. "Let's go, Lexie," he said as he steered her toward Nevermore's front stairs.

"It's been nice meeting you, Lexie," Jeremy called after them. "I look forward to getting to know you."

"Why did you claim to be an aspiring novelist?" Ben asked when they were inside Nevermore.

"You clearly won't get a lot out of Jeremy, so it's up to me," Lexie said. "I figured he'll assume I latched on to you just so I could meet your grandfather and maybe he'll hit on me. I thought it was inspired."

"And unnecessary," Ben said. "You're with me. Jeremy's going to hit on you."

– – –

"*No . . .*"

Lexie bolted up in bed. The word was thin and metallic, scraping down her spine like a steel blade.

Then silence.

She jumped out of bed, grabbed her robe, and raced into the hallway.

CHAPTER 5

"That's Dylan," Ben said as he sprinted down the hallway.

"What's going on?" Lexie asked, running behind him. Her heart was hammering like a woodpecker on speed.

"Damned if I know."

By the time they reached Dylan's doorway, the screams had stopped. Ben opened the unlocked door and flipped on the overhead light. "What's wrong?"

Lexie had been braced to see Dylan's dead body, but he was sitting up in bed, his face nearly as white as the sheet he clutched. His gaze was fixed on an overstuffed chair against the wall.

"Grandfather." His voice was low and wobbly. "Grandfather was here, in this room."

Cecilia hurried from the hallway to her brother. "You were dreaming."

"Or drunk," Jeremy said, stepping into the room and tightening the belt of his black silk robe.

"I wasn't. He woke me up." Dylan pointed at the chair. "He was sitting right there."

Ben walked over to the chair and pointed to the floor lamp beside it. "Are you sure you didn't mistake the lamp for Grandfather? In the dark, the white shade might look like Grandfather's hair."

"It was Grandfather." Dylan's voice was stronger, steadier. "He was sitting, then he got up and disappeared."

"Grandfather's dead, Dylan," Cecilia said softly. She sat down on the bed beside him, her scarlet robe a vivid contrast to his pale face.

"I know that. I meant it was his ghost." Dylan released the sheet and turned to Cecilia. "You remember how we used to hear things when we stayed here. Things that couldn't have been trees or the wind or an old house."

Cecilia nodded. "We always thought Grandfather had staged it."

"But what if he didn't? What if the house was haunted before, and now Grandfather's joined the party?"

"What did he do?" Ben asked. "Just sit and look at you?"

Now that her anxiety about Dylan had lessened, Lexie noticed that Ben was wearing only a pair of running shorts that accentuated a tight butt and a muscular chest with a light dusting of hair. She immediately refocused on Dylan.

He was shaking his head vigorously, his loose hair flapping. "Grandfather told me he knew what I'd done and asked why I'd done it."

"Then what?" Seth asked.

"Then I screamed, and he disappeared."

"I can certainly understand your dreaming about Grandfather, being at Nevermore so soon after his death," Ben said. "We'll probably all dream about him."

Dylan shook his head again. "It wasn't a dream."

"We'll discuss it in the morning." Ben headed for the door.

Dylan grabbed Cecilia's arm with both hands. "I can't sleep here. What if he comes back?"

Ben turned back toward Dylan. "You can sleep in my room. I'll sleep in here."

"Do you think staying here's a good idea, Ben?" Cecilia asked.

He shrugged. "I'm not in the mood to share my bed with Dylan, and Aunt Muriel forbade me from sleeping with Lexie."

Lexie suddenly realized that Muriel was the only family member absent. "Where is your aunt?" she asked.

"Asleep, I assume," Ben said. "She sleeps with earplugs, and her room's at the far end of the hallway." He raised an eyebrow. "Why don't you stay in here with me? Aunt Muriel didn't say a thing about us sharing someone else's room."

"I don't think that would be appropriate," Lexie said, since "no way in hell" definitely wouldn't be appropriate in front of this audience.

"You're probably right," Ben said. "Aunt Muriel's already overwhelmed saying rosaries for Grandfather's sins without having to fit in more for us." He stepped up to Lexie. "How about a kiss in case I don't survive the night?"

He rested his hands on Lexie's shoulders. His bare chest and masculine scent made her pulse jump. His lips brushed over hers, sending a bolt of liquid heat swirling through her stomach and lower.

She frowned.

Ben chuckled, removing his hands. "Don't look so worried. I promise I'll survive."

She was obviously exhausted, Lexie thought as she walked back to her room. She certainly wasn't attracted to Ben—he wasn't at all her type, and she was mature enough that her brain controlled her hormones. Her brain seemed to have taken tonight off, but that had to be due to fatigue, stress, and her recent celibacy. She'd have reacted to any halfway attractive, half-dressed male the same way. After a good night's sleep, she'd be back to viewing Ben as nothing but the necessary evil he was.

And with any luck, she'd soon be on her way back to Philadelphia. Because Dylan's dream could very well have been triggered by a guilty conscience, especially since he'd dreamed that Max had confronted him about what he'd done, which could have been to commit murder. That put Dylan at the top of the suspect list.

– – –

"What do you mean, you won't be able to attend the summer gala? Everyone who's anyone will be there." Elizabeth Barrington sounded as scandalized as if her daughter had just admitted she was staying at Max Windsor's mansion and investigating his possible murder while pretending to be Lexie, the cocktail waitress girlfriend of an auto mechanic.

Catherine sank down on the bed. She'd been on her way to the shower when her cell phone had rung. She'd wanted to ignore it, but she couldn't blow off her mother.

She should have gone with her gut. "I told you I'm out of town working, Mother."

"Where are you?"

"Chicago." Catherine wasn't about to say she was in Minnesota, since her mother would realize her work was related to Max. She'd listened to her mother badmouth him enough when he was alive.

"Do your best to come home by the weekend. I told Steven Wilmington that I was sure you'd be there." Elizabeth sniffed. "I assume he didn't dare ask you to accompany him after how rudely you turned him down before."

"I wasn't rude, Mother. I told Steven I needed more time before I'd be ready to date again, and he understood. My divorce was just final a few months ago." Not that she'd have dated Steven if she'd been divorced for decades. In his mid-thirties, he was already the definition of a stuffed shirt.

"Don't remind me." Her mother's voice sounded pained, as if someone had hammered a nail through it. "The sooner you remarry, the sooner people will forget you were ever divorced. Especially since Neil's already remarried. You have no idea how hard it is for me to have a daughter who's divorced. No one in my family has ever been divorced."

Catherine rolled her eyes. *It hasn't been a piece of cake for me either.* "I can imagine, Mother."

"Steven's from a very good family."

"Neil was from a good family," Catherine couldn't resist pointing out.

"You were too involved with your career to be a proper wife to someone like him, a surgeon who has such a demanding job. He obviously wanted a wife who was willing to stay home and have children, since Deidre's done just that." Her mother sniffed again, her phone equivalent of a condescending look. "I don't know why you insisted on working, since you certainly didn't need the money. I'm sure you won't make that mistake again."

Marrying someone who not only cheats with a twenty-three-year-old massage therapist but also gets her pregnant? "I certainly won't, Mother."

"Good. You know, if you wait too long to start dating again, you'll be too old to be attractive to any man worth having. I'd hate to see you turn out to be a childless spinster like my sister."

Catherine's hand tightened around her cell phone. "Aunt Jessica had a wonderful life."

"She was a disappointment to our family in so many ways."

"She was a bestselling author and in a committed relationship with another bestselling author."

"She wrote trashy romance novels, for heaven's sake," her mother said. "And you know how I felt about Max Windsor. The only good thing is that they never married." She sighed loudly. "But I won't speak ill of the dead. Jessica was my sister, and I loved her."

Catherine chewed her lip to keep from responding. Defending Aunt Jessica to her mother was as big a waste of time as defending Max.

"You know, if you don't show up, people will assume you're still heartbroken over Neil, since he and Deidre will almost certainly be there," her mother continued. "Self-pity is not an attractive characteristic."

"I hope you'll spread the word that work, not self-pity, kept me from attending," Catherine said. "Now I need to go. Give my best to Dad."

"I'll do that. Please change your attitude about dating. A Barrington does not give up because of one failure."

"I know, Mother." Rule Number 23. The one right before Rule 24, no self-pity. "Thanks for calling. I love you."

She did love her mother. Although sometimes she didn't like her much. Probably because her mother seemed to consider her as big a disappointment as Jessica had been.

Catherine tossed her phone onto the unmade bed and headed for the shower.

– – –

"I told you I'd survive, Lexie," Ben said, walking into the dining room where she was savoring a cup of French roast. He dropped a kiss on the top of her head.

Other than feeling a flick against her hair, Lexie's body didn't react to the kiss, thank God. She'd been right—exhaustion had been responsible for last night's more heated response.

"Is Dylan still asleep?" Cecilia asked.

"Yep." Ben slathered a bagel with cream cheese and carried it and his coffee to the table. "He didn't even flinch when I went in to get my stuff. Much as I hate to agree with Jeremy about anything, I think alcohol played a major role in last night's dream." He sat down in the high-backed chair beside Lexie.

"I'm not so sure," Cecilia said, fiddling with the tennis bracelet circling her wrist. "Dylan's right about those noises we heard when we were younger, tapping on the walls and strange footsteps and loud groans, things like that. We thought it was Grandfather, but he always denied it and insisted he'd bought some ghosts to haunt Nevermore. If anyone could arrange for a few ghosts, it would have been Grandfather."

"Provided you believe in ghosts, which I don't," Ben said. "I heard the same kinds of things, especially when I was living here. I figured Grandfather was behind it no matter what he said."

"Did anything ever happen when Grandfather was traveling?" Cecilia asked.

"Sometimes. I assumed he'd rigged it to go off while he was gone," Ben said. "Or that I was imagining things."

"I believe Dylan saw your grandfather's ghost," Lexie said.

"You believe in ghosts?" Ben looked at her incredulously, an understandable reaction to her outrageous statement.

She didn't, but Lexie very well might, and that would give her an excuse to quiz Dylan about exactly what he'd seen and hopefully trip him up. "How can anyone *not* believe in ghosts? I watched this series about haunted houses on the History Channel." Which was true— she'd watched for about two minutes until she'd concluded it was completely lame. Lexie clasped her hands together. "I never expected to ever stay in a haunted house myself. I can't wait to talk to Dylan."

"Whatever makes you happy," Ben said, wrapping an arm around her shoulders and giving her such an indulgent smile that she'd have slugged him if his reaction hadn't been because she was pretending to believe in ghosts. "We can go for a walk before I head off to work. I'd like to show you the lake. Assuming you can stand to wait to talk to Dylan."

"I doubt he'll be up for at least an hour," Cecilia said.

Lexie got to her feet. "Then let's go now."

"It's so nice to know you'd pick Dylan over me," Ben said.

"Only to talk about ghosts to, and you know it," Lexie said. "That fake jealousy just makes you look like an idiot. I'll meet you out front in five minutes."

Cecilia grinned. "The more I see you handle Ben, the more I like you, Lexie. Enjoy your walk."

− − −

Lexie and Ben made their way through the pines and birch trees, taking the path that led down the hill to Forest Lake. The world was cathedral-quiet other than the clomp of their feet and crackle of dry leaves. Every breath of cool, pine-scented air seemed to scrub out Lexie's lungs. After walking maybe five minutes they reached the lake. Sunlight sparkled off the crystal-blue water and made the rocky shoreline glow. A sky the same deep blue as the water provided a stunning backdrop to the velvety green pine trees and silvery birch that covered the hills surrounding the lake.

"This is beautiful," Lexie said quietly. Speaking at a normal volume seemed sacrilegious. "Is all of this Max's property?" Other than a dock and a storage shed, there was no evidence anyone else used the lake.

"Most of it. The rest is national forest." Ben plopped down on a flat-topped gray boulder the size of a loveseat. "I thought you said you don't believe in ghosts."

Lexie sat down beside him. "I don't. But I thought pretending to would give me an excuse to quiz Dylan about last night, since he's the most likely suspect."

"Why do you think that?"

"He said that Max told him he knew what he'd done, which I assume refers to the murder. No one besides us knows Max was murdered. So why would Dylan dream that if he didn't do it?"

"Because alcohol makes people paranoid and irrational, even in nightmares," Ben said. "We also don't know for sure that Grandfather's comment referred to murder."

"True," Lexie said, pulling a notepad from her purse. "But Dylan also has a gambling problem and owes money to someone possibly connected to the Mafia, according to Cecilia. He could be desperate for cash. Does he have a job?"

"He freelances," Ben said. "Believe it or not, he's a computer genius. He could earn a fortune, but he doesn't have the greatest work ethic."

"What a surprise," Lexie said. "Checking into Dylan's finances is the first item on my To Do list."

"I'll talk to Cecilia," Ben said.

"Good idea. Do you want paper and a pen?"

"Why?"

"So you can write a To Do list."

"I think I can remember everything," Ben said.

"Are you sure?" She grabbed her purse and unzipped it. "I've got another pen."

"Lexie, I'm not incompetent," Ben said, sounding offended. "I run a business. And I hate To Do lists."

Lexie rezipped her purse and returned it to the rock. "How do you know what you have to do each day?"

"If it isn't obvious, it obviously isn't important. Since you're clearly a big fan of lists, what's item two?"

She looked down. "Checking into whether other beneficiaries are in desperate need of money. Starting with Cecilia. How did her last divorce leave her financially?"

"We can skip Cecilia. She'd never hurt Grandfather."

"We can't skip her."

"You only suspect her because she's been divorced three times. You figure there's either something wrong with her or she's a gold-digger." Ben's voice had an edge.

"Why would I think that?" Lexie asked. "I don't know her well, but I like her. It sounds like she makes bad decisions about men and has mother issues, which are two things we've got in common. Max wanted my objectivity. That means looking into everyone."

Ben let out a long breath. "Sorry. I guess I'm a little protective of Cecilia. I can pretty much guarantee she needs money. Cecilia's an incurable romantic and always thinks this man is the one she'll be with forever, so she signs lousy prenuptial agreements. But unfortunately she also has lousy taste in men."

"What does she do for a living?"

"She's pretty much a professional wife," Ben said. "She's never had a paying job in her life. Her mother can't survive without a man supporting her, and she's convinced Cecilia that she's the same way. Cecilia's smart and talented and could succeed at any career she tried, but it's hard to overcome years of your mother's influence."

Lexie's lips twisted wryly. "I can relate to that. What about Seth?"

"Seth is supporting a wife and two little boys on what he makes videotaping weddings and bar mitzvahs. They also live in California, which isn't exactly cheap. I'm sure he could use the money,"

Ben said. "But he's got a bigger motive. Seth's share of the trust will allow him to finally break into films or television. And his wife, Joanna, will get to act in something other than local theater and tampon commercials, which I assume is a big part of why she married Seth."

Ben tapped his knuckles against his chin. "Actually, Joanna could be involved, too. She was here with Seth and the kids for Easter. She's always struck me as one of those Lady Macbeth types."

"I take it you don't like her."

"Not so much," Ben said. "I think Joanna is my second favorite suspect."

Presumably Jeremy was his first. Lexie made another note. "How about Muriel?"

"Aunt Muriel inherited quite a bit when her husband died," Ben said. "But she contributes to a lot of religions and might have given more than she can afford. I'll see what I can find out."

"That leaves Jeremy. I'd better talk to him, since he clearly won't tell you the truth."

"If he's having money problems, he'll lie to you, too, if only out of pride," Ben said. "I'll ask my ex-wife. She isn't a big fan of Jeremy's either."

"Doesn't Jeremy live in New York?"

Ben shrugged. "Olivia knows a lot of people."

Lexie looked down at her list. She'd reached the end, and every task had been delegated to Ben. "If you're going to find out all the money stuff, what am I supposed to do?"

"Once you're done discussing Grandfather's ghost with Dylan?" Ben asked, a corner of his mouth quirking. "Why don't you ask everyone about Grandfather? Since he was famous, you'd naturally be curious about him. Maybe someone will admit resenting him."

"Wouldn't I ask you?"

"Tell people I'm too upset to talk about him."

"I guess I can also ask them about you," Lexie said.

"Me?"

"I'm not about to take your word for it that you have no interest in Max's money."

Ben narrowed his eyes at her. "Grandfather trusted me enough to appoint me a co-investigator. You're just trying to get back at me for making you ride on my motorcycle."

That sparked Lexie's temper, and she lifted her chin. "I'm not that petty. I'm trying to be thorough. I can't exclude one beneficiary from the investigation."

"Fine. Ask all you want. But—" He pointed at the path. "Quiet," he whispered.

Lexie heard a couple of footsteps, then silence.

Ben walked over to the path and started back through the woods. "What the hell are you doing spying on us?"

Lexie rushed to the path. Ben had a tight grip on one of Seth's arms.

"I'm not spying on you," Seth said. "I didn't even know you were there." He waved his camera the best he could since Ben was holding his arm. "I'm taking photos of Grandfather's land. Nevermore is probably going to be sold, and this might be my last time here. It's been such an important part of my growing up that I want to make sure I've got photos of it. For myself and to show the boys."

Ben stared at Seth for a moment. After last night's car discussion, Lexie braced herself for a loud argument and maybe even a few thrown punches.

Instead, Ben dropped his cousin's arm, smiling faintly. "You really have gotten sentimental, haven't you?"

"Fatherhood will do it to you. You should try it," Seth said, and then he grimaced. "Sorry."

"No big deal," Ben said.

"You know, I have a feeling that Grandfather got sentimental, too," Seth said. "That's why he wanted us to spend two weeks here, both so we'll appreciate Nevermore and so we'll start to appreciate each other."

"You honestly think that was Grandfather's motivation?"

"It makes sense."

Ben rolled his eyes. "I think you've been in California too long."

– – –

It was almost nine that evening when Ben knocked on Lexie's bedroom door. "Sorry I missed sherry hour and dinner, but I got stuck at work. How was your day?"

"Wonderful," Lexie said, giving him a saccharine smile. "I spent several hours reading and memorizing everything I could about Lexington, Kentucky, in case Seth or someone else decides to quiz me about it. Which wouldn't be a problem if you'd made me from a city I'd actually spent some time in."

"Too late now," Ben said. "How was sherry hour?"

"I didn't show up until the end," Lexie said. "I told everyone I felt uncomfortable about intruding on the family when you aren't around, which is true. But I was there for dinner, and it was lovely. Seth kept taking pictures of everything and everyone. Dylan and Muriel got into a heated argument about whether God exists and Buddha's role in the creation of the universe, since Muriel seems to think he had one. Then Jeremy and Cecilia argued over whether the fact she keeps signing bad prenups indicates she's an incurable romantic or just stupid. Trey tried to keep peace and change the subject, which didn't work. And despite my research, no one asked me a single damn question about Lexington. At least the food was good."

"I think I prefer the burger and fries I ate by myself at Dairy Queen before I came home." Ben took Lexie's arm. "You deserve a break. Let's go."

"Go where?" she asked.

"Trust me."

"*Right.* The last time I did that, I ended up riding a motorcycle and dodging a cop."

Ben grinned. "Relax. I'm just going to introduce you to a Lakeview institution." He opened the door. "We'll take my truck."

CHAPTER 6

Walt's Tavern was a dive located a mile outside Lakeview. Lexie and Ben walked through a cloud of smoke thick enough to slice, courtesy of a dozen men and women with drinks and cigarettes milling around the entrance. Although smoking inside was prohibited by state law, the front door was propped wide open, so a smoky haze encompassed a room packed with men wearing T-shirts, jeans, and swaggers, and women with shrill laughs and too much eye shadow. In a khaki skirt and navy silk T-shirt, Lexie felt overdressed—literally. Every other woman seemed to be wearing a cropped top, paired with either a miniskirt or jeans so tight they were superfluous as a body covering.

Ben put his hand on Lexie's back and directed her to the bar, an expanse of light wood covered with scratches and smoke burns. "What can I get you?" he asked, his voice barely loud enough to be heard over the blaring jukebox and alcohol-loudened conversations.

"I don't suppose they have a decent cabernet," Lexie said.

"I wouldn't try it."

"I assume the mixed drinks are watered down."

Ben grinned. "How else is Walt supposed to make a living?"

"I'll try a gin and tonic."

Lexie surveyed the room as she waited for her drink. From the minute she'd stepped into the place, she'd felt as if every eye was on her, and from the way people were unabashedly staring now, she wasn't just being paranoid. She shouldn't have been surprised—from what she knew of small towns, gossip was a major form of entertainment. She'd bet everyone had heard all about Ben's girlfriend from Kentucky.

"Here's your drink," Ben said, handing her a tall glass filled with a reddish-orange liquid and a few bobbing ice cubes. "It's Walt's special. He insisted. Don't drink it too fast."

"Since you won't buy me another one?"

"I didn't have to pay for this one."

Lexie took a sip. The drink was fruity but not overly sweet. She could barely taste the alcohol—hopefully it contained enough to kill any germs lurking in the glass or water supply.

In contrast to everyone else's interest in Lexie, Ben ignored her, instead scanning the crowd. "I've got to talk to someone," he said after a moment. Then he took off, heading for a blonde who was leaning against the back wall, probably because otherwise her oversized bust would make her fall flat on her face. Ben took the woman's arm and led her to a corner table.

That's why he'd come here, Lexie realized—to meet another woman. Although she had no idea why he'd brought her along. The probability she'd pick up any clues as to Max's killer seemed about as likely as the blonde's boobs being gifts of nature. People certainly wouldn't mention any gossip they'd heard about Ben or his family to his girlfriend. She turned around and set her empty glass on the bar.

"Can I get you another?" the bartender asked immediately.

"I'd love one," she said. "Put it on Ben's tab." After dragging her here and then deserting her, he could damn well pay for her drinks. While she waited, she looked for Ben. He was still at the back table in deep conversation with the blonde, assuming any woman he found attractive was capable of deep conversation.

She turned to the bar just as Walt handed her another drink. She was halfway through it when a man sidled up beside her. "I thought I saw you come in with Ben Gallagher."

"I did, but he's obviously forgotten me."

"That's hard to believe."

"It seems to have happened," she said, giving the man a warm smile. He was good looking, with dark hair and a thick mustache on his deeply tanned face. No wedding ring either, not that he was any more likely to be her type than Ben was.

He pressed his hand over his heart. "My mother would turn over in her grave if I left a lady unattended. I'm in the middle of a game of pool, and I'd be honored if you'd be my good-luck charm."

She glanced at Ben again. She might not care what he did or with whom, but his behavior was starting to piss her off. He'd come up with the girlfriend charade in the first place, then he drags her to a place she'd never have ventured within smelling distance of otherwise and immediately dumps her for another woman?

"I'd love to," she told the man with another smile.

"Get the lady a refill, Walt," the man said. "My name's Sam Harris."

"I'm Lexie."

He took her hand. "I'm delighted to meet you, Lexie. Thanks, Walt," he said as Walt set another drink and a beer on the counter. "The pool tables are in the back room." Sam picked up both the beer and Lexie's glass.

The table in the corner was empty now, and Lexie couldn't see Ben anywhere, making her even happier she'd decided to go with Sam. She followed him through the crowd to a separate room with four busy pool tables.

"I thought you chickened out about finishing, Sam." The speaker, a man with thinning sandy hair and a thickening waistline, waved a pool cue.

"Not when I'm winning. I got distracted. Lexie, this is Eddie."

Eddie gave Lexie a friendly smile. "Pleased to meet you, Lexie." Unlike Sam, he was wearing a gold wedding band. "Where do you hail from?"

"Kentucky. I'm here visiting Ben Gallagher."

Eddie snorted. "Yet another reason the guy's a lucky bastard. Not that Ben had any trouble getting women before, but I'll bet he's got his pick now that he's going to be a multimillionaire. Not that you're with him for his money," he added.

"I was sorry to hear about Ben's grandfather's death," Sam said. "And in an accident like that. It's a damn shame."

"Max was a great guy," Lexie agreed.

"You met him?"

She recovered quickly. "No, but everyone I've talked to says that."

"Well, they're right," Sam said. "He was one of the best."

"Which is high praise considering Max didn't trust Sam with his legal business," Eddie said, sinking a ball in the corner pocket.

"You're a lawyer?" Lexie asked.

Sam nodded. "But Max used some hotshot firm from out east where all the lawyers are specialists. Good thing, since as a small-town general practitioner, I probably would have screwed up the trust provision that makes everyone spend two weeks together to inherit."

"You're lucky you didn't do it," Eddie told Sam. "Everyone in that house would hate you for making them stick together for two weeks, especially Ben and Jeremy. And what if one of them lost out on a fortune because of it? I heard Dylan's in debt t who'd be happy to break a few of your bones. The rest could probably take you out themselves. 'Cept maybe Muriel."

"I came here because Ben was so upset about his grandfather's death," Lexie said, shifting the conversation to a more comfortable subject than her potential future bodily harm. "Even though it was a major hassle to get time off. Then he runs out on me."

"His loss is our gain," Sam said. "Like I said, I have a feeling you're going to be my good-luck charm."

"Maybe you should come over to my side so you can back a winner." Eddie took another shot, missed.

"In your dreams, Eddie," Sam said, picking up a cue.

Lexie leaned against the wall. She felt as if she'd stepped into a bad movie—city girl gets stuck in the country, drinks too much, watches a couple of locals play pool, and finds true love with one of them. The only differences were she wasn't drinking too much or falling in love. Actually, most of those movies also had a bar fight scene—she'd prefer to skip that part, too.

"I assume Ben plans to go ahead and expand his garage the way he wanted. Now that he's inheriting a fortune," Sam said.

"He's planning to expand?" Lexie asked.

"Double it in size. Last winter he had the plans drawn up and hired me to handle the legal issues. Everyone knew about it, so it's not like I'm violating any attorney-client privilege talking about it." Sam took a shot. "Ben planned to do it this spring, but then decided to delay indefinitely."

"Why?"

"He said he needed to resolve a few things first," Sam said.

"Sam's using his attorney double-talk," Eddie said. "Everyone knows Ben had to drop it because he couldn't come up with the cash. That won't be a problem anymore, if he's even gonna work at all now that he's filthy rich. I sure as hell wouldn't."

So she'd found out something useful tonight after all. Of course, Ben's business must be good if he was considering doubling it in size, and how much money did you need to live well in a place like Lakeview? But living in Lakeview gave Ben opportunity, and he now had a possible motive. She wasn't about to accept he was innocent just because Max had made him her co-investigator. Maybe Max had done that because he suspected Ben and assumed that if he and Lexie spent enough time together, Ben would inevitably give himself away.

Sam knocked in another ball. "How's Nevermore, Lexie? Seen any ghosts?"

"Not yet, although I wouldn't be surprised to. The place is spooky."

Sam shot again. "You got that right. Damn," he said when the ball skimmed the side of the pocket but stayed on the table.

"You've been there?" Lexie asked.

"I think everyone in town has driven up there to look at least once, though I've never been inside," Sam said. "Eddie has."

"Just on the first floor. I do glass repair, and Max called me in to fix his front window after some kooks shot it out."

That's right. "You're a friend of Seth's, right? He mentioned you."

"Yeah, we were tight back in high school," Eddie said. "I haven't talked to him in a few years, though." His shot bounced off the side, landing a few inches from the pocket.

"Side pocket," Sam said, then sank the eight ball. "I told you that you didn't have a prayer, not with Lexie on my side. Another game?"

Eddie shook his head, handing Sam a folded bill. "I'd better get home or Miranda will have my ass. It's been a pleasure meeting you, Lexie."

"Do you play pool?" Sam asked as Eddie walked away.

Lexie shook her head. Technically she played billiards, so it wasn't exactly a lie. She certainly couldn't play anything in a bar like Walt's.

"Do you want me to teach you?"

On the other hand, Lexie the cocktail waitress would definitely play pool in a bar, and she needed something to do while she waited for Ben's return. "I'd love to learn."

After Sam had instructed her in the basics, Lexie awkwardly positioned the cue behind the ball. "Now what do I do?" she asked.

"Slide the cue so it hits the ball. Try it."

She intentionally missed the ball and jabbed the table, then turned and made a face. "I don't think that's exactly right."

His smile made him even more attractive. "Not exactly. Let me help you." He moved behind her and leaned over her, putting his hands on hers. His body was warm, his scent of beer and spice. With his help, her shot landed in a corner pocket.

"I think I've got it," she said, moving away from him. She positioned herself and shot. This time she topped the ball, propelling it only a few inches.

"Try again. This time focus."

She hit the ball, landing it exactly where she intended—a couple of inches from the pocket. She was getting tired of being pathetic, but she couldn't suddenly become Minnesota Fats.

She turned toward him. "I did it. Almost."

"You're a natural."

"What the hell are you doing?" Ben was suddenly beside her and glowering as if someone had scratched his precious motorcycle.

"Sam's teaching me to play pool," Lexie said.

"Not anymore he isn't."

She raised her chin. Where did he get off, telling her what to do? "I'm not quitting right when I'm getting the hang of it."

"If you want to learn how to play pool, I'll teach you," Ben said.

She didn't want to do anything with Ben, but if he wasn't going to leave her alone, she might as well enjoy herself. "I don't need any more lessons. Sam's an excellent teacher. But I'll play against you."

"I don't think so," Ben said.

"Afraid I'll beat you?"

"*Right.*" Ben took down a cue. "I'll spot you two balls and let you break."

Lexie picked up her cue, and then remembered. "You have to break. I haven't had that lesson yet."

Ben broke. "Since I spotted you two balls, you can take them off the table before you take your shot."

"I need more to aim at." Lexie positioned her cue and took her first shot. A solid-colored ball went into a side pocket. She didn't stop until she'd cleared the solids and shot the eight ball into the corner pocket.

"Beginner's luck, I guess," Lexie said, giving Sam a warm smile. "I told you Sam was an excellent teacher."

"I'm not *that* good," Sam said. "Where did you learn to play?"

"In my parents' billiard room, of course."

Sam chuckled, clearly thinking she was joking. "Why did you pretend you didn't know how?"

"Because I was enjoying my lesson." She returned her attention to Ben. "I assume you came to tell me I need to find my own way back to Nevermore."

"I'll be happy to drive you there," Sam said.

"For God's sake, I'm driving you," Ben said.

"I'd rather go with Sam," Lexie said. Especially since Ben now looked as if his motorcycle had not just been scratched but totaled.

"He was nice enough to entertain me while you were busy with another woman."

"I'll entertain you now," Ben said.

Ben being entertaining was about as likely as her becoming a professional pool shark. But she couldn't see any way to avoid going with him, short of making a scene, and Barringtons never made scenes. Rule Number 14. Who knows, Ben's ego might even demand one of those damn bar fights.

Lexie gave Sam a rueful look. "Sorry, but I think Ben and I need to talk." She picked her drink off the wooden table she'd left it on when she'd started her pool lessons and took a sip. The ice had melted, and the small amount of liquid remaining tasted like warm Kool-Aid. She returned the glass to the table.

"That was embarrassing as hell," Ben muttered when Sam was out of earshot.

"Being beaten at pool by a girl?"

"Having my girlfriend hanging out with the biggest lech in the state." His voice was so low Lexie had to lean toward him to hear.

"I didn't realize anyone could hold a candle to you in that regard," she shot back, not nearly as quietly. "Besides, you left me to talk to that overinflated blonde. Where is she, by the way?"

"She left."

"Waiting for you at her place," Lexie said, nodding. "Just make sure you show up at Nevermore before one, like the trust requires. No matter how attractive, I doubt she's worth losing a fortune over."

"She left because I told her I wouldn't be seeing her anymore now that you're here," Ben said. "Not that Amber and I were dating seriously, though she apparently thought otherwise."

"I'm sorry I interfered with your relationship."

"Don't be."

Lexie rolled her eyes. "I was being sarcastic. And unlike your real girlfriends, I know what that means. This charade wasn't my idea."

"I meant that it was time to call it quits anyway," Ben said. "Eight weeks of a woman is about all I can handle."

"Maybe if you hadn't sworn off women with careers and intellect you wouldn't get sick of them quite so fast."

"I wasn't complaining," Ben said. "I like variety. Did you really learn to play pool in a billiard room?"

"I made my brothers teach me." Lexie suddenly felt a little light-headed, and she grabbed the table edge to steady herself. "Don't tell my mother. She doesn't think ladies play billiards." Her tongue tangled on her words.

Ben put his arm on her back and urged her toward the main room of the bar.

Lexie stumbled against him. "What are you doing?"

"We're leaving."

She planted her feet. "I don't want to go yet."

Ben reached down and squeezed her butt. "Even with a stick up it, you have an excellent ass."

"Thank you."

"You're thanking me for a rude remark like that?" He chuckled. "I knew it. How much did you have to drink while I was gone?"

"A couple more of Walt's specials. But they're almost all fruice. I mean fruit juice," she said, enunciating more carefully. "It must be jet lag."

"It must be Walt's special. He waters down the other drinks, but he takes pride in his special. It's almost all booze. That's why I told you to drink it slow." He moved his arm around her shoulders. "I think we'd better go. I'll pay you tomorrow, Walt."

The room seemed to be moving. Lexie leaned against Ben, who kept his arm around her and steered her to his pickup. He half lifted her up onto the seat, fastened her seat belt, and she promptly fell asleep.

– – –

Nevermore was dark and Lexie was still sound asleep when Ben pulled his truck to a stop. He looked at her for a minute, shaking his head. Grandfather had been right—Lexie needed to loosen up. She was a lot more fun when she did. He'd never in a million years have guessed she played pool or that she'd condescend to play in a place like Walt's, no matter how much she'd had to drink.

Ben got out of the pickup and walked around to open the passenger door, then unhooked Lexie's seat belt. She still didn't stir.

"Lexie, you need to wake up. I don't think I can carry you upstairs."

"You had enough trouble with my suitcase." Her eyes were still closed. "Maybe you should call Igor."

"I don't think that's such a good idea. Stand up."

Fortunately, the night air seemed to revive her, and the house was silent. Ben had gotten Lexie up the stairs and down the hallway to the door of her bedroom when Jeremy stepped out of his room.

"I'm going to kiss you," Ben whispered. "Go along with me because Jeremy's watching. Then we'll go into your room for a while, just for show."

He moved his lips to hers without waiting for an answer. He'd intended to give her one of those closed-mouth movie kisses, but that intention evaporated when Lexie opened her mouth and flicked her tongue over his closed lips. He deepened the kiss, pressing her against the door.

"We should go inside now, right?" she murmured when he moved his lips from hers.

"Right." He got the door open and her inside, then started kissing her again, his tongue caressing hers. He pulled her close, holding her so tightly there wasn't room for anything but body heat between them.

She pulled his shirt from his jeans, then moved her hands underneath and up his back. God, he wanted to feel her hands stroking him everywhere like that. He maneuvered her so the bed was against the back of her knees, his mouth still devouring hers.

"I'm really glad we left Walt's."

At the sound of Lexie's voice, Ben froze. Jesus, he'd been so lost in lust he'd forgotten who he was with and what he was doing. "I think I'd better leave."

CHAPTER 7

"Why?" Lexie asked.

"I never take advantage of a woman who's had too much to drink." As he answered, Ben somehow forced himself to remove Lexie's hands from under his shirt, to pull away.

Her arms circled his neck, and she rubbed her body against his. "I think I've drunk just enough."

Summoning up an even bigger shot of willpower, he extricated himself again. "You'll regret this in the morning, and that will make it impossible for us to work together." A nice speech, although to be honest, he'd probably have been willing to ignore those potential complications if she weren't drunk.

"Sleep well, Lexie," he said, and then raced out of the room. Once inside his own room, he leaned against the door, his breathing not the only thing that was hard.

What had he been doing? He didn't even like her, and he was old enough that he had some standards when it came to women. Worse yet, he knew exactly what he'd be in for if he slept with her. She'd screw up his life the way only a smart woman could, using both sex appeal and brains to manipulate him. He was never having sex with Lexie. Hell, he shouldn't even be thinking about having sex with Lexie.

He just had to make sure his own brain remembered that. Because he had more than enough problems already.

– – –

The good news was that despite too many Walt's specials, Lexie wasn't a bit hungover the next morning. The bad news was she remembered exactly what she'd done last night, and she couldn't believe it. What had she been thinking, throwing herself at Ben?

Actually, the problem was she'd been too drunk to think, which never would have happened if Ben hadn't told her Walt watered down his drinks. It also had been far too long since she'd kissed anyone, and Ben was world-class when it came to that activity. His claim to be unbelievable in bed might not be false bravado, not that she was ever going to find out.

Her problem now was facing him. The instant they were alone, she'd apologize for being drunk and acting totally out of character. Or maybe she should pretend to have been so drunk she didn't remember the kiss. She'd play it by ear.

At least she hadn't been too drunk to beat him at pool.

To Lexie's relief, when she got to breakfast, only Cecilia and Jeremy were there.

"Ben already left for work," Cecilia said.

"Since Ben's busy today, I'll take you boating," Jeremy said. "A friend from the Cities loaned me his Fountain 38 Lightning to use while I'm here. It's docked at the Lakeview Marina."

The Cities presumably meant the Twin Cities of Minneapolis and St. Paul. Lexie had no idea what a Fountain Lightning was, but it must be some kind of powerboat. Powerboats were nearly as high on her Things to Avoid list as motorcycles. "I can't. Sorry." She should talk to Jeremy sometime, but she planned to do it in a more comfortable setting.

"Why not?" Jeremy asked.

Admitting she was a wimp might be an option for Catherine, but not for Lexie. "I'm taking classes online so I can finish college, and I have a paper due," she improvised. That would also give her an excuse to use her laptop.

"I'll give you a rain check."

"Why do Ben and Jeremy hate each other?" Lexie asked after Jeremy had left. Knowing that might give her insight into both Ben's and Jeremy's possible motives.

"Jeremy grew up in Lakeview. He was the most popular guy in school, the best looking, best at sports, the top student," Cecilia said. "Then Ben's mom died, and Ben moved in with Grandfather. Ben was as smart and athletic as Jeremy, but also a bad boy from Los Angeles, which made him way more interesting than a guy who'd spent his entire life here. Jeremy resented it and tried to prove he was better than Ben, who did his best to prove Jeremy wasn't. From what Seth told me, it got ridiculous. Every girl one of them looked at, the other one went after. Every sport one of them was in, the other started."

"Testosterone makes men act like idiots."

"Doesn't it?" Cecilia said as she refilled Lexie's cup, then her own. "There also was Grandfather. We all idolized him—I mean, he was a cool guy and wrote books that were made into movies that scared our friends to death. When Grandfather took Ben in, it was hard for all of us not to be jealous, but it was hardest for Jeremy. Before then, Jeremy had spent the most time with Grandfather, but suddenly Ben was living with him. Jeremy resented it."

"That all happened when they were kids. Haven't they outgrown it yet?"

"Olivia only happened three years ago," Cecilia said. "Ben's ex-wife. Jeremy convinced her to leave Ben for him."

Lexie's jaw dropped. "He broke up Ben's marriage?" She hadn't seen that one coming.

"Yeah. That went way over the line, in my book. Especially when it seems to have been more competition than true love, since after a couple of months, Jeremy broke things off with Olivia. By then Ben wasn't about to take her back, which is the only good part of the whole scenario. I'll bet Jeremy tries to take you away from Ben out of habit. Not that he wouldn't like you for yourself, of course," she added quickly.

"It's okay. I get your meaning."

Cecilia tilted her head, her dark hair skimming one shoulder. "You could use Jeremy's interest to make Ben jealous. You might be able to get him to commit that way."

"I'm not in the market for commitment."

"Good call." Cecilia made a face. "Take the advice of someone who's just finished with husband number three. Don't get married until you're too old to worry about it ending other than by death do us part. Divorce sucks."

If she were friends with Cecilia, she'd get more information than if they were simply acquaintances. And Lexie knew the perfect topic to bond over. "I'm divorced, too," she admitted. "Only once, but it truly sucked."

"Is that how you can afford your expensive clothes?" Cecilia asked. "I can't believe any consignment store would have this season's Jimmy Choos, but I figured you had a sugar daddy and didn't want Ben to know."

"No, a successful ex-husband." Lexie didn't have to fake her look of distaste. "I dropped out of college after a year to get married and put Neil through med school, then he had seven years of residency. I worked two jobs most of the time. Finally Neil was a cardiac surgeon and making big bucks. So naturally he decided he was in love with a twenty-three-year-old massage therapist and wanted a divorce."

"The shit."

"That describes him. Luckily I had a good lawyer. Neil's going to be paying me off for years." A pity that last part was a lie, since monthly payments would not have made darling Deidre happy. Of course, the part about supporting Neil wasn't true, either—he had even more family money than Lexie did.

"I never believe any woman who claims to be friends with her ex," Cecilia said. "I hate every damn one of them."

"No argument here," Lexie said. "That's why Ben and I don't have anything serious going on. I've sworn off serious."

"Whereas I keep trying. I always think this is the guy who's going to rescue me and make me happy for the rest of my life. I'm always wrong."

"Rescue you?" Lexie's forehead furrowed. "From what?"

Cecilia waved a perfectly manicured hand. "From a life on welfare and food stamps. I dropped out of college after two years to get married, but unlike you, I didn't get a job. I've never had a job in my life, just husbands who supported me."

"Now that you'll be inheriting your grandfather's money, you'll have the opportunity to think about what you really want to do with your life," Lexie said. "Maybe you should consider a career instead of another husband. Not that it's any of my business." They hadn't bonded *that* much.

"Maybe you're right," Cecilia said, apparently unoffended by the unsolicited advice. "I viewed my inheritance as giving me breathing room before I settle on husband number four, but maybe I should go back to school instead." Her attention shifted to Dylan, who was walking into the dining room. "You're up early."

Dylan filled a coffee cup, then sat down at the table. His face was darkly stubbled, his eyes puffy, his Grateful Dead T-shirt wrinkled. "I've been having trouble sleeping since I saw Grandfather. This place gives me the creeps."

"You mean since you dreamed you saw Grandfather," Cecilia said.

"It wasn't a dream."

Seth walked into the dining room, for once without his camera. "What were you saying about seeing Grandfather?"

"That I really saw him, damn it!" Dylan said, slamming his fist on the white damask tablecloth. His cup shuddered, and coffee sloshed onto the saucer. "I didn't just dream it. He was sitting in a chair in my bedroom."

"And told you he knew what you'd done," Seth said, sitting down beside Dylan. "What was he talking about?"

"I don't know," Dylan said. "But first he told me he was sick of the way I've been wasting my life. He said if he hadn't died, he might have disinherited me just so I'd have to get my ass in gear."

"That proves it wasn't Grandfather," Cecilia said. "He'd never have disinherited you."

"I'm not so sure about that," he said, staring into his steaming coffee. "A couple of weeks before he died, he really laid into me and did say he was sick of the way I've been wasting my life. He was pissed because he'd heard a rumor I was in hock to the Mafia. I told him it wasn't true, which it isn't. Although I didn't mention I'd borrowed from an independent lender." He looked up. "Maybe Grandfather found out, and that's what he meant when he said he knew what I'd done."

"And your guilty conscience about that made you dream you saw Grandfather," Cecilia said. "Although Lexie believes you saw his ghost."

Dylan looked at Lexie. "Really?"

"You believe in ghosts?" Seth asked.

"I believe people who die untimely deaths sometimes come back to complete things they didn't finish in their lifetimes," Lexie said. "Did you and your grandfather get along while he was alive, Dylan?"

Dylan shrugged one shoulder. "Well enough. When he wasn't trying to get me to check into some rehab place."

"He was worried about you," Cecilia said. "You need to get your addictions under control, or you're going to die an early death. Like Dad did."

"I think being married to our mother might have hastened his death. Mother can be a real bitch," Dylan told Lexie. "Although luckily she was usually too busy either with her newest husband or hunting for the next to pay much attention to us."

"I'm sure Lexie doesn't want to hear about our family problems," Cecilia said.

"You should meet my mother," Lexie said. Yet another topic she and Cecilia could bond over. "Back to your grandfather's ghost. Maybe he's so worried about you that he came back to try to convince you to change. Especially now that you're inheriting enough to pay off your creditors, stop gambling, and figure out what you want to do with your life." Lexie raised her coffee cup to hide a frown. She wasn't just pretending to believe in ghosts, she was also channeling Dr. Phil.

"I've already figured it out," Dylan said, rocking back in his chair. "I'm going to enjoy myself."

"Until you run out of money," Seth said. "Then what?"

Dylan righted his chair. "I'll worry about that if it happens. It would be worse to die with unspent money."

"You're impossible." Cecilia got to her feet, shaking her head.

"Is this yours?" Lexie picked up a gold and diamond tennis bracelet on the table to the left of Cecilia's plate.

"The clasp must have come undone," Cecilia said, taking it from Lexie. "I love that bracelet. It's the only good thing husband number two left me with." She fastened the clasp, then looked up, her lips twisting ruefully. "You know, my only good memories of my husbands are a few pieces of jewelry. I think you're right—I need to take time for myself."

"You go, girl."

"I just might. Thanks for the advice. And here's some for you—if you want to stay on Ben's good side, stay away from Jeremy."

– – –

After breakfast Lexie retrieved her laptop and a file from the trunk of her car. Too bad she didn't really have a paper to write—the most arcane topic a professor could come up with would be more interesting than her work To Do list.

She was delighted when Igor stopped her the moment she stepped back into the house with a request from Trey that she come to his office. Trey probably wanted her to deliver a message to Ben, but with luck she could drag out their conversation.

Trey's office was a good-sized room just off the kitchen, furnished with a dark wood desk and matching file cabinets, as well as traditional office equipment. The floor covering, however, was decidedly untraditional—a room-sized rug in black, red, and cream, decorated with bloody daggers and spiderwebs.

"Nice carpet," Lexie said.

"A gift from Max. Sit down." Trey indicated a chair in front of his desk.

"How long have you known Ben?" he asked when Lexie was seated.

She should have guessed that Trey would be concerned about protecting the interests of his old friend's grandson. "I met him a month ago at a wedding in Lexington, but we've both agreed it's nothing serious. You don't have to worry I'm a gold-digger."

"I wasn't worried about that."

Maybe he was worried about Ben's feelings. "If I were using Ben to get his grandfather to help with my writing, I wouldn't have bothered coming here after he died," Lexie added. "In case you've heard I'm a writer."

"I hadn't," he said. "But I wouldn't be surprised if you inherited your aunt's talent, in addition to her eyes."

CHAPTER 8

Lexie blinked the eyes in question. "What are you talking about?"

"I suspected who you were when I met you," Trey said. "You really do have your aunt's eyes. When I googled your law firm and saw your photo, I knew I was right."

Denying it would clearly be futile. "Did you know Aunt Jessica well?" Lexie asked.

"Fairly well. I was usually around when she came here to visit Max. She was a charming, talented, beautiful lady. I can see why Max loved her." Trey idly tapped his pen on his legal pad. "My only question is why you're pretending to be Ben's girlfriend. If I had to guess, I'd say it was because Ben isn't satisfied that Max's death was an accident and contacted you about it and the earlier attempts on Max's life."

Lexie thought for a moment, chewing her lower lip. Ben didn't want Trey to know what they were doing out of fear he might give them away, not because he was a suspect. And Trey might be able to help. He'd worked for Max for a long time and knew the family. He'd also be anxious to see his best friend's killer brought to justice.

"Actually, Max contacted me," Lexie admitted, then explained about the letter.

When she'd finished, Trey's mouth twisted wryly. "Max always knew what buttons to push."

"I'm not going along with it just because of my duty as a lawyer," Lexie said. "It's also because Aunt Jessica would have wanted me to do it. And because I liked Max and owed him a lot."

"I can certainly understand that. Max was my best friend for more than thirty years." Trey shook his head. "I'm still having trouble believing he's gone."

"He's lucky to have had you," Lexie said. "He always told me that anything to do with money and numbers bored him so much that without you, he'd have been out on the street for failure to pay his bills."

"True." Trey smiled faintly. "Not that I could ever understand the sentiment, especially when you've got as much money as Max had, but then I'm an accountant."

Lexie laughed. "I never got it, either, but Aunt Jessica was the same way. I think it's one of those left-brain things that affects exceptionally talented artists." Then something Trey had said earlier hit her. "You knew about the prior attempts on Max's life?"

Trey nodded. "I was at Easter dinner when he had what he claimed was a gallbladder attack. A few days later his doctor asked me if Max honestly would have taken poison for a book, which is apparently how Max explained the poison. Bill and I play poker together every Thursday, and he was worried Max might be losing it. He didn't mention the kind of poison, so I assumed it was something mild and reassured the good doctor that Max was completely sane and probably had done it for a book. Max could get a little fanatic about his writing."

"What about the shooting?"

Trey pursed his lips. "I didn't know about that until Max showed me the tabloid article about it. Then I started questioning whether Max really *had* taken the poison intentionally. I didn't feel I could ask him about it since Bill had probably violated some medical privacy law mentioning it to me, although he'd assumed Max had already told me the truth. So I told Max I didn't believe any group had shot out his window, because he hadn't mentioned getting threatening letters to me. He said he didn't tell me everything and to drop it. He was so vehement that I did." Trey closed his eyes for a moment, pain flickering across his features. "God, I wish I hadn't."

"The cops probably wouldn't have found anything," Lexie said. "According to Ben, they give new meaning to 'incompetent.'"

"I might have been able to convince Max to hire a P.I.," Trey said. "Although knowing Max, probably not. And Ben's right about our local law enforcement. I assume that's why Max wanted you to check this out."

"He was also afraid that someone else might discover some unrelated family secrets during their investigation and make them public."

Trey started tapping again. "He had a point. Max has always been so protective of his privacy that the tabloids will pay a fortune for any dirt related to him or his family. They'll pay even more right after his death. But he knew you'd never expose anything, both because you were his attorney and because of your aunt. How did Ben get involved?"

"Max sent him a letter asking him to work with me."

"That doesn't surprise me. Max trusted Ben implicitly."

Something in his voice made Lexie look at him curiously. "Do you know a reason he shouldn't have?"

"Only that I don't think you should trust any beneficiary when you're dealing with as much money as Max had," Trey said. "I like Ben. For what it's worth, he's never tried to cheat me on a car repair, even though he knows I know nothing about cars and would do whatever he recommended and pay whatever he asked."

"Do you know if any family member is desperate for money?" Lexie asked.

"Muriel," Trey said immediately. "She went through all of her inheritance from her late husband making contributions to her favorite religions and is now living on her social security. She hasn't made a mortgage payment for months and is actually in danger of being foreclosed on. Which is ironic considering her late husband, Harold, was president of the bank holding the mortgage."

"Did Max know about that?"

Trey nodded. "She tried to borrow money from Max a couple of months before he died, and I couldn't help overhearing. He told her he wasn't about to finance Billy Graham's ministries, the Vatican, *Buddhism Today*, and that Wicca church or school or whatever the hell it is with his hard-earned cash."

"Would Max really have let her lose her house?"

"Probably," Trey said. "But he'd have made sure she had a place to stay, paid rent for an apartment, or bought her a condo. He might even have bought her house from the bank and let her stay there. He wouldn't want her to be homeless. Just unable to make contributions she couldn't afford."

"Anyone else?"

"Cecilia showed up a couple of days early for Easter," he said. "She seemed agitated. She had a long meeting with Max, and when it was over she was even more agitated."

"She asked him for money?"

"I don't know. I do know that Max was really upset by her most recent divorce and afraid she was turning into her mother. Max also told me that Jeremy asked for money, although not why he wanted it. Probably had some hot investment opportunity. Max turned him down."

"What about Seth?"

"I know the money he's inheriting will help him advance his career," Trey said. "And he's no doubt still furious that Max refused to force the director of *Dark Fire* to hire him as an assistant last year.

"Not that any of them would have killed Max," he added quickly. "And I'm sure Max would have helped anyone who became truly desperate. I got more from Max alive than dead, in case you suspect me."

"All you get from the trust is a year's salary as severance pay. At your insistence," Lexie said. "Max wanted to give you much more. Why did you turn it down?"

"I inherited some family money, and Max has paid me very well, so I've saved quite a bit. I don't need more money." Trey looked rueful. "What I do need is family. My wife died four years ago, and we never had kids. I consider Max's grandkids my family, and I didn't want to risk ruining my relationship with them because they resented how much I got from the trust. Especially when I'd never spend it anyway."

"Will you be looking for another job?"

He shook his head. "I think I'll retire. I'm sixty-three, and after working with Max, any other job would be a major letdown."

"Do you know what family secrets Max was concerned might be uncovered?"

"Other than what you already know, I haven't got a clue." Trey steepled his fingers. "I'm sure you've considered the possibility that when Max arranged to send you the letter, he was trying to create one last great drama, making sure if he died, someone would suspect it was murder."

Lexie nodded. "Can you think of anything else that might be relevant?" she asked.

Trey considered that for a moment, and then shook his head. "If I do, I'll let you know. It's hard for me to believe anyone in the family killed Max. But if one of them did, I want the killer punished."

Lexie got to her feet. "I'd appreciate it. I'd also appreciate it if you'd keep my identity quiet."

"Absolutely," Trey said. "Are you married?"

"Divorced. Why?"

"Because it just occurred to me that Max might have had another reason for wanting you to work with Ben on this. He could have been trying to match up his favorite grandson with Jessica's niece."

Lexie rolled her eyes. "If so, it's a good thing he was such a successful writer. Because he'd never have made it as a matchmaker."

– – –

When Lexie walked into the parlor for sherry hour that evening, everyone except for Ben and Trey was already there. "Have you seen Ben?" she asked Cecilia. "I knocked on his door before I came down, but he didn't answer." She'd also been watching out the window for his return. Much as she'd prefer to avoid him until their kiss was a distant memory, she needed to talk to him about what she'd learned from Trey.

"I don't think he's back from work yet," Cecilia said.

Jeremy draped an arm around Lexie's shoulders. "So you're on your own? Lucky for me."

Lexie deftly extricated herself from Jeremy's arm. "How was boating?"

"Terrific. You'll have to join me tomorrow."

"Do you remember when Grandfather took Dylan and Seth out sailing and convinced them that the lake was haunted and they needed to clap the entire trip to keep the ghosts from tipping over their boat?" Cecilia asked.

Jeremy chuckled. "Grandfather had the special effects crew working on the movie version of one of his books rig up some dry ice specters," he explained to Lexie. "Scared those two to death."

"Attention, everyone. Attention." Muriel was standing in front of the fireplace, waving her hands. She'd traded her habit for a deep purple caftan and silver turban. Seth was busily snapping pictures. "Later tonight I will be holding a séance. My dear brother has tried to speak to us. We need to listen."

"That was the result of the combination of Dylan and alcohol," Jeremy said. "Grandfather had nothing to do with it."

"Some of us aren't quite as narrow-minded as you seem to be, Jeremy." As Muriel waved her hands again, Lexie counted a total of six rings and three bracelets, all gold and studded with jewels.

"Why not do an exorcism?" Jeremy asked. "That way he won't bother anyone else."

"It would be unseemly to banish Maxwell from his own house, especially if he wants to tell us something. I have a special bond with him, you know," Muriel said. "Just before Easter, I predicted he would die soon. A couple of months later, he was dead."

Jeremy snorted. "He was eighty-seven. Predicting he'd die soon was a pretty safe bet."

Muriel ignored him. "The séance will be held in the living room at nine tonight, and all believers are welcome to attend," she said. "Now if you'll excuse me, I must prepare myself. Please eat dinner without me."

"Well, I'm not a believer, but I'll go if you will, Lexie," Cecilia said.

Lexie had even less desire to attend a séance than she did to make another trip to Walt's, but she was supposed to believe in ghosts.

And maybe someone would let something slip during the séance. Something that would enable her to identify Max's murderer and head back to Philadelphia tomorrow.

She didn't have to fake her enthusiasm. "Of course I'll be there. I can't wait!"

CHAPTER 9

Whatever their reasons, every family member had decided to show up at Muriel's séance, Lexie noted as she walked into the packed living room just before nine. Correction—everyone except Ben. He was no doubt stuck at work, helping yet another beautiful, sexy woman needing emergency muffler repair.

The heavy burgundy velvet drapes were drawn, blocking out every bit of dusk, and only the sconces on either side of the fireplace were lit. Muriel was sitting in a dining room chair that had been positioned in front of the fireplace, her eyes closed, her hands clasped together on her lap. Seth had already started taking pictures—documenting his eccentric Great-Aunt Muriel for his sons, no doubt.

"Trey and Ben are both lucky they're busy tonight," Cecilia said as Lexie joined her on the black leather couch.

Before Lexie could respond, Muriel spoke. "Everyone be still." She opened her eyes, stood, and turned toward the fireplace mantel, her purple caftan flowing around her. Lexie winced as she lit an incense burner only inches from the sacred Maltese falcon statue.

Muriel returned to her chair. "I'm about to contact my dear brother." She raised her hands out in front of her. "I summon the spirit of Maxwell Windsor," she singsonged. "Maxwell, if you're here, give me a sign."

Silence.

Muriel waved her hands, her jewelry glittering and flashing in the spotlight. "Maxwell, please give me a sign that you want to talk to us. You've tried before."

"Maybe he'd answer if you called him Max," Jeremy said from a chair the same black leather as the sofa. "He hated Maxwell."

"Shush," Muriel said. "Maxwell, we want to understand what you're concerned about. Max, please."

The house groaned. Lexie caught a whiff of incense.

"Told you he preferred Max," Jeremy said.

"Be still. So you are here, Max," Muriel said. "We know you've appeared to Dylan. Please tell us what you want."

The house groaned louder, like a perfectly cued movie sound effect.

"Max, we're your family. Speak through me, or speak through another who is here."

The house groaned a third time, even louder, then the wind whooshed. The incense odor was strong. The hairs rose on the back of Lexie's neck.

"Max, speak to us. Please."

But even though Muriel eventually got to her feet and paced and gestured like a television evangelist while begging Max to speak, he never said a word through anyone. After fifteen minutes, Muriel lowered her waving hands and planted them on her ample hips, letting out an exasperated sigh. "Max, would it hurt you to do what I wanted just once? You always were obstinate, even when we were kids. I know you think you run everything since you're seven years older than me and this is your house, but you're dead, for God's sake. I'm trying to help you. Come on, Max, talk to me."

Silence, not even a groan from the house.

"If you don't want my help, then tough," Muriel said. "The séance is over."

"I don't know about you, but I could use a drink," Cecilia said.

"My thoughts exactly," Lexie said.

By eleven-thirty they'd finished a bottle of wine and decided to go to bed. Ben still hadn't made it home, and Lexie was annoyed. Not because she cared that he was with some other woman. But because she and Ben were supposed to be partners. How could they be partners when he wasn't around for her to give him valuable information?

"Everyone, come here. I have a message from Maxwell."

Lexie and Cecilia raced up the stairs, then down the hallway. Muriel was standing just outside her open bedroom door. She was still wearing the purple caftan.

Muriel waited until everyone had gathered around her before speaking again. "I was trying to sleep when Maxwell's ghost woke me up!" Unlike Dylan, she seemed more excited than terrified by the encounter.

"Maxwell told me he doesn't do séances. That's why he waited until I was alone to come to me. He was standing at the end of my bed. He even motioned for me to take out my earplugs before he talked to me."

"I'm sure it was just a dream," Cecilia said, patting her aunt's arm. "The séance probably triggered it. Don't be upset."

Muriel raised her double chins. "I'm not a bit upset," she said, taking a couple of steps away from Cecilia. "I tried to summon my brother to the séance, so why would I be upset he finally appeared to me? Maxwell said he wasn't in purgatory, but he couldn't go to heaven or be reincarnated until he found out who murdered him."

"Grandfather claimed he was murdered?" Cecilia asked.

"I wouldn't put too much stock in it, since he's obviously confused," Muriel said, waving a disparaging hand. She'd at least taken off her jewelry before going to bed. "He didn't even know whether he was scheduled to go to heaven or to come back to earth as some animal."

"What else did he tell you?" Dylan asked.

"Nothing important. But he appeared to me. He really did."

"Of course he did, Aunt Muriel," Seth said. "Let's go down to the parlor and get you a little sherry so you'll sleep."

"I'd prefer a little Jack Daniel's," Muriel said, allowing Seth to lead her to the stairs.

"Where's Ben?" Jeremy asked.

"He must still be at work," Lexie said, since Jeremy was looking at her.

Jeremy checked his watch. "At eleven-thirty?"

Lexie yawned. "If the excitement's over, I'm going to bed."

"I think I'll stay up to make sure Ben makes it home before one," Jeremy said. "It would be a pity if he lost out on his share of the inheritance because he decided to"—he paused long enough to give Lexie a significant glance—"*work* all night long."

"Ben wouldn't do that." Cecilia smiled tightly. "He's not like you."

"I'll take that as a compliment. See you at breakfast, Lexie."

– – –

Jeremy was the only person eating breakfast when Lexie walked into the dining room the next morning. "You'll be happy to know Ben made it home at a quarter to one," he announced. "However, he's already gone into work again, which means you have time to go boating with me."

"Actually, I don't. I'm going to see Ben at work."

Jeremy raised an eyebrow. "Do you think that's a good idea? You might not be real happy to discover what he's working on."

"I'll risk it."

After a quick cup of coffee and half a scone, Lexie strode out of the house.

"How's it hanging, Lexie?"

The speaker was a man with thinning dark brown hair and the build, beefy neck, and paunch of a former football player a few decades out of playing condition. He was leaning against a white Cadillac with Ontario plates parked in the circular driveway. Lexie had never seen him before in her life.

"Excuse me, but have we met?" she asked.

"No, but I've heard all about you," he said, walking toward her. He was wearing khakis, a tight scarlet polo shirt, and white loafers. "I like a woman with balls. And my fourth wife was an exotic dancer."

Lexie blinked at the non sequitur as the man extended his hand. He wore a pinky ring with a diamond nearly as large as the rock sported by her mother's best friend, Bitsy Davenport, and exuded a mixture of toughness, spicy cologne, and breath mints. "The name's Jack Pierre Jackson," he said. "J-A-C-K, not Jacques. My mom was from Quebec, but my dad put his foot down on my first name. You can call me J.P."

"Are you here visiting one of the family?" Lexie asked.

"I'm here checking on my investment."

"You invested in Nevermore?" Surely she'd have heard.

"Hell, no. I'm talking about Dylan Windsor. He owed a friend of mine from Vegas money, and I bought the debt. Since I was in the area, I'm checking whether he's fucked up getting his inheritance."

She should have guessed. "So far he hasn't."

"Happy to hear it, especially since I paid nearly face value for the thing. Not including interest, of course."

"Does he owe you a lot?"

"Enough that I'd like to get repaid. Even if I have to break a few bones to do it."

Lexie's heart hit a speed bump, and her eyes widened.

J.P. grinned, holding up his hand. "I was kidding. I don't work that way."

He certainly hadn't sounded as if he were kidding. If she were smart, she'd say good-bye and leave. On the other hand, this was her chance to find out more about Dylan's motive, and he was high on her suspect list. Surely she was safe in broad daylight.

Lexie cleared her throat and plunged. "I hope you won't find this question impolite, but are you with the Mafia?"

J.P. spit on the lush grass that edged the sidewalk, just missing one loafer. "Don't I wish. But the fucking Americans don't give us Canadians no respect, and the Canadian families think you gotta live in Montreal or Toronto to be worth anything. Which is a bunch of shit. I mean, I might be in Thunder Bay, but I ain't no amateur, let me tell you. I've whacked more guys than any of their soldiers." He raised his hand again. "Not no more, of course. My fifth wife's got a soft heart and made me quit. And I never whacked anyone except in self-defense. I wouldn't want you to think badly of me."

"I don't," Lexie said, shaking her head for emphasis. She wasn't about to offend a man who bragged about whacking people for any reason, even self-defense.

"So because everyone's so damned prejudiced, I'm stuck deal-ing with deadbeats like Dylan Windsor with only a half-dozen guys to help me out."

"Maybe you should sue for discrimination."

J.P. chuckled. "Beautiful and got a sense of humor. You really do remind me of my fourth wife."

"Do you want to talk to Dylan?" Lexie asked, changing the subject before he remembered the things he didn't like about his fourth wife. She was an ex, after all.

"I wanna make sure he understands he better not blow his

chance at getting some of his grandfather's money." He glanced at an enormous gold watch. "If you could give him the message, I'd appreciate it. I'm running late."

"I'll tell him."

"I'd also consider it a personal favor if you'd do whatever you can to make sure he don't fuck up."

Just what she needed, being held responsible for an alcoholic gambler. She shifted uncomfortably. "I'm not that close to Dylan."

"Don't worry that I'll blame you if he screws up, 'cause I won't," J.P. said, obviously noticing her discomfiture. "But if you do have the chance to help me, I'd consider it a favor, like I said. I don't forget nobody what does me a favor."

"I'll try. Is it all right if I deliver your message to Dylan later today?" Lexie asked. "He's still asleep, and I need to see Ben."

"No problem. And tell Ben he's a lucky man." J.P. winked. "I can tell you're a hell of a woman, and having been married five times, I'm somewhat of an authority on women."

"I appreciate the support. It's been nice meeting you, J.P."

"The pleasure's all mine, Lexie."

Lexie leaned against Nevermore's cool stone façade to support her weak knees as she watched J.P. get into his Cadillac and drive off. When she'd first arrived at Nevermore, she'd thought she'd slid into a version of Wonderland. She'd been half-joking.

She'd been right.

– – –

Lexie hadn't been in Lakeview since her first day in Minnesota, when she'd been so focused on finding Ben's garage that she'd barely noticed the rest of Main Street. If you ignored Lake Superior—which was hard to do since it filled the horizon—the place resembled

Mayberry from the old *Andy Griffith Shows* she'd watched on cable with their housekeeper, until her mother had found out and informed her Barringtons didn't watch that sort of thing. Cars in vintages spanning the last forty years were angle-parked along both sides of wide Main Street. The stores and cafes didn't appear to have been remodeled since the sixties; two barbershops had red, white, and blue spinning poles; and the movie theater had only one screen. The five bars were all grouped together on the block before the railroad tracks that marked the end of the business district, away from the more family-oriented merchants. There wasn't a coffee bar, fast food restaurant, or bagel place in sight; the only things that would have confounded Aunt Bea were the cell phone dealer and the sign in the window of the hardware store advertising computer repair.

As Lexie stepped into Ben's garage, it was déjà vu all over again, complete with the scent of eau de oil, the blaring country music, and Ben's legs protruding from beneath a vehicle. This time she didn't waste time trying to speak loud enough for him to notice her. Instead she switched off the music, and then pounded on the Camry's hood. "We need to talk, Ben."

He slowly slid out from under the car and sat up. "Can't it wait? I'm a bit busy."

"No, it can't wait." Finding Max's murderer was taking long enough without Ben delaying things. "If you'd ditched whatever woman you were with at a more reasonable hour last night, we could have talked when you got home. Since you didn't—"

"If you're here to tell me about Aunt Muriel's séance and supposed conversation with Grandfather, Cecilia already filled me in."

"I'm not." And she wasn't moving until he talked to her. She planted her hands on her hips.

Ben got the message. He stood, wiping his hands on his jeans. "I guess I can afford a short break. Let's go to my office."

CHAPTER 10

Ben hadn't turned on the air conditioner today, but since the outside temperature was in the low seventies, the office was only a little stuffy. Lexie opened the mini-fridge and checked inside. "You're out of bottled water," she said, and then sat down on one of the folding chairs.

"Sorry, but I wasn't expecting you. Trudy made coffee."

"I'll pass." She'd smelled Trudy's coffee when she'd come in. The stuff was so overheated she was surprised it didn't trigger the smoke alarms. Lexie pulled a notepad out of her purse and opened it to today's To Do list.

Ben shut the door. "What's so damned important?"

"For one thing, I had an interesting conversation with Dylan's loan shark." That wasn't on her list, but it seemed a good place to start.

"When?"

"When I came out of the house this morning. He wanted to warn Dylan not to screw up and lose his share of the trust."

Ben's jaw dropped, and he plopped down on the other folding chair. "I thought you meant you talked to him on the phone. He showed up at Nevermore?"

She nodded. "He's from Thunder Bay and bought Dylan's loan. The good news is that he isn't Mafia, although he'd like to be. J.P. complained that the American and Canadian Mafia families won't let him affiliate, even though he's probably whacked more people than they have."

Ben's jaw dropped a couple more notches. "He what?"

"Killed people, but only in self-defense, he claims. And he's quit now."

Ben rested a hand on her arm. "Did he hurt you? Or threaten you?"

"Not a bit," Lexie said. "He was actually quite pleasant."

"Thank God," Ben said, removing his hand. "Did this J.P. talk to Dylan?"

Lexie shook her head. "I told him I'd relay his message, so he left. I also wanted to tell you that Trey figured out who I really am."

"How?"

"I have my aunt's eyes."

"What's your aunt got to do with anything?"

"She was Jessica Stuart."

Ben looked even more shocked than when she'd told him about Dylan's loan shark. "Your aunt was the famous romance writer?"

"And the love of your grandfather's life. Besides your grandmother, of course."

"Don't bother being tactful," Ben said. "I barely remember my grandmother, and I know for a fact that Grandfather loved Jessica much more. He admitted that he cheated all the time on Grandmother, but never once on Jessica. His greatest regret was that Jessica never married him."

"She wasn't a fan of marriage, which is a little ironic for a romance writer whose books always ended with marriage and happily ever after," Lexie said. "She was my mother's only sister."

"Is that how you met Grandfather? Through your aunt?"

"Indirectly," Lexie said. "I never met him while Aunt Jessica was alive, probably because she knew my mother didn't approve of their romance and might use that as an excuse to keep me from visiting her. But Aunt Jessica had told Max about me and that I was a lawyer in Philadelphia. After she died, I think Max wanted to keep a connection with her family, so he came to me. I was only a third-year associate when I brought in not only Max Windsor's estate-planning business but most of his other business. The partners immediately stopped treating me like toilet paper stuck to the sole of a shoe, and my work life improved immensely. I owe Max big-time for that."

"Is that why you pretended to be a writer? Because of your aunt?"

Lexie shrugged. "For a while I was a writer. Aunt Jessica encouraged me, and I had three romances published. My mother didn't approve, even though I used a pen name. I'm not sure whether it was more because I wrote something she considered lowbrow or because she disapproved of the sex. She was already scandalized by what her sister wrote."

"I met Jessica a few times when I was a kid," Ben said. "Why didn't you tell me she was your aunt?"

"It never came up." To be honest, she'd also feared he'd use that information to guilt her into staying and investigating. "Trey knew Jessica's niece was Max's lawyer, and he also knew my name. He checked out my photo on my law firm website to confirm his suspicions. I doubt anyone else would recognize me simply because of my eyes."

"You're probably right. Especially considering how different your aunt was from you."

"Aunt Jessica definitely didn't have a stick up her ass." Lexie smiled faintly. "Max got that phrase from her. She always used it to describe my mother." Her smile faded. "Trey also gave me information about possible motives." She related what Trey had told her. "Did you learn anything else?"

"Cecilia confirmed that she could use the money, but claims she's got enough to get by for a while," Ben said. "She hasn't gotten back to me with specifics about Dylan's debt, and I haven't had time to call Olivia about Jeremy. So I guess everyone is still a suspect."

Lexie tapped her pen against her To Do list. "Although the more I get to know everyone, the harder it is to believe any one of them would have murdered Max. Maybe no one was trying to kill him at all. Maybe all of this was Max creating his last fictional work."

"The poisoning and shooting weren't accidents."

"Maybe Max staged both incidents, then wrote the letters to us so that when he eventually died, we'd suspect it had been murder. If he'd lived longer, he might have staged even more incidents."

"I can't imagine Grandfather doing that." Ben was drumming his fingers on the paper-strewn desktop.

"Why not? Max earned a fortune setting scenes and manipulating people into suspending disbelief."

Ben's fingers halted. "What are you saying?"

This hadn't been on today's To Do list, either, but talking to Ben had made it clear it should be. "I'm saying that I never thought I was qualified to solve this in the first place, but I owed it to Max to give it a shot. Well, I have, and I'm no closer to figuring out who did it than when I arrived. I'm not even sure there was a murder. I also can't keep charging the trust for my fees when I'm not accomplishing anything. I think it's time to call in a professional."

"I won't hire a private investigator. Grandfather didn't want that."

"It isn't your decision, Ben," Lexie said. "It's the trustee's obligation to make sure Max's murderer, if there is one, doesn't get anything from the trust. I'm sure someone at my firm can recommend a discreet P.I."

Ben stared at the ceiling for a moment. "Look, you like lists," he finally said, meeting her eyes. "How about we make a list of everything we know about every beneficiary, even things that seem irrelevant, then see where we are. We also haven't looked into where everyone was when Grandfather died. Or when the window was shot out."

"As you pointed out, anyone could have hired a killer."

"We should at least find out. There are probably other things we've missed."

"A private investigator would find out the same things," Lexie said. "Plus things we're too inexperienced to realize are important."

"We also haven't uncovered the family secrets Grandfather was afraid would come out. Your aunt would have wanted you to protect his family and his reputation. It's possible some of those secrets concern her."

Her aunt was long dead and would probably have relished a scandal even if she were alive. But Lexie had been right to worry that Ben would try to use Aunt Jessica to guilt her into investigating, and it was working. She let out a resigned breath. "Okay. I'll wait until we've at least discussed it before I advise the trustee to hire a P.I."

Ben got to his feet. "Let's go."

"Go where?"

"To Lee's Market. Apparently I'm out of bottled water."

"I can live without it," Lexie said. "We still have one more thing to discuss."

"After we go to Lee's. I need a couple of other things there anyway. Close the door behind you." He took off.

Lexie could either follow him or go back to Nevermore. She wasn't about to leave town until she'd brought up one last issue. So she followed.

While Ben made his purchases in Lee's Market, Lexie checked out the store. It had a surprisingly good variety of merchandise, including many gourmet ingredients and what appeared to be high-quality meat and vegetables. It also had more flavors of Jell-O and versions of Hamburger, Chicken, and Tuna Helper than she'd dreamed existed.

When she walked up to the counter where Ben was checking out, he draped an arm around her shoulders. "Your secret's out. Ruth knows you aren't a cocktail waitress."

A name tag identified Ruth as the clerk checking Ben out. So much for Lexie's confidence that no one besides Trey would recognize her.

"Amber told her, but Ruth said she should have guessed from the way you walk," Ben added.

"The way I walk?" People had a lot of stereotypes about attorneys in general and even more about female ones, but she'd never heard anything about a distinctive walk.

"Yep. It's obvious you're really an exotic dancer. I told Ruth you preferred that to being called a stripper."

Lexie stared at him, speechless.

"That isn't a problem," Ruth said before Lexie could manage a response. "Most people in town are broad-minded and realize that's just another job. Assuming all you do is take off your clothes and dance."

"If she did more than that, she wouldn't be with me," Ben said.

Ruth nodded, her gray bouffant so heavily lacquered the curls didn't even quiver. "You always did have high morals, Ben. You've also got your pick of women, so she must be a good one."

"She is." He squeezed Lexie's shoulder. "And she does a hell of a pole dance."

Apparently Ruth didn't know what a pole dance was or she considered it permissible, since she seemed to take it in stride. She handed Ben his change. "It's been nice meeting you, Lexie."

"You, too," Lexie got out. "People think I'm a stripper?" she asked the instant they stepped out of the store.

"I'd think you'd be flattered. I told Ruth you were very talented and had even performed in Las Vegas, but moved back to Lexington to take care of your sick mother. You use most of your salary to pay for her medicine and medical expenses."

"And I do a hell of a pole dance."

"I was going to make it a lap dance, but I didn't want Ruth to think I'd have a girlfriend who spent her time wiggling around on top of other men." He grinned. "I don't care who looks, but I'm the only one who gets to touch."

"You're enjoying this, aren't you?"

"I have to admit having a stripper girlfriend will improve my standing with the guys at Walt's."

Lexie rolled her eyes. "I'm so happy to be of service. Who did you say told Ruth?"

"Amber Morris. My most recent ex-girlfriend."

"The one you broke up with the other night?"

"Yep. Although I distinctly remember telling her you were a cocktail waitress. But don't worry. Ruth will spread around that you're also helping out your mother. So even if some people consider you a slut, they'll know that at least you're one with a heart of gold."

Lexie burst out laughing. She couldn't help it—this whole thing was absurd. "Max would have loved this."

"He would have," Ben agreed. "What else do we need to discuss?"

Lexie's smile faded. "Let's wait until we get back to your office."

"What is it?" Ben asked when they were again seated in his office.

Lexie hesitated. This was uncomfortable, but she had to bring it up. "Look, I don't want you to think I've gone off the deep end. But do you think it's possible Max is haunting Nevermore?"

"I thought you didn't believe in ghosts."

"I didn't think I did," Lexie said. "But both Dylan and Muriel swear they saw him. And after Muriel mentioned murder—"

Ben's expression shifted, only for an instant, but long enough that Lexie caught it. "I knew it," she said. "You're wondering the same thing, right?"

"No, but—" The phone interrupted him. "What is it, Trudy?

"For the record, I don't think Nevermore is haunted by anyone," he said after he hung up. "I have to take care of a customer. Anything else we need to discuss?"

"That's it. I just need a couple of minutes to finish my notes," Lexie said. "What time will you be home tonight? So we can analyze possible suspects?"

He got to his feet. "We'll have to do it tomorrow. Tonight we're going to a street dance."

"I'm not going to a street dance."

"Have you ever been to one?"

"No, and I have no desire to. I saw the poster for this one. The band playing is called Miles and the Muleskinners, for God's sake."

"They're very good. I'm going, and it will look strange if you don't come along." Ben opened the office door. "Especially considering you dance for a living."

"As I told you before, I'm on vacation."

"Your loss." Then he left, shutting the door behind him.

Lexie spent a couple of minutes updating her notes and To Do list, then opened the office door to the day's second bout of déjà vu. Just like the first day, Ben was talking to yet another stacked bimbo, this one a brunette dressed in a tight pink T-shirt and denim miniskirt. Okay, so Lexie didn't know for a fact that she was a bimbo, although if life were fair, no one who looked like that would also be brain surgeon material.

The woman was standing so close to Ben that one of her breasts was pressed against his arm. "I'm looking forward to seeing you tonight," she said. "I'll save you a couple of dances."

Lexie strode toward her. "Sorry, but Ben's dance card is full. I'm Lexie. Ben's girlfriend." She extended her hand.

The woman ignored it. "You didn't mention you'd be bringing anyone to the dance, Ben."

Lexie wrapped both hands around Ben's forearm and pulled him away from the other woman. "He probably didn't think it was necessary since the entire town knows I'm here."

"I thought you planned to skip the dance, Lexie," Ben said.

Lexie met the other woman's eyes. "You misunderstood, Ben. I wouldn't miss it."

The woman stared at Lexie for a moment. Then she turned and sauntered away.

"What was that about?" Ben asked. "I thought you refused to go."

"What you do behind my back is your own business, but I don't appreciate you acting like that in front of me," Lexie said. "I'll see you later."

Then she turned and strode out of the garage, frowning. Why the hell had she agreed to go to that dance, especially since she suspected Ben had manipulated her into it? But it was too late to get out of it. Rule Number 6—once an invitation has been accepted, it's as binding as any written contract. She'd bested that woman, but now she was obligated to go to a street dance with Ben. Life just kept getting better and better.

She also didn't have a thing to wear. The four suits she'd brought were out, she was sick of her jeans and her khaki skirt, and the only tops that might be appropriate were dirty and had to be dry-cleaned. She was going to have to check out The Clothes Garden after all. God willing, they'd have something without ruffles and flowers. Her frown deepened. And something that was appropriate for an exotic dancer.

At least they wouldn't be surprised when she paid cash.

– – –

The entire Main Street had been cordoned off for the dance. Porta Potties were strategically placed all around the area. A six-member band with guitars, fiddles, and too much facial hair was twanging up-tempo tunes on a raised wooden stage as dancing couples swirled around them. A refreshment counter set up in front of Lee's Market already had long lines at the four beer windows.

Lexie had been hoping rain—or even a June snowstorm—would force a cancellation, but no such luck. The night was clear and warm, the sun turning the sky a peachy rose and making the scene glow.

"Thanks for coming with me," she told Cecilia as they walked to the edge of the dancing area.

"I was planning to go even before Ben got held up at work," Cecilia said. "I've never been to a street dance, but it's got to be more fun than watching Aunt Muriel say rosaries for Grandfather's soul, or reruns of TV shows that shouldn't have been broadcast the first time. That dress looks great on you, by the way."

Lexie smoothed the skirt of her sapphire cotton sundress. "Thanks. I got it at The Clothes Garden, along with these." She lifted one foot. "I've always wanted silver sandals, and not just because my mother would have a fit if she saw them. Did Ben have any idea when he'd get here?" He hadn't bothered to call her but had instead phoned Cecilia, asking her to drive Lexie and relay the message he was stuck at work and would meet her at the dance.

"He didn't think it would take very long, but who knows?"

Lexie nodded. Who knows how long it would take Ben to satisfy the brunette he'd no doubt arranged to meet at the garage, since his pretend girlfriend had made fun at the dance with the brunette an impossibility. After he'd used said brunette to convince said girlfriend to go to this stupid street dance.

"Ben told me he knew how much you were looking forward to the street dance and didn't want you to miss out on a single minute of it," Cecilia continued.

"How sweet of him," Lexie said. "Let's go get something to drink."

– – –

Ben paced back and forth between the bed and chair. "We've got a problem," he said, raking his fingers through his hair. "Catherine plans to go back to Philadelphia and hire a P.I. to investigate. She doesn't think she should be wasting the trust's money when she isn't accomplishing anything. Especially since she's not even convinced there really was a murder."

Max Windsor smiled. "I told you she was damn smart."

CHAPTER 11

"If Catherine wants to leave, you'll have to convince her to stay," Max continued, rocking back in his chair. "We need her."

Ben stopped pacing and narrowed his eyes at his grandfather. "Just like you could convince her aunt to do something she didn't want to?"

Max grinned, righting his chair. "She told you about Jessica, did she?"

"It would have been nice if you had. I think Catherine inherited the stubborn streak you complained Jessica had."

"Catherine's always been agreeable to me."

"That's because you're her client. Trey figured out who she is, by the way. When he confronted her, she admitted what we're doing."

"That's probably a good thing," Max said. "Trey might be able to help you."

"Of course, Catherine has no clue what we're really doing." Ben didn't even try to hide his disgust. "I think I should tell her the truth. She'd be more help with all the facts. And I feel guilty about keeping her in the dark." So guilty that if he hadn't been interrupted by Tina, he would have told her the truth this morning when she was discussing the possibility Nevermore was haunted.

"You can't tell her," Max said, his tone encased in steel. "The more people who know, the more chance it will leak out."

Ben resumed pacing in the windowless secret room that he'd had no idea existed until Grandfather had proposed playing dead and haunting people by using secret passages Ben also hadn't realized existed. "Catherine's not going to tell anyone. Maybe knowing the truth will make her more willing to stay."

"It could also make her more likely to leave, since if I'm not dead, she doesn't have to worry about who gets the trust. She'll also be upset she was kept in the dark this long."

"We might as well risk it. She plans to leave anyway."

"I'm sure you won't let that happen."

Ben stopped pacing and turned on his grandfather, resting his hand on the microwave atop the dresser. "How the hell am I supposed to prevent it?"

"You could take her to bed. That always made Jessica more agreeable."

Ben snorted. "I think trying that would have the opposite effect on Catherine. Even if she stays, we're at a dead end. Look at this." He walked over to the nightstand, picked up the notebook he'd set on top of a pile of mail, and flipped through it. He handed the open notebook to his grandfather.

"What is this?" Max asked.

"A list of everyone's possible motives."

Max raised an eyebrow. "I thought you were opposed to making lists on principle."

"Only To Do lists, and that's because they can distract you from what's really important. Catherine wants to discuss everything we found out, and I didn't want to risk forgetting anything. By the way, she's addicted to lists. Including To Do lists."

"I'm not surprised."

"The bottom line is that every single trust beneficiary theoretically has motive and opportunity, but there's absolutely no evidence who made the attempts on your life," Ben said. "Catherine thinks we should hire a P.I. to investigate, and I agree."

"I told you why I don't want an outsider involved."

Ben threw up his hands. "Because you're afraid family secrets will come out. Yet you won't tell me *what* family secrets."

"That's because I don't know what they are."

Ben's temper flared, and his tone sharpened. "You mean there aren't any secrets? You just used that possibility to convince us not to hire a P.I.?"

"I didn't say that," Max said calmly. "Considering my family, there could very well be all sorts of secrets out there, especially where my son Allen was involved. Dylan definitely takes after him, and not in a good way. Besides, a P.I. would have a better chance of discovering I'm still alive. You can distract Catherine, but you'd have a tougher time with a P.I. As long as no one knows I'm alive, I'm safe."

"A P.I. would also have a better chance of finding whoever tried to murder you."

"I'm not convinced of that," Max said, rubbing his chin again. "Catherine is extremely perceptive, and the two of you are more likely to get information than a P.I. would. Especially since right now the guilty party doesn't suspect anyone even knows a crime was committed."

"You blew that by telling Aunt Muriel you were murdered," Ben said.

"It slipped out," Max said. "No one takes anything my sister says seriously. But hiring a P.I. would broadcast to everyone that you suspect I was murdered." He let out a long breath. "It would also mean I'd have to turn the guilty party over to the police."

Ben's jaw dropped. He plopped down on the bed and stared at his grandfather. "You might not prosecute whoever's trying to kill you?"

Max shrugged. "It depends on who it is and the circumstances. I want to keep that option open."

"We're talking about attempted murder, not stealing a couple of candlesticks from your parlor," Ben said, gesturing broadly.

"We're also talking about family," Max said. "I don't think Catherine believed me when I said my motivation for the two-week requirement was my hope that you all would realize how important family is and start getting along better."

"Your motivation for that provision was because you wanted to help Catherine and me identify whoever's trying to kill you."

"Partly. But getting older has made me appreciate the importance of family. Especially now that I've faced death twice."

"If we find the guilty party, don't you think Catherine will insist on going to the police?" Ben asked.

"I've got a better chance of convincing her to keep quiet than I do a P.I.," Max said. "I know you didn't like this from the start. But you said you'd do it because you love me—"

"*When* I thought Catherine and I had a reasonable chance of identifying whoever wants to kill you," Ben said. "I've changed my mind. I worry you'll get hurt."

"How can I get hurt when everyone thinks I'm dead?" Max asked. "I want to continue with the original plan. If you won't go along out of love, then do it because I rescued you from your father years ago. I did that because I love you and because you're Rebecca's son, but it doesn't alter the fact that I had to make a lot of changes to accommodate a teenage boy. You owe me. I'm cashing in my chips."

Grandfather's expression was so stony it could have graced Mount Rushmore. Ben knew that look. He'd have more luck arguing with one of the granite presidents. "All right. I'll do my best to keep Catherine from leaving or hiring anyone. Now I'd better get to the street dance."

Like he'd told Lexie, no one could ever convince Grandfather of anything.

— — —

Lexie and Cecilia had been watching the dancers, sipping Diet Cokes, and waiting for Ben for more than an hour when a blond man approached them. He had a typical Scandinavian build and features, attractive but not heart-stoppingly handsome, with a slightly crooked nose that added character. "You must be Cecilia," he said, giving her a smile that shifted him into the heart-stopping category. "Ben's told me about you. I'm Peter Carlson."

"I'm happy to meet you," Cecilia said. "This is Lexie, Ben's girlfriend."

Peter turned his smile on her. "I've heard about you, too."

Lexie rolled her eyes. "I can imagine," she said. "For your information, I am not nor have I ever been an exotic dancer. And my mother hasn't been sick a day in her life."

"What are you talking about?" Cecilia asked. From her confused expression, at least one person didn't inhale Lakeview gossip.

"Ask Ben," Lexie said. "On second thought, don't bother. He's enjoying this too much."

"Where is Ben anyway?" Peter asked.

"He got stuck at work, and Cecilia was nice enough to babysit me," Lexie said. "If you two want to dance, go ahead." If Ben had told Peter about Cecilia, he'd probably been trying to fix them up.

"I'm enjoying talking to both of you," Peter said gallantly.

"I think the point of a street dance is to dance," Lexie said. Despite the band's unfortunate name, it was pretty good and more country pop than hardcore country western. Especially now that their only female member had shown up, a Carrie Underwood look-and-sound-alike who'd been delayed by babysitter problems.

"While I wait for Ben, I'll check on Dylan," Lexie added. "Make sure he isn't drunk enough to have decided to take off to a casino for the night." A legitimate concern, as they were within easy driving distance of a couple of Native American–operated casinos. J.P. might not hold her responsible for Dylan's behavior, but he'd probably appreciate it if she made an effort. Even though he claimed to have stopped whacking people, she'd like to stay on J.P.'s good side.

"Thanks," Cecilia said. "I don't see Dylan dancing, so I'll bet he's near the beer."

Lexie was halfway to the beer stand when she ran into Jeremy. In black trousers and an olive silk shirt—both perfectly tailored and obviously expensive—he looked more like he belonged at her country club than a street dance.

"Where's Ben?" Jeremy asked.

"At work. I came with Cecilia, who's out dancing."

"Let's join her." He took Lexie's arm. "I heard you're an exotic dancer," he said as they made their way to the dancing area.

"Sorry, but it isn't true. My mother would probably keel over dead if I were."

"Your sick mother," Jeremy said.

"Not sick, just stuffy and snobbish. That rumor's false, too." She grinned. "Do you still want to dance with me?"

"Absolutely."

A hand clamped over Lexie's free arm. "I'm claiming this dance."

Lexie turned toward Ben, who'd managed to sneak up on her. He was wearing a pair of tight jeans, a camp shirt that matched his eyes, and cowboy boots. Unlike Jeremy, he definitely fit in with tonight's crowd.

"She's dancing with me," Jeremy said, his hand tightening on Lexie's arm.

"Wrong," Ben said. "Since she's here as my date, she dances with me. Her mother would be appalled if she didn't. Right, Lexie?"

Rule Number 33. Lexie sighed. "He's right, Jeremy. Sorry. Maybe later."

Jeremy released her arm as Ben led her toward the dancers. "How do you know my mother would be appalled if I ever refused my date's request to dance?" she asked.

"I'm starting to figure her out. She's big on manners and propriety and that kind of crap, right?"

"Manners and propriety aren't crap. They're essential to a civilized society."

He snorted.

"Although you're right about my mother," Lexie admitted. "On my eighth birthday, she gave me a leather-bound notebook containing thirty rules of good manners, proper social behavior, and appropriate dress. The book also had blank pages so I could add new rules whenever the situation warranted. Rules Mother came up with and ordered me to write down."

Ben dropped her arm. "You've got to be kidding."

Lexie held up her hand. "Swear to God. My sister got one, too. I actually still write in it, although now I put in my own rules. I'm up to number 148."

"Like what?"

Like never getting involved with any man who calls you "babe," but mentioning that one to the man who'd inspired it would violate several other rules. "Like never drink anything with tequila or an umbrella in it," she said instead. "Or one of Walt's specials, I guess

I should add. Never eat sushi in a restaurant that misspells it on the menu." She grimaced. "And never get a massage."

"What do you have against massages?"

"Long story."

Fortunately Ben let it go, since Lexie wasn't in the mood to discuss her failed marriage. He took her into his arms and started dancing what must be a two-step. She'd never attempted it in her life, but thanks to years of ballroom dance lessons, she picked it up fast. It helped that Ben was an excellent dancer.

"You don't have to worry about any of that now, since only Trey and I know who you really are," Ben said as he steered her through the other dancers. "You get to act like a cocktail waitress who doesn't give a damn about what your mother considers appropriate behavior."

"Pretending to be a college dropout cocktail waitress who's having an affair with a mechanic would already offend my mother's idea of appropriate behavior so much that anything else I do is superfluous," Lexie said. "She's kind of a snob."

"I got that impression," Ben said. "Tell me honestly—aren't you enjoying not having to live up to her standards?"

She pondered that for a moment. "It's fun, but only in the short term. It's like taking a vacation somewhere you enjoy visiting but would never want to live."

"You might be surprised."

"I don't think so," Lexie said. "I can't overcome the way I was raised."

"I assume your aunt was raised the same way as your mother and managed to overcome it."

Lexie chewed her lip. "I'd feel too guilty about how much I was upsetting my mother. Even if I don't like some of the things she does, I still love her. Where does your dad live?" Her mother was up there with her marriage on tonight's Do Not Discuss list.

"In California," Ben said. "I'm a complete failure in his eyes. But I'm not in the mood to discuss that bastard."

The dance had ended, and the group started playing a ballad. Ben wrapped his arms around Lexie, and then pulled her close. "Act like you're crazy about me. We need to convince the local gossips we're a real couple. Especially the ones who noticed you were about to dance with Jeremy. Think you can pull it off?"

"How can you ask that? Considering the exceptional job I've been doing playing your dippy girlfriend."

A smile ruffled his mouth. "To be honest, you've had problems with the dippy part. But thanks to the exotic dancer rumor, most people are too busy looking at you to listen to what you're saying." He pulled her tighter against him, crushing her breasts against his chest and moving one hand to her butt. "You really do have an exceptional ass."

She removed his hand. "If you touch it again, I'm having you arrested for assault."

"Obviously you aren't drunk." He kissed her neck, then his tone lowered and roughened. "Which is a good thing, since the way you look tonight, I feel like doing more than just dancing with you. And I don't take advantage of drunk women." He put his lips to her ear. "Pretend like you're turned on."

His touch, his tone, and his words did make Lexie's body heat, but she certainly wasn't about to admit it. "I'm not that good an actress."

"Give it a shot." He caressed her bare upper back, triggering goose bumps. His body had responded, too, although that just meant Ben was male—a stiff breeze could trigger the same reaction.

Ben reached down and cupped her butt again, pressing her harder against him. It felt so good Lexie didn't even consider telling him to move it or lose it. Her entire body was throbbing, just as it had when she'd blamed it on being drunk. Except now she was sober.

"How am I doing?" she asked, attempting to lighten the mood. "My acting, I mean." To her disgust, she sounded breathless.

"Babe, you deserve an Oscar." He kissed her neck.

Remember Rule 148. Guys who call you "babe" are bad news. Lexie's brain told her that, but she ignored it. "Good," she got out just before his lips met hers.

He tasted of mint, which she'd never realized was an aphrodisiac. Although her sprinting heart and melting body were probably due more to the soft pressure and heat of Ben's lips and tongue as he expertly kissed her.

His fingers slipped under one strap of her sundress, caressing the crest of her breast. The Clothes Garden hadn't stocked strapless bras, so Lexie was braless tonight. Her nipple pearled, and she shifted against Ben, silently urging him to move his fingers lower.

"I think we should get out of here," he murmured, his lips a fraction of an inch from hers.

"Because people would expect us to."

"Right. Cecilia drove, didn't she?" He kissed her again.

"Sorry to interrupt, Ben, but Cecilia needs help."

Peter's voice broke through Lexie's lust-induced stupor.

"Dylan's about to get into a fight with Lyle Martin," he continued. "Cecilia's trying to calm him down, but it isn't working."

Ben released Lexie. "Damn. Where is he?"

"In Lee's parking lot," Peter said.

Lexie followed Ben and Peter off the dance floor. It was amazing how fast her mind focused and her hormones cooled down. Probably because she didn't want any beneficiary besides the one she was sure had killed Max to end up in jail overnight and therefore lose out on the trust, since that could trigger a lawsuit that would upset the trustee. And she especially didn't want that to happen to Dylan, which would also upset J.P.

A dozen people had gathered to watch the show going on in the blacktopped parking lot of Lee's Market.

"Ben. Thank God," Cecilia said when she spotted him. "He won't listen to me."

"I'm going to knock you on your fat ass," Dylan said. His hair was halfway out of his ponytail, and he was nose to nose with a guy who was bigger and presumably just as drunk as he was.

"Who are you calling a fat ass?"

Ben stepped up and took Dylan's arm, pulling him away from his opponent. "Dylan, it's time to leave."

"I was dancing with Mary Lynn, and he butted in. I have to defend my honor. And Mary Lynn's honor."

"I don't think that's a good idea."

"Why not?"

"He's too chicken to fight me," Lyle said.

"I'm not chicken. Ben, this asshole claims he's gonna bust my pretty face, but I'll show him. I'll beat the shit out of him." Dylan tried unsuccessfully to shake free of Ben's arm.

In response, Ben grabbed Dylan's other arm. "Maybe you will, but if you beat the shit out of Lyle, you'll be hauled to jail." His calm tone was a marked contrast to Dylan's belligerence. "We won't be able to get you out until tomorrow, so you'll miss out on spending tonight at Nevermore. You know what that means, don't you?"

"That I'll lose Grandfather's money?"

"At least you're sober enough to remember that," Ben said. "Do you honestly think punching out this guy is worth all those millions?"

"I forgot the bastard's loaded," Lyle said. "Hell, I'm going to sue him for threatening me."

"Trust me, you don't have a case," Lexie said.

Lyle looked at her and snorted. "You're the stripper, aren't you? What the hell do you know about suing people?"

Lexie lifted her chin. "Actually, I'm a cocktail waitress. Some of my best customers are lawyers, so I've learned a lot about lawsuits. You bring a frivolous one, and the judge won't like it. You'll end up paying a whole lot of attorneys' fees and court costs. You'll probably also end up paying Dylan a fortune, since from what I heard, you threatened him more than he did you. In front of a lot of witnesses."

Ben smiled at the petite redhead who was watching the fight with interest. "You'll have to stick with your fiancé tonight, Mary Lynn. Dylan has to go." He turned his attention to Cecilia. "Lexie and I were about to leave, so we'll take him home."

"Mary Lynn is engaged to that bozo?" Dylan asked as he, Ben, and Lexie made their way to Ben's truck.

"Yep."

"Why'd she come and ask me to dance?"

"Maybe because her fiancé isn't about to inherit a fortune," Ben said.

"And because you're much sexier than he is," Lexie added. Alcoholics frequently had self-image problems. Letting Dylan think his only attraction was his bank balance wouldn't help that.

Dylan put his arm around Lexie. "I'm also a lot sexier than Ben. And I've never made it with a stripper."

Okay, so a poor self-image wasn't the reason Dylan drank too much.

"Get your hands off my woman, or I'll be forced to beat the shit out of you," Ben said before Lexie could respond.

Dylan released Lexie. "Then you'd end up in jail and miss out on Grandfather's money."

"Here's the truck, Dylan," Ben said. "Let's get you into the back."

"Isn't it illegal for a person to ride in the back?" Lexie asked as Ben helped Dylan into the bed of his pickup.

"You want him squished between us?" Ben asked. "He could puke any minute."

"You've got a point."

When Lexie and Ben were seated in the pickup, she gave him a saccharine smile. "It's so sweet you'd give up your inheritance for me."

"I've never made it with a stripper, either." He started the truck.

The drive home was silent, except for snores loud enough to be heard over the pickup's engine. Lexie watched through the back window, concerned Dylan might jump or fall out. But he was lying so still that if he hadn't been snoring, she'd have worried he was dead.

"I'd better make sure Dylan gets into bed," Ben said when they'd arrived at Nevermore. "The trust doesn't specify that he stay inside the house, but he could decide he needs to take a leak and wander into the next county."

"That's a good idea." Lexie opened the passenger door. "Do you need my help?"

"I can handle him. Go to bed."

She waited until Ben was out of the pickup before heading into the house. "Thanks for convincing me to go to the dance and giving me a ride home."

"I'm glad you enjoyed it," Ben said, coming up beside her.

"It was—interesting."

"It was. You're a hell of an actress." Ben smiled slowly and ran a finger down her cheek. "Assuming you were acting."

His touch shot heat through Lexie's body. She took a step backward, away from his finger. "I was."

His smile grew. "Right. Sleep well, Lexie."

– – –

Ben's smile faded as he dragged Dylan upstairs and deposited him on his bed, and not just because Dylan was damn heavy. To be honest, he was grateful to Dylan, since otherwise he'd have been in danger of doing something really asinine, like taking Lexie to bed. He'd only kissed her to convince the crowd—and Jeremy—that she was at Nevermore because she was his girlfriend. For some reason he'd gotten carried away, just like he had that night after Walt's.

But he was not sleeping with Lexie, even though she'd turned out to be a lot different than he'd expected, even though he enjoyed talking to her, even though she made him hotter than any woman in recent memory. A one-night stand with her would be a bad idea for all sorts of reasons. As he'd told Grandfather, he had a feeling it was also more likely to make her leave than stick around.

And she was going to be furious enough when she found out he'd lied to her.

CHAPTER 12

Thank God for Dylan. Lexie woke up mentally repeating the same mantra that had lulled her to sleep last night. Because if Dylan hadn't been stupid enough to get drunk and into a fight, she'd probably have done something even stupider.

What had she been thinking? Granted, there wasn't any ethical reason not to sleep with Ben. He wasn't her client, and First Trust knew she was working with him. He also wasn't a suspect. She'd realized almost immediately that her theory that Max might have had her work with Ben in hopes he'd trip up didn't make sense. Max didn't want his murderer to realize he knew he'd been murdered, so he certainly wouldn't have alerted Ben if he suspected him. More important, Max would never have endangered Jessica's niece by putting her in close contact with someone he considered capable of murder.

Just because sleeping with Ben wouldn't jeopardize her career didn't make it a good idea, though. She didn't do one-night stands, and no way would Ben ever fall into the relationship category. Her ideal man was the intellectual, professional type, someone with more brains than brawn, who shared her interests and desire to get ahead. Even though he'd proven to be a lot smarter and more evolved than she'd originally feared, and ambitious enough to want to expand his business, Ben wasn't in the same book as those guys, let alone on the same page. Her mother would have a fit.

Which was the point.

Lexie sat up in bed, the explanation so obvious she couldn't believe she hadn't figured it out before. Sleeping with Ben would simply be another of her periodic mini-rebellions against her mother, like buying shoes in a non-neutral color or eating at a restaurant that didn't have a wine list or, worse yet, at a Burger King. Some of it could also be her vacation mentality where she got to pretend to be a cocktail waitress and do things she'd otherwise never have considered.

But she wasn't a cocktail waitress or on vacation, and if she wanted to rebel against her mother, she'd buy some more things from The Clothes Garden. She was here to do a job, and she couldn't let anything jeopardize that. She got out of bed and hurriedly dressed. She was going to make it clear to Ben she wasn't interested in being one of his conquests, just his partner in finding Max's murderer.

When she got to the dining room, Cecilia was alone there eating a blueberry scone. She had her dark hair in a ponytail, emphasizing her classically beautiful features.

"Has Ben already left?" Lexie asked.

Cecilia nodded. "His pickup was gone when I came down. I want to apologize for my brother. I'm sorry he ruined last night for you two."

"He didn't," Lexie said, probably more vehemently than she should have.

Cecilia grinned. "Good. I'm glad you and Ben had a chance to finish what you started at the street dance."

Lexie felt her cheeks heating. "Did you have fun?"

"Actually I did," Cecilia said. "But now I have a big problem. Peter asked me to dinner tonight. I couldn't think of a good reason to turn him down, so I said yes."

Lexie filled a coffee cup, then sat down at the table. "Don't you like him?"

"It's not that." Cecilia's features tightened. "He's a doctor and trained in Chicago, but came back here a couple of years ago to take over his dad's practice. He's committed to staying in Lakeview, and I'd die in a small town like this."

"You're just going on one date."

"I don't work that way," Cecilia said, waving her half-eaten scone. "Every date I've had since I turned eighteen has been with a man I'm hoping to marry. I can't be like you and date a guy when I know nothing will come of it."

If Ben had encouraged Peter to meet Cecilia, he must think Peter would be good for her in at least the short term. It was worth trying to convince her to give him a shot. "I'll bet the reason you've only dated men you considered marriage material is because you thought you needed a man to support you financially," Lexie said. "Now that you don't, you can date for fun, lots of different guys, since your only concern is whether you're having a good enough time for a next date."

"I never thought of it that way."

"Try going out on a casual date. If you don't like dating for fun, you can always go back to being serious."

Cecilia nodded but looked even tenser. "Except I told Peter I was divorced." She set her scone on her plate.

"That obviously isn't a problem for him."

"He thinks I only meant once. He doesn't know I've been divorced three times."

Lexie's forehead creased. "How could he not know, the way gossip travels around here?"

"I've never lived here, so no one knows that much about me. Just Ben, Grandfather, and Aunt Muriel, and none of them gossips. At least not about family."

"Has Peter ever been married?"

Cecilia shook her head. "Although he lived with a woman for a couple of years."

"So he understands that sometimes serious relationships don't work out."

"Three times?"

"Go out tonight and see what happens," Lexie said. "If he's a doctor, he might have a God complex like my ex, and you'll decide you never want to see him again."

"Then I won't have to care what he thinks," Cecilia said, her expression relaxing. "I wish you and Ben did have something serious going on. Not just because I think you're good for him, but because I'd like it if you were part of our family. I'll miss you when we leave Nevermore."

"I'll miss you, too." That was true, although she had a feeling Cecilia wouldn't feel the same once she found out why Lexie was really at Nevermore. "We can still keep in touch even if I'm no longer with Ben."

"I'd like that," Cecilia said. She got to her feet. "Thanks for the advice."

"Any time," Lexie said. Like she was in a position to give advice on relationships. Not with one humiliating divorce under her belt and a major case of lust for a man who gave new meaning to the word "inappropriate," even if it was simply a form of rebellion.

Cecilia had only been gone a minute when Jeremy waltzed into the dining room.

"Just the woman I was looking for," he said. "It's a beautiful day for boating, and I don't feel like going alone. Come with me."

"I didn't finish my paper," Lexie said, thankful she had the excuse ready.

"Work on it this morning. We'll go out this afternoon." He took her hand and looked down at her, his dark eyes smoldering. "I promise you'll love it."

Her brain told her Jeremy was one of the sexiest men she'd met in ages. Despite that, her heart rate didn't accelerate, her temperature didn't spike, and her stomach didn't flit, let alone flutter. Then again, her mother would probably approve of Jeremy.

Lexie still had no desire to ride on a speedboat, but riding in the open water was a lot safer than on a motorcycle. Ben hadn't gotten any information about Jeremy's finances—probably because he was afraid he'd learn Jeremy didn't have a motive. Knowing Ben, he'd use that failure as an excuse to delay hiring a P.I. And she needed to hire one and get back to Philadelphia ASAP, before her rebellious hormones made her do something she regretted.

"What time do we leave?"

– – –

At just after noon, the air was warm, the sky cloudless and magnificently blue, the bright sun making Lake Superior glitter like a multifaceted sapphire. According to the marina owner, days like this were why residents were willing to put up with nearly six months of winter.

Lexie would have given anything for some threatening gray clouds and an approaching thunderstorm. Because at the moment she was staring at the largest powerboat at the Lakeview Marina, her heart in her throat. From its pointed nose, sleek body, racing stripes, and the fact it was called "Lightning," she could guarantee this one wasn't big because it was a slow family vehicle.

"Isn't she a beauty?" Jeremy handed her a life jacket. "You're in for a treat. This baby can do over a hundred."

Lexie swallowed hard. "Miles per hour?"

"Yep. Like I said, you'll love it."

Wrong. At least motorcycles had to comply with posted speed limits. Sure, she could swim and would be wearing a life jacket, but she'd read about people being paralyzed and even killed by the force of hitting the water after being thrown from a boat going too damn fast. Lake Superior also was cold, so cold that dead bodies sank in it. Even if she didn't drown, she could die of hypothermia and be on the lake bottom with the shipwrecks before anyone missed her.

She opened her mouth to tell Jeremy she'd changed her mind, and then closed it. She had a job to finish, and this could be her best chance to talk to him and rule him in or out as a suspect. She put on her life jacket, then carefully got into the tippy boat and positioned herself on the padded seat beside his.

She closed her eyes, taking theoretically relaxing breaths as Jeremy fiddled with a couple of things. Even with the rhythmic waves as a calming background, her heart was still pummeling her chest and stomach when he started the engine. "Here we go."

Lexie opened her eyes and gripped the side of the boat as he steered through the sailboats and smaller powerboats surrounding them. When they'd cleared the harbor, he sped up, as did Lexie's breathing. A glance at the speedometer showed they hadn't even hit thirty, and her knuckles were already as white as the boat.

It was going to be a very long afternoon.

– – –

"Thanks for taking me out," Lexie said as she and Jeremy walked from his car to Nevermore late that afternoon. "I had a great time."

To her surprise, that was true. She'd eventually stopped hyperventilating long enough to realize that Jeremy was a safe and skilled driver, the boat was built to be stable at high speeds, and there wasn't much other traffic to run into. Once she'd gotten to that point, she'd stopped being scared and started appreciating being out on the water on such a beautiful day.

Actually, she hadn't just stopped being scared—she'd started to love going fast, feeling the wind against her cheeks and the fresh air cleansing her lungs. The boat sliced the water so smoothly they could have been flying above it. When Jeremy had let her drive, she'd had it over sixty before she'd realized it.

"We'll go out again tomorrow, and you can do more driving," Jeremy said. "I didn't know you were such a speed demon."

"Neither did I. I'll try to control myself."

He took her hand and grinned at her. "Please don't. I like women when they're out of control."

"Lexie. I've been looking for you."

Lexie turned to see Ben striding toward them. His faded jeans were ripped at the knee, he was wearing an oil-stained Budweiser T-shirt and a Twins cap, and he still made her body heat. This rebellion thing was getting out of hand.

She glanced at her watch. It was four thirty-five, and he usually didn't show up at Nevermore until just before sherry hour. Or just before one in the morning.

"I thought you were working," she said.

"I came home at three thirty today. I was looking forward to spending time with you, but you weren't around." His voice vibrated with anger.

Lexie's own temper spiked. He had no right to be angry when he hadn't bothered mentioning he'd be coming home early, pre-sumably to analyze what they knew. She narrowed her eyes behind her sunglasses. "Jeremy took me out on his friend's powerboat."

"Seth told me."

Lexie gave Jeremy a warm smile. "Thanks for taking me."

"My pleasure. Let me know what time you want to go out tomorrow."

"She's going sailing with me tomorrow." Ben's hands fisted at his sides.

"Is that what you want, Lexie?" Jeremy asked.

What she wanted was to get out of here without Ben slugging Jeremy, so she swallowed her own annoyance and nodded. "Maybe we can go out some other day."

"Or not," Ben said.

"I'll see you later," Jeremy said, and then he started up Nevermore's front steps.

The instant Jeremy was inside the house, Lexie planted her hands on her hips and raised her chin. "I feel like I just witnessed a junior high pissing contest." She kept her voice low, practically hissing out the words. "What's the big deal if I went boating with Jeremy? It's not like I'm really your girlfriend. And it was a good opportunity to find out whether he has a financial motive to murder your grandfather."

"Olivia said his last couple of deals fell apart," Ben said.

So she'd risked her life on the boat for nothing—that she'd ended up enjoying it was irrelevant. "You could have told me that."

"I thought I did."

"You didn't, but Jeremy did. That doesn't mean he's in dire enough need of money to kill anyone. He said he's got another deal about to close that will more than make up for those failures. His lifestyle certainly isn't suffering."

"How do you know that?"

From Ben's dark look, he wouldn't be happy to hear about Jeremy's invitation to fly her to New York to check out his condo. "He just got back from a two-week vacation on the French Riviera."

"So he claims," Ben said. "Even if he's telling the truth, it doesn't prove he isn't living on credit. Maybe he knew he didn't have to worry about money because he'd already paid someone to knock off Grandfather."

"You're going to suspect Jeremy no matter what you find out," Lexie said. "I don't think—"

"Who the hell is that?" Ben asked, interrupting her. He was looking over her shoulder.

Lexie turned to see a white Cadillac pulling up behind her. "Oh, God."

A plot twist this scene did not need.

"Who is it?" Ben asked again.

Before she could answer, J.P. got out of the car. He was dressed the same as when she'd met him, except today's polo shirt was lime green.

"Nice to see you in person, Lexie," J.P. said, walking toward her. "I figured I'd have to leave you a message. I was in the area and thought I'd stop by since I don't have your cell phone number. Not that I couldn't have got your number even if it's unlisted, but I respect people's privacy."

"This is J.P. Jackson," Lexie told Ben. "I told you I talked to him before. This is Ben."

A muscle twitched in Ben's clenched jaw. "What do you want?"

"Relax," J.P. said, holding up both hands. "I'm here to thank you. I heard about what you both did last night to keep Dylan from ending up in jail and losing his share of his grandfather's fortune. I also wanted to give you something." He reached into his pocket, then handed Lexie a business card for J.P.'s Construction and Cement Work, located in Thunder Bay. A phone number was handwritten under the printed one. "That's my cell phone. Like I told you, Lexie, I never forget a favor. If either of you ever needs my help, call. Anytime, day or night."

"We appreciate that," Lexie said.

"I'd appreciate it if you'd keep watching out for Dylan."

"We will. Thank you."

J.P. nodded, then turned to Ben. "You be good to this one. She's a keeper." He winked. "I hear she does a hell of a pole dance."

"Did we just get a mafioso's private number?" Ben asked when J.P. had gotten into his car and pulled away.

"I told you he's just a Mafia wannabe. That's probably why he keeps coming here himself—he figures being associated with Max Windsor will get the Mafia's respect."

"Or because Dylan owes him a hell of a lot," Ben said. "Thank God we're on his good side. I don't want to find out firsthand what kind of cement work he does."

Lexie looked at the card for a minute, and then shook her head. "A week ago I was a respectable Philadelphia lawyer handling mundane trust and estate cases. Now I'm apparently living someone else's life."

"I'll bet you're having a lot more fun."

"It's different." To be honest, she was so far out of her comfort zone she wasn't sure what she was feeling.

"You're right that I'm biased against Jeremy," Ben said. "It's not just because we haven't gotten along since junior high." He let out a long breath. "Jeremy had an affair with my wife."

"Cecilia told me."

"That's why I see him as the most likely to commit murder, I guess, because of what he did to me. That's also why I got so upset when you went out with him, since he'll think he's stolen another woman away from me." Ben looked down at the grass. "I know you're not really my girlfriend, but my ego would appreciate it if you didn't take up with Jeremy until we've gotten this resolved."

Lexie's eyes widened. She'd dismissed Ben's issues with Jeremy over her as simple male competition. It had never occurred to her that his ego might also be involved, probably because he seemed supremely confident when it came to women. "I don't plan on getting involved with Jeremy at any time," she said. "He isn't my type."

"Your type isn't handsome, rich, intelligent, and successful?"

"Usually, but something about Jeremy is a little too smooth," she admitted. Spending the afternoon with him had clarified the reason he didn't appeal to her. "My bullshit meter goes wild around him."

"You have a bullshit meter?"

"Try practicing law without one." Memory twisted her lips. "Although it occasionally malfunctions, since I didn't have a clue my ex was cheating on me." If Ben trusted her enough to share his insecurities, she could do the same. "The reason I hate massages? Because my surgeon husband left me for a twenty-three-year-old massage therapist. You know what it's like for a lawyer to be left for a massage therapist? Not that I'm a snob, but a lot of people I know are," she added quickly. "And Deidre's twelve years younger than me and so perky and sweet I'm tempted to douse her with water to see if she melts."

"Like the witch in *The Wizard of Oz*."

"I was thinking more like a sugar cube, but the witch analogy works for me, too."

"Divorce sucks."

"You've got that right," she said. "Look, you don't have to take me sailing. I won't go boating again with Jeremy."

"Have you ever been sailing?"

She shook her head.

"Grandfather would never forgive me if I didn't make sure you experienced it. He loves sailing as much as I do. I mean he loved sailing." Ben grimaced. "I'm still having problems accepting he's gone."

"Do you have time to analyze what we've learned about his murder now?"

He glanced at his watch. "Let's do it after dinner. I know you'd hate to be late for sherry hour."

— — —

They didn't get around to it after dinner because mid-meal Ben was called into work to do an emergency car repair for the mayor, who was driving to Minneapolis for a conference the next morning.

As Lexie watched Ben leave, however, she realized she didn't need his help. This was her decision—okay, it was technically the trustee's, but First Trust would follow her advice. She ran upstairs and grabbed her notes, a fresh legal pad, and sat cross-legged on the bed.

Two hours later she was even more convinced they had absolutely nothing, not even clear evidence a murder had been committed, let alone who'd committed it. Everyone had a theoretical motive, but she couldn't believe anyone would have been desperate enough to kill Max instead of approaching him for help. Everyone also could have hired a killer, if not done the deed personally, but she couldn't believe anyone would have done either.

That's why she was wrong for this investigation, because she couldn't contemplate that anyone who wasn't a complete monster would ever commit a murder. This case needed someone who had experience with seemingly nice people who'd been driven to do horrible things. She didn't need to discuss this with Ben.

Tomorrow she was going back to Philadelphia. And the trustee was hiring a P.I.

She booked an afternoon flight out of Duluth. Then she went to bed.

– – –

Lexie woke abruptly, opening her eyes in the total blackness, her heart hammering. It must have been a nightmare, one she couldn't remember even though it must have scared her to death. She glanced at the clock: 11:47. She closed her eyes again.

"I'm counting on you to find out who killed me."

Her blood turned to ice. "Who is it?" she asked, unnecessarily, since she knew that distinctive voice.

"You know who I am, Catherine. Just remember the money is the key. Because I really was murdered."

She was finally alert enough to think to switch on the bedside lamp. For an instant she swore she saw Max Windsor standing across the room by the dresser, studying her.

But it couldn't be. She blinked twice.

When she focused on the spot by the dresser again, it was empty.

CHAPTER 13

She'd been dreaming. That had to be it. Analyzing everything possibly relevant to identifying Max's murderer—including the ghost appearances—had triggered a nightmare.

Except she was wide-awake now, and she was positive she'd been equally wide-awake when she'd seen Max and he'd spoken to her. But that was impossible. Max was dead, and despite what she'd suggested to Ben, she really didn't believe in ghosts. So what had just happened?

Of course. She hopped out of bed, stormed to Ben's room, and pounded on the door.

"What?" he asked from behind her. He was dressed in a black T-shirt, jeans, and Nikes. She caught a whiff of motor oil.

"Where have you been?" she asked.

"I just got back from work. Why?"

"You know darn well why." She grabbed his arm and dragged him into her bedroom, then shut the door. "I just saw Max, who assured me he was murdered. What do you know about that?"

"What the hell are you talking about?"

"I told you yesterday that I don't believe Max was murdered, and I'm thinking about leaving. Then tonight I coincidentally get a visit from Max. Or more likely, a holograph of Max that you created."

"You honestly think I know how to create a holograph?"

"You're good at mechanical things."

"Like making a holograph is the same as fixing a transmission," Ben said. "I'm flattered by your high opinion of my abilities, but anything like that is way beyond me. I think you were dreaming, and it was your subconscious talking. You feel guilty you're considering running away without solving this thing."

"I was awake, and I saw Max in my room," Lexie said. "He told me he really was murdered and that the money is the key to who did it. The point obviously was to convince me to stick around and keep investigating your great-aunt and cousins, which is what you want me to do. Of course you were responsible."

"I had nothing to do with it," Ben said firmly. "You must have dreamed it. Or maybe it really was Grandfather."

"Don't make fun of me."

"I'm serious." He held out his hands, palms up. "I'm willing to entertain the possibility you truly saw my grandfather. Maybe he somehow knows you're getting frustrated and appeared to reassure you he was murdered so you'll stick around. He could plan a return appearance with more information if we don't figure it out ourselves. Grandfather was always big on pacing."

"Or maybe he doesn't know who killed him," Lexie said. "Being dead might not make you omniscient."

"Does this mean you believe he was murdered and plan to stay?"

"I don't know," she said honestly. "I'll let you know in the morning."

"I don't think you should stay alone in here tonight," Ben said.

"Why not? Even if it *was* Max's ghost, he certainly doesn't want to hurt me."

"The murderer might have figured out your identity and set up a holograph to scare you back to Philadelphia."

"By creating a holograph in which Max confirms he was murdered?" Lexie asked. "That would be pretty dumb."

"I think I should stay with you," Ben said. "Grandfather would never forgive me if I left you alone and something happened to you."

"Your grandfather's dead, for God's sake. And nothing's going to happen to me."

Ben raked his fingers through his hair. "Of course nothing's going to happen to you."

"Then why are you pretending?"

"Because I don't want to leave. Because you look so damn sexy in that T-shirt that I'm having a hell of a time keeping my hands off you. Because although it pisses me off, I really want to make love to you."

Lexie stared at him as her stomach somersaulted.

Ben's mouth twisted ruefully. "I'll take that as a no. At least I have the satisfaction of managing to leave a lawyer speechless." He turned and started out of the room.

Her brain told her hormones to cool it. Instead her body heated. "Although it annoys me more than you can imagine, I seem to feel the same way."

He stopped. Then he turned and started back toward her, a corner of his mouth quirking. "Admit it. It more than annoys you. It pisses you off as much as it does me."

"All right, it pisses me off," Lexie said. "I don't sleep with a guy unless we're in a relationship. Which is never going to happen with us, even if I hadn't sworn off relationships."

"True," Ben said. He reached out and fingered her loose hair. "I swore I'd never sleep with another smart professional like my ex-wife. But we've got a problem here. There's a lot of sexual tension between us, and because we're fighting it, we're building it up in our minds." His fingers moved from her hair to her neck, then slowly down the front of her T-shirt. "It's probably interfering with our ability to find Grandfather's murderer. If we'd just have sex once, we'd get it out of our systems and realize it wasn't that big a deal." He fondled her breast through the thin cotton. "Then we'll be able to focus all our attention on the murder."

"Sounds like a line to me," Lexie said, trying to ignore the way her body quivered and softened under his touch. This was a bad idea on so many levels. "A creative one, I'll admit, but I don't fall for lines. Rule 79." She said the words without one iota of conviction.

Ben moved toward her, and then kissed her. Between the heat and her hammering heart, she was breathless when he finally released her and barely got out the words. "To hell with Rule 79."

He chuckled deep in his throat, the sound making her nerve endings sizzle. Then he was kissing her again. The smooth pressure of his lips and tongue had her mind spinning until she couldn't think, could only feel. His hands stroked her T-shirted back, and then he yanked the T-shirt over her head so she was naked except for her silk panties. He moved away for a moment, his eyes slowly raking over her body. "You're so damn beautiful," he said.

Insecurity reared its head, and Lexie covered her breasts with her arm. "I'm a lot older than your last girlfriend." And than her husband's new wife.

He moved her arm away. "You're obviously like a fine wine that gets better with age."

Her arm returned, and she rolled her eyes. "Another line, and a dumb one at that."

Ben moved her arm away again, this time directing her hand to his straining erection. She could feel its hard heat through his jeans. "I obviously meant it. Looking at you must have drained my brain of all creativity." He reached out and stroked her breasts.

If he was lying, so what? He still wanted her, and she wanted him more than she'd ever wanted anyone. "That was better."

His lips fastened on one of her breasts, sucking her nipple hard enough that she felt the sensation deep in her pelvis.

"Much better," she murmured as he switched to her other breast. He reached down to her panties, but she pushed his hand away. "I'm not going to be nude while you're fully clothed."

His slow smile made her shiver. "We can take care of that." He pulled his T-shirt over his head as she tried to unbuckle his belt. She'd barely started when he put his hands over hers. "I can do it faster." In seconds he'd discarded his jeans and briefs.

"Now you're the one who's overdressed," he said, pulling off her panties. They pooled at her feet, and she kicked them off.

He kept kissing her as he backed her up until she was against the bed, and then urged her down onto the smooth sheets. He moved on top of her and kissed the valley between her breasts. Then his tongue and lips began working their way down her body, down her chest, then her abdomen, then lower. He paused, his lips close enough that she could feel his hot breath on her. He lowered his mouth to kiss her, teasing her with his tongue as she arched and moaned on the bed. Then he closed his lips around her and sucked.

"Oh." That was the only thing Lexie could get out as her body spasmed in the biggest orgasm of her life, uncoiling with a force that shook her. She felt like she was flying, sparks and heat erupting like the grand finale at a Fourth of July fireworks display.

Ben moved up her body again and kissed her. She could taste herself on his lips.

Maybe it was just her competitive spirit, but she wanted to make him feel the same. "My turn," she said, closing her fingers around him. He felt like hot iron.

He grabbed her hand. "Not now, or this is going to be over too soon. And I need to be inside you." He grabbed a condom from his jeans pocket, ripped open the package with his teeth, and put it on. Then he rolled over and pulled her on top of him. "Since you're supposedly a stripper, I'd like a lap dance."

"I thought pole dancing was my specialty."

He grinned. "That works for me, too. And don't tell me this isn't the type of pole you meant."

She looked down at his erection and laughed.

"Not the reaction I was hoping for," Ben said.

"You can't pull off false modesty, so don't bother trying." He was definitely impressive. She ran one finger down him. "Although size doesn't matter."

"And men like Hooters for their hot wings," Ben said. "I heard that in a country song. That's not really why men like Hooters."

"What a surprise," she said, laughing again. Then she positioned herself, her body stretching and throbbing as she lowered herself onto him.

She looked down into his eyes. They were dark, intense. "I've never seen anyone do a lap or pole dance," she said. "What do I do next?"

"Brace yourself on my shoulders." His voice was a low rumble. "Then you move."

She leaned forward enough so she could rest her hands on his shoulders, and then flexed her knees as she moved up and down his length a few times. "Like this?"

"Exactly like that." He put his hand on her back and urged her forward so his lips could fasten on her nipple.

She moved faster.

He sucked on her nipple, and then caught it lightly between his teeth as he reached between them and rubbed her with the pad of his thumb. She could feel another orgasm building, building, then exploding inside her. She heard someone scream—it must have been her, although she'd never screamed during sex before. Ben bucked hard beneath her, and then pulled her down on top of him, her head resting on his chest.

She had no idea how long they lay there, panting together, before Ben finally spoke.

"I was right. You do a hell of a pole dance."

− − −

"I need to shower," Ben said, slipping out from under the covers a while later and grabbing his clothes. "I'm a mess from work." He brushed his lips over hers. "I'll be back soon." He stood up beside the bed and grabbed his clothes.

An alarm sounded somewhere in her brain, and she pulled the sheet over her. "I thought we were just doing it once to get it out of our systems," Lexie said.

"How's that working for you?"

"Not so well," she admitted. She couldn't remember sex ever being so hot and intense, which was surprising since she'd never laughed and joked during sex before. She'd always considered sex serious, but Ben had shown her it could be fun. That didn't make it right, though. Actually, most things that were fun ended up being somehow bad for you.

"We can't keep doing this," she said. She kept her gaze on his face, since looking at his muscular chest and equally impressive lower half might destroy her resolve.

"Of course we can," Ben said. "I'm a mechanic who loves living in a small town. You're a Philadelphia lawyer. It would never work between us, which makes this perfect."

"Perfect?"

"Yep." He stroked her neck, raising goose bumps. "It's more of your vacation mentality while you're pretending to be Lexie." He moved his fingers under the sheet and stroked her breasts. "View it as a vacation fling that we agree will end the instant you go home."

"I don't have flings." She could feel her resolve fading.

"But I created Lexie, and trust me, she loves flings." He leaned over and kissed her, making the last of her resolve evaporate. "Get some sleep until I get back. You're going to need your energy. I'm not just creative when it comes to lines."

– – –

"How would you like to go for an early morning sail on Forest Lake?" Ben asked.

Lexie opened her eyes and glanced at the clock. Six minutes after five. It felt as if she'd just gone to sleep. Maybe she had—Ben was right about his creativity.

"Isn't it too dark to go sailing?" she asked.

"The sun will be up soon," Ben said. "There's nothing like being on the water at dawn, the colors, the peace and quiet, everything. And I promised to take you out today."

What she'd really like was to spend more time in bed with Ben, but she didn't want him thinking his skill had turned her into a nymphomaniac. His ego in that regard was big enough already. "Okay. I need to shower first."

"The boat's in the storage shed, so it will take me at least half an hour to get it ready. Then I'll come back and get you. That will also give you time to have coffee before we go." He traced his finger around her nipple. It pearled immediately. "Unless you want to stay in bed. I'm up for that, too."

"I'd much rather go sailing," she said.

He chuckled. "Liar. I'll see you soon."

– – –

Lexie was downstairs in sixteen minutes, having showered, pulled her wet hair back into a ponytail, and dressed in nearly record time. Despite the little sleep she'd had, she was so wide-awake that for the first time she could remember she didn't need caffeine to function. Good sex must be energizing.

She was far too antsy to sit around waiting for Ben, so she decided to go find him. Maybe she could help with something. She went into the kitchen and grabbed one of the half-dozen flashlights she knew were kept in the pantry. After checking to make sure it worked, she headed for the front door.

She stepped out of Nevermore into the pale gray coolness of early dawn, crossed the dewy grass, and then walked into the trees to the path that led to the lake. She'd been smart to bring a flashlight—the trees were so dense she definitely needed it. The springy ground, pine scent, and silence were relaxing muscles she hadn't realized were tensed. She smiled faintly. Or maybe a night of terrific sex had done it. She'd forgotten how good sex could be, or maybe she'd never realized before today. Once she left Nevermore and reverted back to Catherine, she was going to have to work on a new relationship. She was never going without sex for long again.

The world grew a little lighter, and she paused, looking up. The trees had thinned enough that she could see hints of sky, the gray now touched with pale pink. She was starting to understand why Max had been able to give up urban life for a place like this. She felt as if she were in a cathedral, the dimly lit silence peaceful. The kind of place that fed one's soul.

After a few minutes, Lexie reached the end of the trees. Directly ahead was Forest Lake, lapping gently against the shoreline. A loon trilled, followed by the caws of a couple of seagulls. Even more muscles relaxed. She was very glad she hadn't insisted they stay in bed. She was looking forward to experiencing an early morning sail.

She stepped out of the trees onto the rocky lakeshore—and froze, her blood icing to slush.

Ben was there, and the sailboat was tied up to the dock. But he wasn't getting the boat ready. Instead he was dragging something toward the open shed door.

The body of Max Windsor.

CHAPTER 14

"What in God's name is going on?" Lexie got out between stiff lips. Her hand was shaking, her wobbling flashlight fixed on a dark stain on Max's blue work shirt.

"Help me get his body into the shed," Ben said, still tugging at Max's corpse. "Someone could come down here. I don't want anyone stumbling over him before I figure out what to do."

"He's been dead more than a week." Lexie's legs felt like giant ice blocks, too heavy to lift. "His body was incinerated. What is it doing here?"

"He wasn't dead," Ben said. "He just pretended to be, hoping he'd be able to smoke out whoever made the two attempts on his life. I've been helping him. When I came down this morning, I discovered his body. I didn't see it at first, not until I went out on the dock." He pointed. "It was on the other side of those boulders."

"You can't move his body." Lexie's brain had resumed functioning enough to know that. "We have to call the police. And an ambulance."

"I've already moved the body, and it's too late for an ambulance. I need to think this through before the police arrive and mess things up. Give me an hour." He held up a finger. "One hour. Please."

"I can't." She didn't have her phone, so she turned and race-walked back to Nevermore, a hollow ache in her chest and gut.

Max hadn't been dead, but he hadn't bothered telling her. He'd let Ben in on his joke, but Ben hadn't bothered telling her, either.

Except it was no longer a joke because Max really had been murdered.

She ran into Nevermore and used the phone in the foyer to call 911. Then she went outside and plopped down on the front steps to wait.

After a couple of minutes, Ben sat down beside her. "We need to talk about this."

She met his eyes, the man she'd thought she'd known and liked, the man she'd been so wrong about. Grief, shock, and anger had her insides quivering. "Not now. When the police ask if we've discussed it, I'd like to be able to truthfully say no. I'm sick of lying to everyone about who I am and why I'm here." She turned her head, staring across the lawn. "But I guess I'm not the only one who's been lying."

"I didn't want to lie to you." Ben rested his hand on her arm. "Grandfather—"

"As I said, I don't want to discuss this now." Lexie shook off his hand, the emotions his touch elicited tangled and painful. She got up and walked over to her rental car, then stood leaning against it, her arms crossed. She couldn't bear to look at Ben.

– – –

The police arrived twenty minutes later, lights flashing and sirens blaring. Two cars pulled to a stop in the driveway, then three uniformed men got out.

"What's going on?" one of the uniformed men asked as he approached Ben.

"Thanks for coming, Jim," Ben said. "Although isn't this the sheriff's jurisdiction?"

"He's on vacation for two weeks, so the Lakeview police are covering the county, too," Jim said. "What happened?"

"Someone shot Grandfather and left his body by the lake," Ben said.

"I thought he died in a car crash."

"He didn't," Ben said. "Follow me."

As Jim, Ben, and another cop walked back into the trees, Lexie plopped down on Nevermore's front steps. She had no desire to see Max's dead body again. When the other family members came outside, she referred everyone to the policeman stationed in front of Nevermore to explain what had happened. As they made their way en masse across the yard to the path, the peaches, tangerines, and roses of the dawn sky and the flashing red lights of two cop cars reflected off nightwear and pale, tense faces.

When the family members emerged from the trees several minutes later, they all looked even paler and tenser. Cecilia was sobbing.

"What's your problem, Cecilia?" Dylan asked. "You already thought he was dead."

"I know it doesn't make any sense for me to cry like this now. But seeing his body—" Cecilia broke off, wiping her face with her palms.

"Jesus, Seth, don't take a picture of her," Dylan said. "It's bad enough you took photos of Grandfather's body."

"Sorry," Seth said, setting down his camera.

Actually, Cecilia's tears made perfect sense to Lexie. What she couldn't understand was everyone else's lack of tears. Even if you already thought your grandfather was dead, wouldn't you still be saddened seeing his murdered body? Her own eyes had certainly welled up once the shock had worn off. But no—the others' main concern was likely whether this would restart the two-week period they had to stay at Nevermore to inherit.

And one of them wasn't a bit upset or even surprised to find Max's body. One of them had killed him.

Ben and the policeman he'd identified as Jim were also back in front of Nevermore. "Explain this to me, Ben," Jim said, resting a pen on his clipboard. "I thought Max died in a car accident."

"That's what we wanted everyone to think," Ben said. "Grandfather was convinced someone was trying to kill him. He figured pretending to be dead would help him figure out who."

"That sounds a little far-fetched."

"That's what I said, but he was determined. You know Grandfather." Ben shook his head. "When he built Nevermore, he put in secret passages, although I didn't realize that until he told me a few weeks ago. He planned to sneak around and listen to what people were saying. He also appeared to people to make them think he was haunting them, hoping it might motivate someone to confess. Or to let something slip, something that indicated the person knew about the previous attempts on his life."

Jim stopped his note taking. "What previous attempts?"

Ben explained.

"What about the car crash?" Jim asked when Ben had finished.

"I helped stage it," Ben said. "I had someone teach me how to hack into Grandfather's dental records, claiming Grandfather wanted to know how it was done so he could use it in a book. Once I could get in, I replaced Grandfather's records with ones that conformed with a skull he'd bought years ago for research. We put the skull into the car before we burned it up."

"Max burned his Ferrari on purpose?" Jim asked.

"He figured it was worth it to save his life. He could always buy another Ferrari."

"Then you just happened to stumble over Max's dead body this morning," Jim said.

"That's exactly what happened. I was going to take Lexie sailing."

"The Lexie who called to report finding Max's body?" Jim asked.

"That's me," Lexie said, approaching them. "Ben went down to the lake to get the boat ready. I got there about fifteen minutes later and found Ben with the body."

"What's your last name?" Jim was taking notes again.

"My nickname is Lexie, but my full name's Catherine Alexandra Barrington. I'm from Philadelphia and was Max's estate planning lawyer. I also represent First Trust in Minneapolis, the current trustee of his trust." The charade had to end now. She had no choice.

From the family members' shocked expressions, no one besides Trey had suspected she wasn't a cocktail waitress.

"I thought you were Ben's girlfriend," Cecilia said.

"After Max supposedly died in the car crash, he had Ben forward a letter to me claiming he'd most likely been murdered, and he wanted me to work with Ben to find out who did it," Lexie told the cop. "I was pretending to be Ben's girlfriend, hoping to get information."

"What did you learn?" Jim asked.

"That everyone in the family had motive and opportunity. So far we hadn't found any evidence as to who did it." She shot Ben a withering look. "Probably because Max wasn't even dead."

"I would have told you if I could, but Grandfather swore me to secrecy, Lexie," Ben said.

"Are you the only person who knew Max was alive, Ben?" Jim asked.

"Besides his killer," Ben said. "Grandfather was staying in a secret room, which he told me he'd had constructed when he built the house to give him a totally private place to write. The room is soundproof and has a bed, refrigerator, microwave, and bathroom. I left food and supplies for Grandfather in the armoire in his bedroom. He also left me messages in the armoire. I checked it twice a day, in the morning and right after dinner."

"Why didn't you leave things in your bedroom?" Jim asked. "Or in his secret room?"

"Grandfather was afraid someone might see me if I used the secret passages," Ben said. "Or find things left in my room, since the master key kept in the pantry works on that door. The only room the master key can't open is Grandfather's bedroom."

"Who else knew about the secret room and passages?" Jim asked.

"No one, not even Trey. Grandfather said the only person he told was Jessica Stuart, but she's been dead for seven years."

"Eight years," Lexie said. "She was my aunt."

"Where were you last night, Ben?" Jim asked.

"Am I a suspect?"

"You knew Max was alive, and you inherit from him once he's dead."

"I don't need his money."

"I hardly think even the outrageous salary you earned as an I-banker compares to what Grandfather left you," Jeremy said.

Lexie blinked. "You were an investment banker?" Had he told her the truth about anything?

"Ben, do you have an alibi for last night?" Jim asked.

"The mayor called with an emergency car repair while I was eating dinner," he said. "I left the house around seven thirty and finished at eleven fifteen, which the mayor can confirm. I came back to Nevermore, stopped to check for messages in Grandfather's bedroom, and then was about to open my bedroom door when Lexie stopped me. She said Grandfather had appeared to her."

"Max appeared to you?" Jim asked.

Lexie nodded. "At eleven forty-seven. He said he really had been murdered and was counting on me to find out who did it."

"I went into her room to discuss it with her."

"Then you went back to your room?" Jim asked.

"He spent the night with me," Lexie said when Ben didn't answer. After all the lies he'd told, she couldn't believe he was going to be a gentleman about this. "He was there until just after five this morning, when he went to get the sailboat ready."

"Was he with you the entire night?"

"I left for about fifteen minutes to shower," Ben said. "Around twelve thirty."

Jim returned his attention to Lexie. "Can you confirm how long he was gone? Or what time he got back?"

"I can't because I fell asleep," she said. "He woke me when he got back, but I never checked the clock."

"I need to look around," Jim said. "Okay if I search the house?"

"It's okay with me, but I'm not the only owner," Ben said.

Lexie cleared her throat. She'd failed to prevent Max's murder, but she still had a job to do. "The trustee is currently the legal owner of Nevermore and won't agree to a search without a warrant."

"Things always go to hell whenever a lawyer gets involved," Jim muttered. "I'll go call the county attorney. Then I'll be back to question everyone, so stick around."

— — —

Fifteen minutes later, Ben sat on the living room couch, the pain in his gut so intense he could barely breathe. Once again, he'd let Grandfather down. And this time Grandfather was dead.

He poured himself another cup of coffee from the pot Igor had brought into the living room. "Want a refill?" he asked Lexie, who was the only other person in the room. Everyone else was either upstairs dressing or in the dining room having breakfast.

"No, thanks." Her voice and expression were so cold he wouldn't have been surprised to see her breath. She was clearly furious. No surprise there.

He needed her help, which meant he had to make her understand why he'd kept her in the dark. "Did your aunt or maybe Grandfather tell you about when I came to live with him?" he asked.

When Lexie didn't answer, he went on. "My dad was a real bastard. Still is, far as I know, although I haven't seen him in years. He's one of those driven corporate types, always too busy working to have time for his family. And he cheated on my mom all the time. I don't know why she didn't divorce him.

"My mom was terrific, though. Every summer she and I spent a month with Grandfather at Nevermore. It was the best time of my life. Grandfather was everything Dad wasn't. He was way richer than Dad, but he didn't care much about money. He was happiest when he was out on his sailboat or hiking through the woods identifying every tree and plant. Or writing, of course."

Lexie was staring straight ahead. Her expressionless face gave no indication she was even listening, let alone understanding.

Despite the lack of encouragement, he forced himself to continue. "When I was twelve, my mom was killed in a car accident. A drunk driver hit her. Afterward my dad didn't want a damn thing to do with me. I figured it was because he blamed me for my mom's death since she'd been driving to pick me up after soccer practice. Hell, I blamed myself. Then two months after Mom died, Dad told me he was getting married. Andrea was only twenty-five and not up to having a twelve-year-old son, so he was sending me to boarding school out east."

He closed his eyes. Even after all these years, remembering that time made him feel like he was engulfed in a black pit. "I was upset, to put it mildly. I mean, not only had I just lost my mom, but then I was torn away from my friends to go to school across the country. I'd always been a fairly good kid, but I started sneaking out after curfew and drinking beer. I thought if I was bad enough they'd kick me out of boarding school, and I'd get to go back to L.A. I didn't know that if you've got enough money, when one school kicks you out, another will take you in, especially when your grandfather's famous. So I went to another school, got kicked out, and then tried a third. By then I'd realized my dad would never let me move back to L.A. so I decided to run away. I stole a car. I'd figured out how to hot-wire it and decided to drive to Mexico. But I'd only gone fifty miles before I got caught and arrested. They called my dad. He said he couldn't control me and thought a stint in juvenile detention would do me good, so I was on my own."

Lexie got up and walked over to the front window, looking out at Nevermore's front lawn. At least she hadn't left the room.

"Then Grandfather stepped in. He hired a great attorney who made it all go away. I had to do community service and was on probation a couple of years, but then it got erased from my record. Grandfather also agreed to let me come live with him."

Ben shook his head. "I figured Grandfather had only gotten involved because he'd never liked my dad and wanted to piss him off. I assumed Grandfather would soon get tired of me and kick me out, so I might as well speed up the process. But no matter what I did, he didn't kick me out, just grounded me and made me do all sorts of chores as punishment. And unlike my dad, he loved me and made sure I knew it."

He felt moisture on his cheeks, wiped it away with the back of his hand. "My point is that Grandfather saved me, and I know it. If it hadn't been for him, I'd probably have turned into a career criminal, to spite my dad if nothing else. So I'd do anything for him. Including keep you in the dark when he asked, even though I wanted to tell you."

Lexie finally turned away from the window and looked at him. "If you'd told me, he'd still be alive." Then she walked out of the room.

And Ben realized that he hadn't just been trying to convince Lexie that his silence had been justified. He'd been trying to convince himself. It hadn't worked, and he felt worse than ever. Because he knew she was probably right.

– – –

Half an hour later, Jim came into the living room, waving a sheet of paper. "I've got my warrant. Lexie said it's all in order."

"Where is she?" Ben asked.

"I told her she could leave after she let us check out her car to make sure no one stashed something inside. We confirmed who she is, and she said she couldn't advise anyone during questioning since that would be a conflict of interest," Jim said. "Could you get everyone else down here, Ben? Have them leave their rooms unlocked and bring their car keys. My warrant covers the house, grounds, and all vehicles."

The family members waited in the living room as the cops did their search. Ben shook his head. He'd been deceiving all his relatives both about Grandfather being alive and about Lexie's identity, and none of them seemed upset with him. The only person upset was Lexie.

He looked up as Jim walked into the living room. He was carrying a plastic bag with a handgun inside. "Is this your gun, Ben?"

"Why do you think that?"

Jim stopped directly in front of Ben and handed him the bag. "Answer the question. Is this your gun?"

Ben examined the weapon. "It looks a lot like one I bought five years ago. Grandfather wanted to know how easy it was to buy a gun illegally in New York City, so I tried, and it was damn easy. I gave it to Grandfather right after I bought it and never saw it again."

"Grandfather mentioned in several interviews that he'd had Ben do that," Cecilia said.

"As I asked before, why do you think it's the gun I bought?" Ben asked.

"Because we found it under the passenger seat of your truck. It's been fired twice."

Jim's words stabbed Ben through the gut. One of his relatives had not only killed Grandfather but had also tried to frame him for it.

"I didn't put it there," he said. "I leave my truck unlocked, so anyone could have planted it. And anyone could have found the gun. Grandfather kept it out in the open in the basement, on some shelves where he stored most of the things he'd bought as research for his books."

"We also found this." Jim showed Ben a piece of paper stuck inside a smaller plastic bag. "I assume it's from your grandfather."

Ben looked at the note, recognizing his grandfather's handwriting. It said, "Need to talk. One a.m. tonight at the dock. M."

"Grandfather must have left it in his bedroom after I checked."

"It wasn't in Max's bedroom. It was on your nightstand, where I presume you left it."

"I've never seen it before," Ben said. "Grandfather must have needed to talk to me and been afraid I'd already made my nightly check of his bedroom and wouldn't find the note in time if he left it there. But I went into my room just long enough to take a quick shower and change. I never went over by the bed." The knife already stabbing his gut twisted, and he rubbed his face with his hands. "Jesus, I wish I had. Grandfather must have discovered something important, maybe even who was trying to kill him. If I'd have met Grandfather, he'd still be alive."

"Or maybe you found the note, met him, and killed him."

Ben dropped his hands from his face and stared at Jim. "You're crazy. If I'd killed him, wouldn't I have gotten rid of the note? And the gun?"

"Maybe you planned to later, but the cops showed up too soon."

"Because Lexie found me moving the body and called them. Why would I have invited her to go sailing, knowing she could very well stumble over Grandfather's body?"

"Because for some reason you couldn't move the body last night after you killed Max. Going sailing gave you an excuse to do it this morning, which is why you decided to go when the sun was barely up. You figured you'd have time to hide the body, maybe dump it into the water before Lexie got there," Jim said. "Ben, I need to ask you a few questions at the station."

"Am I under arrest?"

"I'd like you to come voluntarily. If you won't, I'll have to arrest you."

Ben got to his feet. "Then I guess I'll go voluntarily."

— — —

Lexie sat on the bed in her room at the Lakeview Inn, trying to watch an old rerun of *Oprah* on the TV in the fake wood armoire.

Even twenty minutes into the show, she didn't have the faintest idea what topic Oprah had decided should be important to the women of America that day. But she couldn't turn it off. That would leave her alone with her thoughts, thoughts that were painful even with a TV audience for company.

Max was dead. She'd grieved when she'd originally thought he'd died, but Cecilia was right. It became more real when you actually saw the body, especially with that bloody bullet hole. It was even worse because he'd been killed while she'd been enjoying herself with Ben.

Ben, the man who was supposed to be her partner in finding Max's murderer. She'd have been a lot more help if she'd had all the facts—like the little one about Max still being alive.

That hadn't been Ben's only lie. He'd also pretended to be a small-town mechanic, but a call to Trey had established that he'd not only worked on Wall Street until three years ago but also had his undergrad degree and MBA from Harvard. He was the kind of guy people could have understood having an intelligent girlfriend, no matter what type of women he'd preferred in his recent past. Yet he'd convinced her she needed to pretend to be an undereducated cocktail waitress, either because he found it entertaining or to prove he could manipulate her. Probably both.

None of that mattered, though, since she was officially off the case. Tomorrow she'd be heading back to Philadelphia on her rebooked flight. The local cops seemed a lot more competent than Ben had led her to believe. Even if they weren't, the trustee could pressure them to call in the FBI or state police. This was Max Windsor, after all.

A crawler announcing breaking news rolled under Oprah and her guest. Lexie read it, and then walked up to the TV, squatting so the crawler was at eye level as it repeated. She read it again. Okay, so her first impression of the local cops had been wrong. They were not only incompetent, they were idiots.

Because they'd just arrested Ben for Max's murder.

– – –

Ben flipped his phone off as he paced the jail cell they were keeping him in until he posted bail. The cop in charge of the jail today was Mike Hamilton, who'd been a friend since they'd played high school football together.

Mike had let him keep his cell phone and hadn't limited him to one call, thank God, since trying to raise his bail had proven more difficult than he'd anticipated. The judge had set it at two million, meaning he needed two hundred thousand in cash. He had more than enough investments, but nothing he could liquidate before tomorrow. Right now he was working on convincing one of the local banks to give him a quick mortgage on his house and garage, both of which were fully paid for and worth far more than two hundred thousand dollars. Everyone was pretending to need days if not weeks to process a loan, although he'd bet their real reason for stalling was they didn't want to be seen aiding the man who'd possibly killed Lakeview's beloved Max Windsor.

"I got here as soon as I could, Ben."

Ben turned toward the woman standing outside his jail cell, dressed in a designer suit and thousand-dollar shoes and holding an even more expensive purse. The absolute last person he'd expected to ever see in Lakeview again.

"Olivia. What the hell are you doing here?"

CHAPTER 15

"I know you didn't want me to come before," Olivia said. "But when I heard Max had been murdered and you'd been trying to prevent it, I knew you'd be devastated. I booked the first flight I could get to Duluth, and then drove to Lakeview. I can't believe they arrested you."

His ex-wife looked the same as the last time Ben had seen her, nearly three years ago—chin-length platinum hair framing enormous violet eyes and the face of an angel, with a Victoria's Secret model-worthy body under that stylishly conservative suit. Just looking at her used to turn him hot and hard, but today his body didn't even twitch. Maybe being in jail had something to do with it. "I should be able to raise bail by mortgaging the garage and my house," he said.

Olivia looked down her nose at him. "You should never have paid cash for those. Think of the investment opportunities you missed."

Or maybe his body's lack of reaction had more to do with their history. "I didn't want any debts, and I'm tired of investments." And of rehashing these old arguments.

"You're wasting your talent."

Her echoing his grandfather's words triggered a flash of pain. "I really don't feel like talking about that right now, Olivia."

"I'm sorry," she said, her tone switching to conciliatory. "You don't have to worry about mortgaging anything. I'll pay your bail. I've got more than enough available cash."

"Don't bother. I'll get the money tomorrow at the latest."

"If you're stuck in jail overnight, won't you lose your share of the trust?"

He hadn't even thought about that. "That's the least of my concerns," Ben said honestly. "Proving I didn't kill Grandfather and finding out who did is a lot more important."

"Of course you didn't kill Max," Olivia said. "Once you're found innocent, getting your share of the trust will be important. Besides, I owe you. I should never have cheated on you, and certainly not with Jeremy."

"I told you I've forgiven you for that."

"I can't forgive myself. Let me do this for you, Ben."

He didn't want Olivia doing him any favors. But for a lot of reasons he didn't want to spend tonight in jail, and she was looking like his only ticket out. "I'll pay you back tomorrow."

— — —

Lexie smoothed both the skirt of her navy silk suit and her French twist, and then strode into the police station. "I'm here to see Ben Gallagher," she told the police officer manning the desk.

"Who are you?"

"I'm Catherine Barrington, the attorney for the trustee of Max Windsor's trust. I'm here to make sure Ben can arrange bail." She needed to make sure he didn't lose his share of the trust because of the cops' stupidity—she'd stake her reputation he wasn't guilty.

The door behind the desk opened, and a stunning blonde stepped into the reception area. "I've already taken care of Ben's bail," she said. "I've also hired an attorney from New York to represent him."

"And you are?" Lexie asked.

"Olivia Gallagher. I'm Ben's wife."

"I thought Ben was divorced," Lexie said.

"That was only because we thought we wanted different things, and I stupidly wouldn't compromise," Olivia said. "Things have changed. I've changed."

"I see." At least Ben hadn't also lied about his marital status. "As long as his bail is taken care of, I don't need to see him."

Olivia smiled. "Don't worry about Ben. I'll take very good care of more than just his bail."

At least one good thing had come of this whole fiasco, Lexie thought as she walked out of the police station and toward her car. Ben and his ex-wife had been reunited. She should be happy for him. It had nothing to do with her, since their affair had ended the minute she'd seen Ben with Max's body, and not just because he'd lied. But because at that instant vacation time had ended, and she'd turned back into Catherine, no matter what people were calling her. The twinge of pain she felt was just hurt pride.

She had no time for hurt pride, though. She might be mad at Ben for lying, but no way had he killed Max. Unfortunately Ben's arrest had changed her plan to have the trustee hire a P.I. or call in the FBI. She couldn't advise the trustee to do that unless there was tangible evidence casting doubt on Ben's guilt. Otherwise the trustee could appear to be trying to clear Ben and therefore favoring one beneficiary over the others.

But she certainly wasn't about to leave the investigation to the local cops. What she needed to do was convince the trustee that she should stick around and monitor things. That would also give her time and opportunity to find Max's real killer—or at least uncover enough evidence that Ben might not be guilty to justify having the trustee hire outside help.

She owed it to Max.

– – –

The last thing Ben wanted was to spend time with Olivia, but when she'd asked to stay at Nevermore, he couldn't say no. The nicest place in town—the Lakeview Inn—had the same standards and amenities as a Super 8. Olivia wasn't the Super 8 type.

He hauled two suitcases heavier than Lexie's plus a garment bag up the front stairs and into the foyer, where he and Olivia were met by Igor.

"I'm Ben's wife," Olivia told Igor. "Please take my things to his room."

Igor was staring at her with his mouth open, even though that probably violated the code of butlering. Olivia had that effect on most men.

"She's my ex-wife," Ben said, setting her suitcases on the floor. "Take her things to one of the vacant rooms."

Igor managed to shift his attention to Ben. "The room next to yours is vacant," he said.

"Lexie's room?" Ben asked.

Igor nodded. "She left."

"Do you know where she went?"

"She did not say."

"The room next to Ben's would be perfect," Olivia said.

"Would that be satisfactory, Mr. Gallagher?"

So Lexie had concluded he was guilty, maybe even thought he'd been using her to give himself an alibi. She thought he was capable of killing his grandfather, the person he loved more than anyone in the world, for some cash. He hadn't thought that between his grandfather's death and his own arrest he could feel any worse, but that had done it.

Ben realized Igor was looking at him, waiting for an answer to his question. He let out a long breath. "Put Olivia in the room next to mine."

– – –

"My God, Catherine. How could you let yourself get involved in Max Windsor's murder? And when everyone already thought he was dead, for heaven's sake."

Catherine frowned at her cell phone. She'd come out of the bathroom after showering and blow-drying her hair to find it ringing and stupidly answered without first checking who was calling. "I'm not involved in Max's murder, Mother," she said, plopping down on the bed. "I happened to be at his place, at his request, when he was murdered."

"You could have at least told me about it yesterday," Elizabeth Barrington said. "Bitsy Davenport saw you on the news this morning and called me. It was humiliating to have to admit I knew nothing about it."

"I've been a little busy, Mother."

"You should never be too busy to call your mother," Elizabeth said. "They reported that you were with that mechanic who killed Max, and you both discovered the body at around six in the morning. What were you doing with him that early?"

"We were going sailing, Mother. Ben didn't murder Max. Ben's his grandson."

"It doesn't mean he isn't a murderer. I mean, what do you expect of a mechanic? He probably saw the chance to inherit all that money and was willing to do whatever it took to get it."

Her mother's words sparked her temper, but years of practice helped Catherine keep her voice level. "That's unfair, Mother. You don't even know him."

"He's a mechanic. What more is there to know?" Elizabeth sighed. "I blame myself for your lapses in judgment. I should never have allowed you to spend time with my sister when you were young and impressionable."

"Aunt Jessica was a wonderful woman, Mother."

"My sister was an embarrassment to her family and a terrible role model for a young girl. Max Windsor wasn't any better, and I don't care how much money he made. He wasn't one of us. I want you out of there."

Catherine's fingers fisted around the bedspread. "Just because you're a snob doesn't mean I am." The words shot out. "Max was a great man, and I'm not leaving until his real murderer is identified. I owe it to him and to Aunt Jessica, who was the *best* role model I could have had."

"I don't think—"

"And I wasn't just with Ben because we were going sailing," Catherine continued. "I'd spent the night with him. You know what? Mechanics are a lot better in bed than surgeons from good families." Then she hung up.

So she'd just violated a whole lot of rules, including 1 and 2—be polite no matter what, and always respect your elders, which was shorthand for "your mother is always right." She'd probably be disowned.

She might as well find out if she was also out of a job. It was the first item on today's To Do list anyway.

"Why would you be?" Melissa Carter asked. Melissa was one of her best friends and also a fellow partner at Whitney and Benson.

"According to my mother, I've scandalized the family. I can't imagine the senior partners are any happier about what's happened."

"Guess again," Melissa said. "Haven't you checked your e-mail?"

"Not yet. Why?"

"Because you'll find a copy of the statement the firm issued this morning. They're using your actions to show how dedicated our attorneys are to carrying out our clients' wishes."

"Maybe that will placate my mother," Catherine said. "She was appalled I found Max's body and was with the prime suspect. I'm sure she was even more appalled when I told her I was there with Ben because I'd spent the night with him."

"You slept with the guy who killed Max?"

"He didn't do it," Catherine said. "Although to be honest, Mother seemed more concerned that he's a mechanic than a possible murderer. She also said some nasty things about Max and Aunt Jessica. So I laid into her about being a snob, then hung up on her."

"Good for you."

Now that Catherine's anger had faded, it had been replaced by guilt. "I need to call her back and apologize," she said, adding that to the bottom of her To Do list. "I shouldn't have talked to my mother like that."

"It's about time you did, and I don't care how many damn rules you violated," Melissa said. "You can't please her no matter what you do, and trying to just drives you crazy."

"I should be able to. My brothers and my sister can."

"You're not like them, and your mother should accept you for who you are. But you've never given her a chance to because she doesn't know what you're really like. You do exactly what she wants you to, including marrying a man you didn't really love."

"I loved Neil."

"I was there, Catherine," Melissa said. "You were more upset about your mother's reaction to the whole cheating and divorce thing than about the fact that Neil cheated on you. He was too stuffy and arrogant for the real you, the one who likes Jimmy Choos and writing romance novels. And who couldn't care less whether someone's ancestors came over on the *Mayflower* or even what someone does for a living."

Melissa was wrong—she had loved Neil, but Catherine wasn't in the mood to argue about it. "Actually Ben isn't just an auto mechanic," she admitted. "He's got an MBA from Harvard and used to be a Wall Street investment banker. I didn't tell Mother that because I was mad, which is petty."

"You can tell her the truth at your wedding."

"I'm not marrying him, for heaven's sake. We just had a casual fling."

"You don't do casual flings."

"He's getting back with his ex anyway," Catherine said. "She flew to his rescue when he was arrested."

"Too bad," Melissa said. "He looks hot. But I still want you to promise you won't even think of apologizing to your mother."

"I don't know . . ."

"Do you honestly want to apologize for defending auto mechanics and your aunt?"

Catherine was silent for a moment. Melissa had a point. And it wasn't as if an apology would change much. Her mother's memory for slights made elephants look forgetful. She crossed the last item off her To Do list. "You're right. I promise."

The next item had seemed like a good idea when she'd written her To Do list last night, but now she was reconsidering. He probably wouldn't be any more unpleasant than her mother, but if she offended him, his retaliation wouldn't be limited to icy stares and pained silences at family gatherings. He'd liked her, but that was when he'd thought she was an exotic dancer.

But she needed to check out everything if she was going to identify Max's killer. Maybe he hadn't heard she was a lawyer. She punched in the phone number and held her breath.

CHAPTER 16

J.P. picked up the phone on the first ring. "I hear you're really a lawyer," he said.

She grimaced. "I apologize for misleading you."

"Yeah, well, normally people who lie to me end up having a few problems. But you got a good excuse since you worked for Max Windsor. Lawyers got to keep stuff confidential."

"I appreciate your understanding," Lexie said. "I assume you've heard that Max was shot and Ben was arrested."

"Yep. I thought people only died twice on soap operas," J.P. said. "Wife number two was a big fan of the soaps. You need money to bail Ben out of jail?"

"He's already out," Lexie said. "I called because I'm looking for information. I assume you have someone watching Dylan, since you found out about the fight at the street dance. I was wondering if that person noticed anyone outside Nevermore the night Max was killed."

"Are you sure you aren't asking whether maybe my spy found out Max was alive, and I had him deep-sixed myself?" J.P. asked. "If he ain't dead, I don't get my money."

Lexie opened her mouth to deny it, and then closed it again. She was sick of lying. "Okay, I'll admit that crossed my mind."

He chuckled. "Like I told you before, you got balls. The short answer is I didn't know Max was alive 'cause I got no one watching

Dylan. I don't got enough men to do that. I heard about the fight 'cause one of my guys has a sister who lives in Lakeview."

"Oh."

"I'll ask around, see if I can find out anything," J.P. said.

"I appreciate it."

"I gotta tell you, I don't like lawyers. Then again, I've never known one what could pass for an exotic dancer."

"Thanks." At least Lexie thought it was a compliment.

"I also got a word of warning for you," J.P. said. "From what I heard, it don't look like whoever hit Max Windsor was a professional. That's bad news, because a professional ain't gonna worry much about getting caught. He'll know he did everything right and won't be. But someone else might hear you're nosing around and panic. So be careful."

Lexie hung up the phone, the muscles in the back of her neck even tenser than before she'd called J.P. She'd never considered that the murderer might decide she was a threat. She'd definitely be careful.

Items three and four on her list involved taking advantage of the small-town gossip network. Lexie went over to the closet and pulled out her navy silk suit, then reconsidered. People would be more comfortable talking to her if she didn't look so much like a lawyer.

She glanced at the bag containing a skirt and tank top she'd impulsively bought the same time she'd gotten her sundress and silver sandals. She'd planned to return them—they were both solid colors, but red. Red was too flashy to be worn other than as an accent color.

Although it was going to be warm today, and she'd accomplish more if she was comfortable.

She took the skirt and tank top out of the bag.

Red actually was a flattering color for her, she thought as she observed herself in the full-length mirror on the bathroom door. She pulled her hair back into a low ponytail and slipped on her brown sandals—wearing the silver ones during the day would be too much of a stretch. Then she headed to Lee's Market.

The store was nearly deserted, and Ruth was working at the front register. "I apologize for thinking you were an exotic dancer," she said when she spotted Lexie. From her cool expression and tone, she was uncomfortable about her misconception.

"No problem. Why wouldn't you believe it, when Ben confirmed it?" Lexie gave her a warm smile.

It didn't thaw Ruth. "I heard you're still here because you want to make sure the cops prove Ben's guilty." Her words were as hard and cold as ice chips.

"I don't think Ben's guilty," Lexie said. "I'm trying to find out the truth so that whoever's guilty doesn't inherit from the trust. And because I want Max's murderer punished."

"Because you're a lawyer, and he paid your law firm a whole lot of money."

"Because I liked Max a lot," Lexie said. "And because my Aunt Jessica loved him, and I loved her."

Ruth studied her with narrowed eyes for a moment. Then her features relaxed, and she grinned, shaking her head. "Well, I'll be. I can't believe I didn't see it before, but you've got her eyes. Your aunt was a real nice lady. I was a big fan of her books. More my type than Max's are, to tell the truth."

"That's why I'm trying to find the real murderer," Lexie said. "Not that I don't have faith in your police—"

Ruth's snort interrupted her. "Our police couldn't find their way out of one of these things," she said, waving a tan-and-blue grocery bag. "I've known Ben a long time, and he would never have hurt his grandfather."

"Do you know anyone in town who might have hated Max?" Lexie asked. "I've assumed he was killed for a share of the trust, but maybe it's something completely different. Someone with a vendetta against him. Or maybe someone thought Max used him in a book and resented it."

"I can't think of anyone offhand, but I'll ask around," Ruth said. "I don't know much about the family, other than Ben and Muriel. Muriel's having money problems."

"I've heard."

"When her husband was alive they were good members of Zion Lutheran," Ruth said. "Now she's into everything, Catholic, Baptist, Methodist, even that yoga and Buddhist stuff. She gives money to all of them, even though she can't afford it. Maybe because she's got a guilty conscience."

"Why would she feel guilty?"

Ruth leaned toward Lexie and lowered her voice. "Muriel came home from a Circle meeting at church one afternoon and found her husband dead of a heart attack. The thing is, she didn't call an ambulance until four thirty. But when Harold had his attack, he fell on his watch, and it stopped at three forty-five, like in one of those mystery stories. According to a neighbor, Muriel got home just after three. She said she didn't go into the house when she got home but instead walked around the neighborhood for more than an hour, said that her Circle meeting gave her lots of stuff to think about. But no one saw her walking, and people kind of wondered if she was in the house when Harold had his attack and let him die. Not that anyone would much blame her, since he wasn't the nicest man. But it could be the reason for all those contributions of hers."

And if Muriel had let her husband die, would it have been that much more of a stretch to kill her brother?

"Hi, Lexie. I mean Catherine."

Lexie started as Seth stepped out of the aisle beside the checkout and greeted her.

"Lexie's fine," she said. "What are you doing here?"

He followed her out the automatic glass door. "I saw you come in and thought I'd try to talk to you. Since you aren't staying at Nevermore anymore."

"About your grandfather's murder?" Lexie asked.

"Actually I wanted to talk about your aunt."

"Why?"

"Because she was such an important part of Grandfather's life. And no one seems to know much about their relationship."

"To be honest, I don't know much about their relationship," Lexie said. "I never saw them together. Not even when I was an adult and my mother couldn't forbid it anymore, which is kind of sad." She'd never thought of that before, but now that she had, she regretted it.

"Your mother disapproved of their relationship?" Seth asked.

"Look, I don't know much, and I'm kind of busy today. Sorry."

She hated to be rude to anyone and especially to one of the trust beneficiaries, but helping Seth document family memories for his kids wasn't her problem. Finding Max's killer was.

She headed for The Clothes Garden.

– – –

Lexie had gone to The Clothes Garden on the assumption the clerks probably heard a lot of gossip. She was right, but unfortunately she didn't learn anything helpful there. She did pick up more clothes, including a pair of red fabric and straw sandals that coordinated nicely with her current outfit. She put on the sandals, and then stopped at Dairy Queen for a burger and fries before heading to Walt's.

At just after noon, Walt's had a half-dozen customers—all male—sitting at a couple of the tables. They stared at Lexie when she walked in, but she ignored them, going directly to the bar. "I'll have a glass of white wine," she told Walt. She usually didn't drink before five, but she thought she should order something.

"All we got is white zinfandel," Walt said.

"Perfect." Lexie detested white zinfandel, but no way was she risking getting plastered on one of Walt's concoctions.

"I heard you're really a lawyer," Walt said as he poured her rose-colored wine.

She nodded. "I'm trying to find out who killed Max since I don't think Ben did. I assume you know a lot of what goes on in Lakeview."

"You got that right." Walt winked. "Including things people would rather I forgot. But I don't know anything about who might have killed Max."

"What are you doing here?"

Lexie turned to see Dylan walking up to the bar. "If you mean in Lakeview, the trustee wants me to stick around a while, so I'm staying at the Lakeview Inn," she said. "I'm in Walt's because I wanted to ask a few questions. How about you?"

"I'm getting drunk. My usual, Walt," Dylan said, then returned his attention to Lexie. "I'm entitled, considering my grandfather's dead and they arrested the only decent member of my family besides my sister."

"You don't think Ben did it?"

"Of course he didn't do it," Dylan said. "He got along with Grandfather better than the rest of us did. Plus he's got money of his own. Nowhere near as much as he'd get from Grandfather, but how much do you need in a podunk place like this?"

"What about the guy you owe money to?" Lexie wasn't about to take J.P.'s word for his innocence. "Have you heard from him?"

Dylan shook his head. "Not since you gave me that message. Maybe Jeremy and Olivia did it."

"Together? Why would you think that?"

"Olivia showed up because Jeremy told her about Grandfather being shot and Ben being a suspect."

"I thought she heard about it on the news."

"Jeremy's news network. I overheard him call her right after the police took Ben in for questioning. Another, Walt."

Lexie's forehead creased. "I thought Olivia hated Jeremy for dumping her after she left Ben."

"If she did, she got over it," Dylan said. "A few months ago I was in Manhattan visiting a friend. We were at Gramercy Tavern, and I spotted Jeremy and Olivia leaving, although they didn't see me. I didn't talk to them because they seemed to be in a hurry to get away. They looked pretty friendly, if you get my meaning."

"When was that?" Lexie asked.

"Right before Easter. We were all at Nevermore for Easter, and I kept waiting for Jeremy to needle Ben about being back with Olivia. But he never did."

Lexie walked out of Walt's a few minutes later, slipping on her sunglasses against the bright sunlight. Maybe Jeremy and Olivia's lunch had been professional, and Dylan had misread the situation. Maybe it had nothing to do with Max's murder.

Except the first attempt on Max's life had been made at Easter dinner, just after Dylan claimed to have seen Jeremy and Olivia together.

She opened her purse and pulled out her cell phone.

CHAPTER 17

Ben was the first to arrive at sherry hour that evening. He poured himself a large Scotch from the bottle in the parlor's liquor cabinet, adding only a single cube from the ice bucket. Usually he preferred a few more rocks, but he was counting on alcohol to make him feel better.

He'd spent the day at work hoping it would distract him. He'd also been hoping that while he was fixing a leaky carburetor on a Yamaha Blaster, his subconscious might come up with a few ideas for how to find Grandfather's killer. Unfortunately his subconscious hadn't had any better luck than his conscious brain had, maybe because work hadn't distracted him from grief and worry. He took a bracing sip of Scotch.

"Is Olivia gone yet?" Cecilia asked as she strode into the parlor. From her tone, more than three years' absence hadn't made her any fonder of his ex-wife.

Ben shook his head. "She's planning to stick around for a while."

"Can't you get rid of her?"

"She did post my bail," Ben said. Although he'd already paid her back. The truth was that at the moment, he couldn't handle the drama trying to convince Olivia to leave would undoubtedly cntail. It was easier to let her stay.

"Could you two tell everyone I won't be at dinner tonight?" Jeremy was standing in the parlor doorway. "I'm taking Lexie to Cleo's." He grinned. "I told her I didn't appreciate that she'd lied to me about who she really is and especially that she'd pretended to be Ben's girlfriend when she wasn't. She's promised to make it up to me. I'll be back at Nevermore by one, although it's going to be a sacrifice."

"I thought Lexie went back to Philadelphia," Ben said when Jeremy had left.

"Dylan said she's staying at the Lakeview Inn," Cecilia said. "Haven't you talked to her?"

"No. You look beautiful tonight, Olivia," Ben told his ex-wife as she paused in the parlor doorway before making her entrance.

"I'm feeling exceptionally well," Olivia said, walking over to him. "It must be getting out of the city." She flashed a cover-girl smile, resting her hand on Ben's sleeve. "Or maybe it's something else."

"You know, I can't face another family dinner," he said. "Why don't we go to Cleo's? The owner's a friend, so I know we can get a table."

"That sounds wonderful," Olivia said. "I'll get my purse."

"What's that about?" Cecilia asked when Olivia had left the parlor.

To be honest, Ben was hoping that seeing Lexie at the restaurant might break the ice, that she'd tell him she didn't believe he was guilty and was willing to discuss things with him. But he wasn't about to share that with Cecilia, if only because it might end up being wishful thinking. "As I said, I'm not up to a family dinner."

Cecilia narrowed her eyes at him. "There are other restaurants."

"Not that meet Olivia's standards."

"So take me. You don't want to go with Olivia."

Ben actually would have preferred Cecilia's company. However, pride wouldn't let him show up with his cousin when Jeremy had a date with Lexie. "Please don't tell me how to run my personal life."

Cecilia waved her hand. "Why not? I'm an expert at screwing up my own. I want you to benefit from my mistakes. I won't let you get back with Olivia in a moment of weakness. Especially not when you can have someone like Lexie."

"Lexie and I had a one-night stand. My only interest in her now is that she's the attorney for Grandfather's trust and wants to identify his killer. That's why I hate it that she thinks I'm guilty."

"I'm sure she doesn't," Cecilia said. "If you won't call her, I will."

"Don't," Ben said firmly. "I don't want you putting her in a difficult situation. I've done enough already."

"And you think showing up at Cleo's with Olivia will make things easier for her?" Cecilia shook her head. "Enjoy your dinner."

– – –

After talking to Dylan, Lexie had called Jeremy, claiming the trustee wanted her to meet with each beneficiary. Jeremy had suggested meeting over dinner at Cleo's, and she'd had no reason to turn him down. She had to eat, and two fast food meals in one day probably wasn't a good idea. Although she doubted a Lakeview restaurant would be much of a step up.

Cleo's surprised her. The décor was simple—cedar-paneled walls covered with framed photos of area scenery, surrounding wooden tables and chairs that were more sturdy than decorative. However, one wall was virtually all windows and provided a spectacular view of Lake Superior. The menu was inventive and the wine list interesting. The restaurant was less than half full tonight, but Jeremy said on weekends it was packed, people driving from Duluth and Thunder Bay just to eat there despite hours-long waits and a no-reservations policy.

Lexie had stuck to small talk since Jeremy had picked her up at her motel. Now that they'd ordered and their wine had been served, it was time to get to the point of this dinner.

"Who do you think killed your grandfather?" she asked. The real point was to confirm what Dylan had told her about Jeremy and Olivia, but Lexie didn't want to open with that. Besides, Jeremy was intelligent and knew the players better than she did, so he might be able to help her find the real killer.

"Probably Ben, since the gun and note can be traced to him and he's the only person who knew Grandfather was alive."

Assuming she could shake Jeremy's knee-jerk prejudice against Ben, that is. "Why would Ben have waited to kill Max if he wanted him dead?" Lexie asked. "Doesn't it make more sense that the murderer was someone who'd just found out Max was alive?"

"Maybe Ben and Grandfather had a falling-out," Jeremy said. "To be honest, it's hard for me to believe Ben's capable of murder, but the evidence points to him. And I don't know who else would have done it."

"Did you have a clue that Max was alive?" she asked, watching him intently. "Was I the only one in the dark?"

Jeremy shook his head, his eyes wide. "God, no. I couldn't believe it when I saw him lying on the ground."

Lexie took a sip of the excellent pinot noir Jeremy had ordered. His claim to have been shocked had sounded and even looked truthful, but he might be an exceptionally good liar. God knows she'd seen some lawyers convincingly spouting positions that should have had their noses hanging down to their knees.

"Look who's here," Jeremy said.

Lexie followed Jeremy's gaze and choked on her wine. Ben and Olivia were walking into the restaurant. What an unpleasant coincidence.

"I mentioned to Ben that we were having dinner here. He's obviously showing me that Olivia now prefers him."

Okay, so it wasn't a coincidence. And what Ben really intended to demonstrate was that things were over between them. "It doesn't bother you to see him with her?" Ben and Olivia's arrival did provide the perfect segue to quiz Jeremy about his relationship with Olivia.

"Not a bit," Jeremy said. "Once I got to know her, I discovered I was much more attracted to her looks than to her personality. Ben's welcome to her."

"You've kept in touch with her, though."

"Nope. I haven't seen or even talked to Olivia since we broke things off." He took Lexie's hand. "I much prefer sexy Philadelphia lawyers."

"Especially since I slept with Ben."

Jeremy had the grace to look embarrassed. "Okay, I'll admit that in the past I was a little competitive with Ben, but I've outgrown that. My interest in you has nothing to do with Ben."

Maybe Jeremy's interest was because he thought he'd be able to convince her of Ben's guilt as a way of covering up his own. He'd lied about his contacts with Olivia.

Assuming Dylan hadn't lied about seeing Jeremy and Olivia together in Manhattan to cover his own guilt.

Lexie glanced toward Ben and Olivia just in time to see them being seated at a corner table, obviously anxious for privacy. She returned her attention to Jeremy. "I think we've talked enough about Ben. Tell me about your new business venture."

– – –

By the time they'd finished dinner, Lexie knew enough about Jeremy's new business venture to check it out. Even without checking, it sounded viable to her. He also was traveling to London to watch Wimbledon at the end of the month—he was an avid tennis player—and was waiting for a Porsche he'd special-ordered nine weeks ago. He'd insisted on paying for dinner and used a platinum Visa that was accepted without a problem. Combined with what she'd learned the afternoon they'd spent on the speedboat, Jeremy didn't sound at all hurting for money.

On the other hand, appearances could be deceiving. Jeremy also clearly had expensive tastes. He could have been willing to kill for the chance to be filthy rich, as opposed to simply extremely well off.

"Before we leave, we should stop by and acknowledge Ben and Olivia," Jeremy said after he'd signed the credit card receipt.

That was the last thing Lexie wanted to do, but she couldn't object. She certainly didn't want Ben thinking she was crushed about his reconciliation with his wife.

"I was surprised to see you here tonight, Ben," Jeremy said when he and Lexie had reached the cozy corner table. Ben was sitting on one side with Olivia directly to his left.

Ben set down his fork. He'd nearly finished his steak and scallops, but Olivia appeared to have only taken a couple of bites of her lemongrass-crusted salmon with watercress ginger sauce. Either she was a slow eater or one of those annoying women who only pretended to eat, even when the food was fantastic—as Lexie knew it was since she'd ordered the same thing and wolfed it down.

"When you mentioned eating out, I realized that for once you had a good idea," Ben told Jeremy, and then he met Lexie's eyes. "How are you, Catherine?"

"Everyone's still calling me Lexie," she said. "It's easier."

"Lexie, then. How long are you going to be around?"

"That's up in the air right now."

"It's nice to see the two of you together again," Jeremy said.

Ben snorted. "Right."

"I'm serious," Jeremy said. "I regret the part I played in the breakup of your marriage. I hope you can work things out."

Olivia rested a possessive hand on Ben's arm. "We intend to."

Lexie had to admit she was disappointed as she accompanied Jeremy out of the restaurant. She'd hoped Ben would have suggested getting together to discuss the murder, since she could use his help. He not only hadn't, but he hadn't even acted as if they were friends. Now that he was back with his wife, he probably considered any contact with his one-night stand awkward. Or maybe he didn't think she'd be any help finding Max's murderer. After all, she hadn't been able to do it in time to save Max's life.

In either case, she could take a hint. If she was going to find Max's murderer, she was on her own.

– – –

The next morning, Lexie headed to Nevermore.

After she'd gotten back to the motel and rid herself of Jeremy—which had proven a bigger challenge than she'd anticipated—she'd realized that even without Ben, she didn't have to do this alone. Trey would want his best friend's murderer punished, and Cecilia would want to help Ben. Assuming Cecilia wasn't guilty, but Lexie couldn't believe she was, and not just because she liked her. If Cecilia had done it, she wouldn't have framed Ben.

Lexie sped up when she got out of town. A sparkling Lake Superior filled her rearview mirror, and thick pines and birch trees surrounded the hilly road with green velvet and touches of silver. She'd disliked this road, but that's when she'd thought it was where Max had died. Now she could appreciate its beauty. She pushed the brake to take a curve.

The car didn't slow.

She pushed the pedal down again and again. Nothing happened. The car kept careening forward, rounding the curve, and then speeding up as she descended a steep hill.

Lexie's heart was pounding, pumping cold panic through her body. A yellow warning sign announced a winding road and recommended a speed of thirty. She was going seventy. She fumbled for the emergency brake and pulled it, bracing herself for a fast stop.

The car continued speeding downhill.

She should downshift, but the car was already entering a curve. She needed both hands on the wheel to stay on the road, didn't dare take one off for even a second. Her hammering heart was pummeling her lungs, making it hard to breathe. She was going so fast she could barely read the sign warning this wasn't a single curve but several.

The other lane was blessedly empty, so Lexie muscled the steering wheel around the first curve, going wide. The car was traveling even faster as she jerked the steering wheel as hard as she could the other way, trying to make the next curve.

She didn't.

Max might not have died this way, but she was about to.

That was her last thought before the car split the wire cord barrier and plunged into the ravine.

CHAPTER 18

"Catherine Barrington's been in a car accident."

Ben's gut had clenched when Mike showed up at the garage wearing his police uniform, but his words twisted it inside out. "Is she okay?" Ben asked.

"Just a little bruised," Mike said. "She's damn lucky. She hit one of the few trees that would have stopped her car, and the airbag kept her from getting hurt worse."

Thank God. Ben's conscience couldn't handle another death or even serious injury, and this one would have definitely been on his conscience. If he'd talked Grandfather out of his stupid plan in the first place, Lexie would never have been involved. "What happened?"

Mike leaned against the wall beneath one of the dozen posters that decorated the garage, this one an old ad featuring the Michelin Man. "That's what I need to ask you," he said.

"What do you mean?"

"A couple of hours ago when Catherine was driving up to Nevermore, her brakes went out. The emergency brake didn't work, either. That all seems a little unlikely when she's driving a new rental car, not unless they had some help. Did you give them that help?"

This time it was Ben's fist that clenched. "You think I tampered with Lexie's brakes? Why the hell would I do that?"

Mike crossed his arms, accentuating his stomach rolls. With all the weight he'd gained since high school, he looked a little like the Michelin Man himself, stuffed into a cop uniform. "Everyone in town knows she's trying to find out who killed Max."

"Since I didn't kill Grandfather, I *want* her to find the truth," Ben said. "Besides, you guys already think I did it. Why would I be concerned about Lexie?"

"You know we might not have enough evidence to convict you, not with that slick New York City lawyer you got defending you. But Ms. Barrington's a big-city lawyer herself, so she could probably find enough new evidence to put you away."

Ben pressed his fists against his sides, resisting the urge to beat some sense into Mike. He couldn't believe that the cops actually thought he'd ever hurt Lexie. "Were Lexie's brakes tampered with last night?" he asked, managing to keep his tone level. "Because I had dinner at Cleo's, then went back to Nevermore. I've got witnesses."

"We don't rightly know when it was done," Mike said. "Ms. Barrington hasn't driven her car since two days ago, and it's been sitting in the lot behind the Lakeview Inn."

"So anyone could have done it," Ben pointed out.

"Assuming someone else knew what to do, which I doubt."

"I'm sure there are Internet sites that explain how to drain brake fluid or cut the brake line." Ben's voice had an edge—he was losing his battle to control his temper.

Mike's eyes narrowed. "How do you know that's what was done?"

"I don't," Ben said. "Those are the easiest ways to tamper with brakes."

"We just happened to find the emergency brake cut and a puddle of fluid in the parking lot where her car had been."

Ben raised his chin and narrowed his own eyes. "Are you charging me with this?" He sounded as belligerent as he felt.

Mike unfolded his arms and took a step away from the wall, his flaccid features stony. Ben should have remembered a challenge always made Mike dig in. "Not yet. But I'd advise you to stay away from Catherine Barrington. Because if anything else happens to her, I'll be back."

– – –

Lexie answered a knock on her motel room door later that morning to find Cecilia standing there.

"Could I talk to you for a minute, Lexie? Sorry, I mean Catherine."

"Lexie's fine. Come in." Lexie gestured to the shabby tan upholstered chair in the corner. "Have a seat."

Cecilia sat down, and then surveyed the room. "This is supposed to be the only decent motel in town. I guess 'decent' is a relative term."

Which was true. Between its monochromatic color scheme, stark furnishings, and slight odor of disinfectant, it had all the ambiance of a public restroom. "On the plus side, it's clean," Lexie said. At least as clean as you could get a room with carpeting and furnishings she'd bet were older than she was.

She sat down on the edge of the bed. "What can I do for you?"

"I heard about your accident," Cecilia said. "We could hear the ambulance and police cars at Nevermore, so Jeremy and I drove down to check what had happened. The cops refused to tell us anything, even who'd been hurt, until I recognized your rental car. Then they said you were fine and had been brought to your motel."

"I got a couple of bruises, but nothing serious." Lexie frowned, which made the bruise on her forehead ache. "It's a little ironic how close I came to re-creating the way we originally thought Max died."

"It's horrible," Cecilia said. "I stopped by to make sure you really are okay and see if you need anything. A ride to pick up a replacement car? Or anywhere else?"

"Thanks, but the rental company's having another car delivered here, since the brake failure could have been a problem they missed when they last checked the car."

Cecilia's dark eyes widened, and she pressed her fingers against her lips. "Oh my God. Your brakes went out? I assumed you were going too fast and missed the curve."

Lexie shook her head. "When I pushed on the brakes, they wouldn't work."

Cecilia touched Lexie's arm. "I'm so glad you're all right."

"Me, too," Lexie said, and then met Cecilia's eyes. "I want to apologize for lying about my identity."

"I understand. You were doing it for Grandfather," Cecilia said. "I am a little hurt that you haven't called me since you moved out of Nevermore. I thought we were friends, but maybe you were just pretending so you could figure out if I killed Grandfather."

"I figured out pretty early that you weren't guilty, and I'd honestly like to be your friend," Lexie said. "I didn't call because I wasn't sure you'd want to talk to me after the way I misled you."

"Like I said, I understand," Cecilia said. "Do you think Ben's guilty? Is that why you haven't talked to him?"

Lexie blinked. She'd never considered that anyone might think that. "Of course he isn't guilty. I haven't talked to him because I don't have any reason to." She smiled humorlessly. "I thought we were working together to find Max's murderer, but he withheld the little detail that Max wasn't even dead."

"So he lied to you the same way you lied to me," Cecilia said. "I'm willing to forgive you because you did it for Grandfather, because you felt like you owed it to him. That's the same way Ben felt."

"I've been trying to find out who killed Max, since I know Ben didn't," Lexie said. "I was on my way to Nevermore this morning to ask you a couple of questions."

"Shoot."

Lexie smiled faintly. "You must have read my mind, because my first question is about the murder weapon. The cops said Max kept the gun in the basement. Who knew that?"

"I assume everyone did," Cecilia said. "Grandfather had bookshelves full of things related to his writing. The gun was there in plain sight for years, along with ammunition. You had to pass by it to get to the laundry room, the wine cellar, and the beer refrigerator."

"Did anyone ever say or do anything that might indicate he or she knew your grandfather was alive? Or do anything else suspicious?"

Cecilia chewed her lower lip for a moment. "Not that I can think of," she finally said. "It's hard to imagine any of my relatives giving Grandfather arsenic or shooting through Nevermore's window, let alone shooting him at close range. What about Dylan's loan shark?"

"I'm checking him out," Lexie said. "If you think of anything that might be related to Max's murder, even something insignificant, please call me."

"I will. I'll do whatever I can to help Ben."

"By the way, did you ever go out with Peter?"

Cecilia nodded, chewing her lower lip again. "It was a disaster."

"I'm sorry. Did he turn out to be a jerk or just boring?"

"He turned out to be wonderful."

Lexie's eyebrows rose. "I think I missed something here."

"He's the nicest, most considerate man I've ever met." Cecilia was wringing her hands together. "He's traveled all over and is interested in all sorts of things. He made me laugh and asked my opinion about things and really listened to what I said. And he's the world's best kisser. Probably the best at everything else, too, although we didn't do anything more than kiss."

"Why's that a problem?" Cecilia's distraught tone and obvious agitation were at complete odds with her words.

"I was supposed to have a lousy time, so then I wouldn't have to worry about telling him I've been divorced three times. Instead I'm going out with him again tonight. What should I do?"

Lexie had forgotten that concern. "If you like him, you need to tell him the truth," she said. "Explain that your mother convinced you that you were like her and needed a man to support you. So you'd marry one wrong man, get divorced, and immediately latch on to another because you were afraid you'd starve otherwise."

Cecilia's hands halted. "That sounds like something Ben would say."

"Ben did say it. You can also tell Peter that you've changed and are determined to do something more with your life. Volunteer work or maybe go back to college and have a career. If he still rejects you because of your past, he doesn't deserve you. But I'll bet he'll understand."

Lexie's lecture was interrupted by her cell phone. "I should take that. It's the police." She answered. "I see," she said when the cop on the other end finished talking. "Thanks."

"Is something wrong?" Cecilia asked after Lexie had hung up.

Lexie's stomach was whirling like a Jacuzzi on overdrive, but she shook her head. "I need to sign another form, but it can wait until my new rental shows up."

Cecilia got to her feet. "I almost forgot—I also wanted to invite you to sherry hour and dinner tomorrow night. Grandfather didn't want a funeral, but we wanted to do something to celebrate him and his life. I don't know why we didn't think of that before."

"Seeing his dead body makes his death a lot more real," Lexie said. "I'll be there."

After Cecilia left, Lexie bent over, her head between her legs. The churning in her stomach had spread, and she was feeling a little dizzy. Panicky.

She didn't know why she hadn't told Cecilia the truth. It was bound to come out. But saying the words would make it real, the same way seeing Max's dead body had. And she didn't want this to be real.

According to the cops, someone had made a hole in her brake line and also cut the emergency brake. J.P. was right. She'd managed to upset someone, and that someone had tried to kill her.

– – –

"How's Lexie doing?" Walt asked, setting an open bottle of Summit in front of Ben. "I heard about her accident."

After Mike had left, Ben had needed to get out of the garage. He'd told Trudy he was going to get an early lunch and headed to Walt's. He was in the mood for a liquid lunch. "I haven't talked to her, but apparently she's fine. She was lucky it wasn't worse." Ben took a long swig of Summit pale ale.

"I heard that, too," Walt said. He tapped his knuckles against his chin a few times, looking unusually serious. "I'm not all that sure it was luck."

"What do you mean?"

"I think maybe your grandfather had a hand in saving her."

"Grandfather's dead," Ben said. "Really dead, this time."

Walt rested his beefy hands on the bar in front of Ben and leaned over it. "I'm talking about his ghost," he whispered.

"You believe in ghosts?"

Before answering, Walt looked across the room at the only other customers, two men with buzz cuts and beer guts who were sitting at one of the tables. They were involved in an animated conversation of their own. "Not usually, but Max always was a determined bastard," Walt said, his voice still low. "He's also bound to feel like he should protect Lexie, seeing as how he got her into this. Especially since her trouble happened on his property."

"I didn't have anything to do with it, no matter what you heard." Ben took another drink.

"Course you didn't," Walt said in a normal tone. "You'd never do something like that. And why the hell would you want to hurt Lexie when she's trying to clear you?"

Ben slammed his bottle down on the bar. "Lexie's trying to clear me?"

Walt nodded. "She asked me to let her know if I heard anything that might be related to Max's murder. Asked Ruby and the gals at The Clothes Garden to do the same thing. She said she knows you aren't guilty, and our cops are idiots, so it's up to her to find out who did it. She didn't exactly come out and call the cops idiots, but that's what she meant."

Lexie didn't think he'd killed Grandfather. The vise that had been crushing Ben's chest since his arrest loosened a little.

"It's probably none of my business, but I think you're as big an idiot as our cops," Walt continued. "Taking back your ex-wife instead of sticking with Lexie. I mean, Lexie might be a big-city lawyer, but she's nice and not a bit stuck-up. She's a lot like her aunt was. And I don't know her real well, but I can't see Lexie taking up with Jeremy the way that ex-wife of yours did. Though like I said, it's none of my business."

Ben grinned for probably the first time since he'd seen his grandfather's murdered body. "When has that ever stopped you?"

Walt grinned back, wide enough to expose a missing tooth. "Probably never, least not when it comes to people I care about."

"Thanks, Walt." For more than the beer. Ben put a five on the bar.

Walt handed the bill back to him. "It's on the house. Take care of yourself."

– – –

"I wanted to tell you that I didn't tamper with your brakes. No matter what the cops think."

Lexie felt a hint of disappointment that Ben's call hadn't been motivated by concern about her. However, her predominant emotion was annoyance. "I should have guessed they'd assume that since you're an auto mechanic, you must be guilty. They're too dumb to realize that if you wanted to hurt someone, you'd *never* do it that way because you'd be the first person suspected. And what's your motive for wanting me dead?"

"To get rid of you before you find more evidence I'm guilty."

"Except I know you didn't do it," she said. "I'm looking for evidence that someone else did it. I'll call the cops and tell them that."

"A waste of time."

"You're probably right." Lexie heard a car drive up outside and checked out the window. A UPS truck that she doubted was delivering her new rental.

"How do you know I'm not guilty?" Ben asked.

"If you were, you'd have been smart enough to destroy Max's note and hide the gun somewhere besides your pickup. More important, you loved your grandfather too much to ever kill him."

"Thanks. It's a relief to have you on my side."

She couldn't believe he'd honestly thought she suspected him, even after what Cecilia had implied. "Don't be too relieved," she said. "I haven't found out much. Do you have time to meet? I'd like your advice about what I should investigate next."

"My advice is that you quit investigating and go back to Philadelphia," Ben said. "Not because I'm scared you'll find evidence implicating me, but for your own safety. Someone tried to kill you."

"I doubt the intent was to kill me," Lexie said. "The brakes could just as well have gone out when I was driving slowly and on level ground." A few hours had made her more rational about that—or maybe just more willing to engage in wishful thinking.

"Well, someone wanted to scare you and didn't care if you got hurt," Ben said. "I'll hire a P.I. to investigate. My lawyer wants me to anyway."

"People around here will talk to me more than they will a P.I.," Lexie said. "If someone's worried about me, I must be getting close. I'll be careful, but I need to do this. I owe it to Max. And I could use your help."

Ben was silent for a moment. "We'll need to meet privately," he finally said. "When the cops questioned me about your brakes, they also warned me to stay away from you."

That sparked Lexie's temper yet again. "They have no legal right to do that." Maybe it was being stuck in this depressing motel room all day waiting for that damn car, but the local cops seemed more irritating than usual.

"I know they don't have a right, but I'd rather not piss them off," Ben said. "And isn't talking to me some sort of conflict of interest?"

"I'm talking to all the beneficiaries, at the request of the trustee."

"I'm the one accused of murder."

"You haven't been convicted of anything."

"I've got some paperwork to do after the garage closes, so I'm skipping sherry hour and dinner tonight," Ben said. "Could you come by at six thirty?"

She could if her rental had arrived by then. Although if it hadn't, she just might have to call the cops, tell them what she thought about their suspicions of Ben, and ask them to do something useful for a change—like give her a ride to his garage. "I'll see you at six thirty."

CHAPTER 19

At 6:28 p.m., Lexie pulled her new rental car into Ben's garage, parking beside a rusty white pickup. She was a little apprehensive about seeing him, but that was only natural. She was embarrassed about their one-night stand now that she'd reverted to Catherine, especially since he was back with his wife. She was also still upset about the way he'd misled her.

Her top priority was finding Max's murderer, though, and Ben was the person most likely to be able to help. She grabbed her purse and notepad and got out of the car.

"How are you feeling?" Ben's voice and expression held genuine concern, but it was undoubtedly motivated by guilt—guilt that her accident wouldn't have happened if he'd told her the truth about Max, not because he was the one who'd tampered with her brakes.

"Not bad," she said as she accompanied him to his office. "I was very lucky."

"Walt's convinced it was more than luck," Ben said. "He thinks Grandfather had a hand in saving you since he was responsible for getting you involved in this."

Lexie sat down on a folding chair. "I think Walt's been sampling his special a little too freely."

Ben opened the refrigerator and got her a water. Then he popped open a can of Coke and sat down on the other chair.

"Do you want to tell me your ideas first, or should I tell you what I've learned?" Lexie asked, pleased she sounded coolly professional. She needed to treat this like the business meeting it essentially was.

Ben met her eyes. "First I want to apologize. I'm sorry I didn't tell you Grandfather was alive. For what it's worth, I tried several times to convince him to let you in on it, but he refused. I could have told you anyway, I guess, but Grandfather told me I owed him for taking me in when I was thirteen."

"Max was good with the guilt card," Lexie said. "As Cecilia pointed out, I was doing the exact same thing, lying to everyone in the house because your grandfather wanted me to. But you certainly could have told me you were an ex-I-banker and Harvard grad."

"Why's that a big deal? Did you sleep with me just to get back at your mother since you thought I was a mere mechanic?" His blue eyes had turned stormy, his tone anger-meets-bitterness.

"Of course not," Lexie said, anger at his assumption edging her own voice. "But it would have made sense for you to have a smart girlfriend no matter who you normally dated, so I wouldn't have made a fool out of myself pretending to be someone I wasn't." Memory clogged her throat, and she took a hard swallow of water. "The whole thing made me feel like when I found out my husband had been cheating. I swore I'd never be that foolish again."

"Why did you feel foolish?" Ben asked. "Olivia's cheating made me feel a lot of things, but not that, even though her partner was my own cousin."

"Because I learned about it from my mother, who'd heard it at our country club. She wanted to know why I hadn't mentioned it and what I was doing to win Neil back, since Barringtons didn't get divorced." Lexie's hand tightened around her bottled water. "Do you have any idea how embarrassing it was to admit I hadn't told her because I didn't have a clue it was going on? Especially since it was apparently common knowledge at the country club."

Ben grimaced. "I wasn't trying to embarrass you," he said. "The cocktail waitress girlfriend thing was actually Grandfather's inspiration, and I couldn't talk him out of it."

"Because he thought people would be less likely to suspect I was really his lawyer?"

"So he claimed. I think it was more because he was trying to manipulate both of us. He thought pretending to be a cocktail waitress would force you to be more laid back, and he was hoping you'd like it. The girlfriend part was to force me into close contact with someone intelligent, which he hoped would make me realize I missed using my brain and decide to go back to Wall Street."

That sounded exactly like Max, thinking he could mold real lives the way he did fictional ones. "You left New York and your job because of your divorce, right?" Lexie hadn't even left the country club Neil and Deidre also belonged to. Maybe Melissa was right that she hadn't loved Neil enough.

"It's more complicated than that," Ben said. "A close friend dropped dead of a heart attack. He was only thirty-eight, and it freaked me out so much that I reevaluated my life. I realized I was burned out, sick of working long hours making money for people who didn't need or deserve it. I wanted to do something that might pay less but would be more rewarding in other ways. And would give me time to spend with a family. Unfortunately Olivia wasn't thrilled with the idea."

"About your changing jobs?"

"Or having a family." He picked a pen off the desk, gripping it like a knife and stabbing the blotter as he spoke. "When we got married, I assumed she wanted kids someday. I'd either read her wrong or she'd changed her mind, because she didn't want kids or anything else that would alter our lifestyle. We argued about it a lot, although I was sure we'd work it out. Then she left me for Jeremy, and I snapped. I'd worked as a mechanic in high school and college summers and liked it. So I decided I was going to change my whole life, starting by moving back to Lakeview and becoming the world's most fair and honest auto mechanic."

He dropped the pen. "Grandfather's murder must be related to whatever he wanted to talk to me about that night."

Lexie accepted Ben's abrupt change of subject. Memory Lane wasn't her favorite street, either. Although now she understood his refusal to date any woman who might want a career. From his history with his father and his ex-wife, he assumed that someone career-driven wouldn't be able to focus on both him and having a family. He was wrong, but she could understand it now.

"If so, wouldn't Max have given me a hint when he appeared to me?" she asked.

"Not if he wasn't positive he was right and planned to meet me a couple of hours later to discuss it," Ben said. "He might have intended to confront the person he thought was guilty and invited that person to the meeting, too, thinking I'd be there to protect him if necessary." His features clenched, as if he were fighting a cramp. "When I didn't show up, Grandfather confronted the killer alone and ended up dead."

"Maybe he just wanted to tell you that he'd appeared to me so I wouldn't catch you off-guard," Lexie said. "When he went outside to wait for you, someone saw him, panicked, and killed him."

Ben shot her an I-don't-buy-it look. "I know you're trying to make me feel better, and I appreciate it." At least he didn't appear quite so pained. "Let's assume Grandfather learned something important, probably related to the previous attempts on his life.

You should check out the secret passages and the room he stayed in for clues. The cops have done it and so have I, but maybe you'll notice something I missed."

"We should also check his laptop."

"The police have it now, but I checked it out first," Ben said. "The only things on it are letters to his agent and publishers and his newest work in progress. A great premise, but no clues there. You said you've learned something?"

Lexie told him what she'd learned about Muriel. "And Dylan told me something, but I'm not sure it's true."

"What?"

"He claims he overheard Jeremy call Olivia and tell her about Max's murder and your arrest."

"Jeremy probably did call her, figuring it would cause problems between you and me."

"The thing is, Dylan also claims he saw Jeremy and Olivia lunching together in New York, just before Easter."

"After Dylan's had a winning streak, he spends a lot of time in Manhattan, so he could have seen them."

"Dylan said that the way they were acting, he assumed they'd gotten back together," Lexie said. "But Jeremy told me that he hadn't talked to Olivia since they broke up, so Dylan could have made the whole thing up, trying to deflect suspicion from himself." If they were going to find Max's murderer, she needed to be straight with Ben, but he was down enough without thinking he'd lost Olivia once again.

Ben rocked back in his chair, steepling his fingers. "Maybe Jeremy and Olivia are together but keeping it secret. Maybe Jeremy killed Grandfather, and she's trying to stay close enough to me to make sure I'm convicted."

"I can't believe that," Lexie said. Ben sounded remarkably complacent about his theory, but pride naturally had him hiding how much the possibility hurt. "When I ran into Olivia at the jail, she told me she'd changed and realized she wanted you enough to compromise."

Ben righted his chair. "I have a feeling that learning I'm about to inherit a fortune has a lot to do with Olivia's renewed interest in me. She called the day after everyone thought Grandfather had been killed in a car accident, which was the first time I'd talked to her since our divorce. She claimed she'd wanted to get back together for a while, but hadn't proposed it to me because she knew Grandfather wouldn't approve after her affair with Jeremy. That doesn't sound like Olivia, though. She'd have assumed she could convince me to defy Grandfather."

"You're willing to take her back even though you believe she's only after your money?" That Ben loved Olivia that much made Lexie's chest ache, but it was just from hurt pride. "Sorry, that's none of my business," she quickly added.

Ben was looking at her as if she'd spoken in tongues, not just tactlessly. "Who said I'm willing to take her back?"

"Olivia said you're getting back together. She's also staying at Nevermore with you."

"Not in my room. She's only at Nevermore because I didn't think I could refuse her request to stay there after she loaned me bail money when I was having trouble getting the cash." He picked up the pen again, turning it over in his fingers. "The truth is, I've realized Jeremy did me a favor breaking up our marriage. Olivia and I really don't have that much in common."

Lexie nodded slowly. "Because she's a smart, ambitious professional woman, and you're done with that kind of life."

"No, because Olivia cares more about money than people," Ben said. "Plus she's a little too bitchy for my taste." He was flicking the pen against his thigh now. "Against all my convictions, I've discovered I'm attracted to another smart, ambitious professional woman. Which shows what a masochist I am, since she clearly prefers Jeremy."

Lexie's eyes widened. "I only went to dinner with Jeremy to ask about his relationship with Olivia. As I told you before, he isn't my type."

Ben stood, then took her hand and pulled her to her feet. The smile he gave her made desire coil in her stomach. "I want to show you something."

She followed him out of the office to a red convertible with a tan interior parked in the back of the garage. "Nice car," she said. "Although I don't know much about cars."

"This is a beauty. It's a 1967 Corvette, to my mind one of the hottest Corvettes ever made, with great performance features. This one has been completely rebuilt with a close-ratio four-speed transmission and a three-fifty-horsepower engine." Ben patted the hood, then released her hand and circled the car as he continued. "It's got nineteen factory options, including power everything, a speed-warning dashboard, and headrest seats. It might not be a trailer queen—"

"A what?"

"A car that's rarely driven and usually transported by trailer," Ben said. "But it's been perfectly maintained. It's a hell of a car." He stopped walking when he was directly in front of her. "Now I have a question for you."

"About the car?" Her heart was hammering, and she was a little breathless.

"Sort of." He moved toward her, backing her against the passenger door. She could feel him already hard against her, and her body heated in response.

"Here's the question." His voice was low and a little rough. "Have you ever done it in a '67 Corvette?"

– – –

So now she could add sneaking around to her list of sins, Lexie thought as she pulled out of Ben's garage a couple of hours later. Not that she had any real reason to sneak around, since she and Ben were both single, but it still was undoubtedly something a proper Barrington didn't do, so obvious her mother hadn't considered a specific rule necessary. She could guarantee that having sex with a suspected murderer fell into the obvious category, no matter how convinced she was of Ben's innocence.

Yet she had absolutely no qualms about what she'd done, which worried her. She was supposed to feel at least a little guilty about her improper behavior. She was starting to think maybe she wasn't a Barrington at all, that her parents had brought the wrong baby home from the hospital. Or maybe she'd really been born to her Aunt Jessica, who'd decided she didn't want a child. Although it was hard to imagine Jessica consenting to have her biological daughter named Catherine Alcxandra, let alone raised by her stuffy sister.

Lexie smiled faintly. She was still very glad she'd been born years before Jessica had taken up with Max. Discovering she was Max's long-lost daughter while having a fling with his grandson was a complication this already convoluted adventure did not need.

CHAPTER 20

Trey called at eight the next morning. "I hope I didn't wake you," he said. "I need to talk to you."

That was convenient, since Lexie had planned to call him. Even though she was now working with Ben, she still intended to ask Trey for help. According to Ben, Max had recommended it. "Should I meet you at Nevermore?" she asked.

"Could you come to my house? I don't want to risk anyone overhearing us."

The tension underlying his tone kicked Lexie's pulse up a notch. She'd assumed Trey had a question related to the trust. But why would he worry about that being overheard? "Is this about Max's murder?" she asked.

"It might be."

— — —

A half hour later Lexie was inside a large Victorian house perched on a bluff overlooking Lake Superior. "This is beautiful," she said as she walked into a living room that could have been featured in a decorating magazine. Enormous windows on one side let in sunlight and a stunning lake view. A sofa the same sapphire as the lake and two scarlet chairs were atop a Persian carpet featuring the same colors; dark wood coffee and end tables sported needlework cloths and flower-filled vases. "Elegant, yet homey."

"All thanks to my late wife," Trey said. "She was a talented decorator."

"Several people mentioned what a wonderful woman she was, all the work she did for the hospital," Lexie said.

"And First Baptist Church, the garden club, the Girl Scouts, and a dozen other groups." Pride warmed Trey's voice. "Maria was a very giving woman. We weren't able to have children, so she gave all her energy to projects. She died four years ago."

"I'm very sorry."

"Thanks. She had a heart attack, so at least she didn't suffer. Although I certainly did." Pain flickered across his features. "Max was a big help, since he understood how hard it is to lose the woman you love." Trey gestured to the sofa. "Please sit down."

"You said you might know something relevant?" Lexie asked when they were both seated.

Trey was silent for a moment, studying the Persian carpet as if seeing it for the first time. "Something that could be damaging to Ben." His gaze was still on the carpet. "I'm not sure whether I should tell the police about it. I'm not sure I should tell you, either, since it won't be protected by attorney-client privilege."

"If you know something, you should tell the police." Much as she hated the idea of more evidence against Ben, she felt obligated to say that. It was probably nothing, anyway, and Trey was just being an overcautious accountant. If any major evidence against Ben were out there, Ben would certainly have mentioned it to her.

Trey finally looked up. "I like Ben a lot." There was weariness in his face, in his tone. "I've known him since he was a kid, and we've always had a good relationship. He's as close as I've got to a son. I guess that's why I discounted this before and didn't mention it when you asked about everyone's motives, especially since Max had chosen Ben to work with you. But now that Max has been murdered and Ben's the prime suspect . . ."

"What do you know?"

Trey was quiet for a moment longer, then let out a long breath. "Ben and Max had a huge argument a couple of months ago. I normally would have been gone by then, but I'd stuck around late because I wanted to finish Max's taxes. I doubt either of them knew I was still in my office, since I had the door and blinds closed." He gave her a rueful half smile. "To be honest, I didn't want Max to know I was around because he'd come in and want to talk, and I wanted to finish the damn taxes."

"So Ben doesn't know you overheard them?"

"I doubt it," Trey said. "Max told Ben that he wanted him to quit working at the garage and get a job where he used his brains and God-given talents. Max thought it was unforgivable for anyone to waste those things. Guess he didn't think Ben's mechanical talents were in the same category. They'd argued about that before, but this time was different."

"Why?"

"Max had just found out that Ben planned to expand the garage. Max was furious because he'd assumed Ben was just taking a few years off from finance, but expanding the garage made it look like he wasn't planning to go back ever. Max told Ben if he didn't get a more appropriate job, he'd be disinherited. As far as I know, he'd never made that threat before."

"When did Max and Ben have this conversation?" Although Lexie had a feeling she knew what was coming. The income tax part had given it away.

"A couple of days before Easter. I remember thinking that I hoped it didn't make the holiday any more unpleasant than family gatherings usually were."

"This past Easter?"

"Yep. The Easter when Max was poisoned."

– – –

After leaving Trey's house, Lexie sat in her idling car for a moment, her muscles so tight even her scalp hurt. When she'd played pool with Ben's lawyer, he'd mentioned Ben had given up his plan to expand the garage. That made it sound as if Ben had taken Max's threat seriously. Had it also upset him enough to kill his grandfather? If the incident hadn't been a big deal, why hadn't Ben mentioned it?

Maybe she'd been wrong when she'd concluded Ben was innocent. Maybe he'd fooled Max and was now playing her, making it appear so obvious he was being framed that she'd conclude he was innocent. Maybe he'd made love to her to manipulate her so she wouldn't believe anything incriminating she heard about him.

Lexie shook her head. She still couldn't believe Ben was guilty. If she were lucky, at least one of the items on today's To Do list would prove she was right.

When she reached Nevermore, all but one of the rental cars usually parked around the circular driveway were gone. She drove around back and parked beside the carriage house. According to Ben, her car would be visible only if someone happened to look out the entertainment room window, but that room was rarely used during the day. If she were lucky, no one would know she was here.

Grabbing the flashlight she'd discovered in the glove compartment of her new rental, Lexie got out of the car and headed to

Nevermore's back door. She used the key she'd gotten from Ben, hoping to avoid alerting anyone she was there. Once inside the house, she tiptoed to the library.

Lexie had never been inside the library before. The west wall was entirely glass that would showcase a stunning view of the sun setting over the woods. Floor-to-ceiling shelves jam-packed with books covered the remaining walls. She headed to the bookshelf on the north wall.

Ben had told her that the lever to get into the secret passages was located—appropriately enough—behind Max's book *Deadly Passages*. Lexie found the book, pulled the lever, and the bookshelf opened, exposing a dark passage. She grinned. She felt as if she'd stepped back into an old Nancy Drew mystery, since she'd never have believed anything like this existed in real life. One more unique experience she could thank Max for.

She switched on her flashlight, took a deep breath, and walked into the passage. She shone her light to the right of the door until she found the red button, and then pushed it. The wall closed.

A wave of cold panic engulfed her, the dark making her claustrophobic. Lexie punched the button again. The wall swung open, exposing the library. She took a couple of deep breaths and reclosed the wall. Then she followed Ben's instructions to Max's secret room.

If she'd had any doubts, the room Max had stayed in would have convinced Lexie that he really had feared someone was trying to kill him. It was gloomy and depressing, windowless with bare cream walls and a plywood floor. She dug through a pile of magazines on the nightstand beside the bed, smiling faintly when she reached a couple of financial statements that Max had been bored enough to open. They were hiding something Max claimed to have even less use for—two books by his rival, Stephen King, one with a bookmark showing he'd been more than halfway through it. She shook her head. Even a bestselling author couldn't write around the clock. The hauntings had probably been the highlights of the last week of Max's life.

She opened the drawer of the nightstand. A notepad, a pen, and a picture of Max and Jessica, standing in front of Nevermore. Her aunt must have been sixty, but she looked a couple of decades younger, her long blonde hair and flowing floral dress evidencing how very different she was from Lexie's mother. Jessica and Max had their arms around each other and were smiling for the camera.

Lexie's eyes filled. She couldn't believe her aunt had been dead eight years. She still missed her so much, missed having someone to encourage her to do what she loved and live life on her own terms even when her mother disapproved. At least Jessica and Max were together again now.

Lexie set the photo back down in the drawer, then picked it up again. Something about it bothered her, but she couldn't put her finger on it. It was probably that this was the first picture she'd ever seen of Max and Jessica together. Their romance hadn't been secret, but it had been private. Jessica had never talked much about Max, and other than being vaguely interested in him because he was famous, Lexie hadn't cared enough to ask.

She returned the photo to the drawer, and then searched the rest of the room and the small attached bathroom. No hidden notes, pages, or anything else that could conceivably be a clue.

She could check out all the passages, but Ben had done that and found nothing. To be honest, she wasn't anxious to search them. With her shaky sense of direction, she'd probably get lost and spend the rest of her life wandering around the nether regions of Nevermore.

She retraced her steps back through the main passage to the door, opened it, and stepped into the empty library. Then she sneaked up to the third floor to inspect Max's bedroom.

Lexie had never been in Max's bedroom before, so it didn't remind her of him, which made things easier. She crossed the room to the dark wood armoire where Ben said he'd left messages for Max and opened the doors. Memories now bombarded her, triggered by the clothes hanging in the armoire, clothes that looked and smelled so much like Max. She made a quick check inside. Nothing. With a sigh of relief, she closed the doors, and then systematically examined the hardwood floor, the rug, the chair, inside the drawers, even under the mattress. More nothing. She got down on her hands and knees and shone her flashlight under the bed.

She found a button on the floor underneath the edge of the bed. She grabbed it and studied it for a moment. Small, white, and with four holes, it looked like it had come from a man's shirt. In mystery books, buttons were always significant, but they usually weren't quite so generic. Although who knows? Maybe she'd get lucky.

First she should make sure it wasn't from one of Max's shirts. The shirt he'd been wearing when he was killed had been blue denim with blue buttons—she'd never forget that. She hadn't noticed any shirts in the secret room, so presumably he kept them all in here. Taking a deep breath, she went back to the armoire and opened the doors again.

Max had several shirts with buttons similar to the one she'd found, but none were missing, not even any of the spare buttons on the bottom of each shirt. She left his bedroom, taking the button with her and locking the door behind her.

She made it to Nevermore's main floor without anyone spotting her, and then headed for the back door.

"Are you staying here again?"

Lexie stopped and turned to see Igor standing beside the door to the parlor, his features expressionless. His usual butler face, but today it triggered a chill that slithered up Lexie's spine. He was strong enough to do her serious damage, and as far as she knew, she was otherwise alone at Nevermore with him.

And he could very well have murdered Max.

Why hadn't she thought of that before? According to Cecilia, the housekeeper and cook were both longtime employees and almost family. Cecilia hadn't mentioned Igor, though, and if he were the eighth butler, he might not have been at Nevermore long. Lexie didn't know a thing about him, not even his real name. "I stopped by to talk to Cecilia, but she doesn't seem to be around. I used the trustee's key because I didn't want to bother you." If Igor were guilty, she certainly didn't want him to suspect she'd been investigating or was working with Ben.

"Everyone is gone except for Seth. He's in the dining room."

The words warmed away Lexie's chill—Igor would hardly risk murdering her with Seth so near. "How long have you worked here?"

He blinked. "Almost four months." He blinked again.

"How did you get this job?"

More blinking. "Why?"

"I was curious how someone came to work for Max Windsor," Lexie said.

"I applied for the job, and he hired me." Igor's face stayed butler expressionless, but he was blinking quite a bit, so maybe her questions were making him agitated. On the other hand, she'd never paid that much attention to him. Maybe he wore uncomfortable contacts.

"Are you a professional butler?" Lexie asked.

"Have I acted improperly?"

"Not at all. I was curious since I've never met a real butler before. Do you have to go to school for it? There's a butlering school in London, isn't there?"

"I don't know. If you don't need anything, I should return to my duties."

She held out the button. "Is this yours? It looks like it's from one of your shirts."

He didn't even bother looking down his nose at it. "I am not missing any buttons." Then he turned and glided into the parlor.

"The butler did it" might be a cliché, but Igor was now officially on Lexie's suspect list. He could have taken this job because for some unknown reason he hated Max. Igor served meals and would have had no trouble poisoning Max's Easter dinner. He also could have shot out the living room window. He would have known about the gun that was kept in the basement. He had the soundless butler walk down, so he could easily have seen Max without Max realizing it.

Besides, Lexie didn't trust anyone so organized he could swear he wasn't missing a single button.

Trey had hired him and would know more about him. She'd ask him when she returned for dinner tonight.

Right now she needed to check out one last thing—the lakeshore where Max's body had been found. She wasn't about to trust that the police had been thorough. Who knows—she might even find a matching button.

Lexie followed the path, then stepped out of the trees onto the lakeshore and paused, her chest tightening. In her mind she could see Max lying there, a bloody hole in his chest. She closed her eyes, took a couple of deep breaths. Then she headed for the rocks and grass where Ben said he'd discovered the body. She looked around, found nothing.

When she'd finished, she sat down on the boulder she'd selected the first day she and Ben had met about the murder, staring at the sparkling water in front of her, at the lush forest across the lake.

Her heart felt bruised. Max was dead, and it seemed somehow worse that he'd been murdered somewhere he obviously loved, somewhere this peaceful.

Somewhere this deserted.

Lexie shivered, wrapping her arms around herself, the sunny day suddenly ominous. Igor said the family was all gone, but someone could have returned. Or maybe Igor had followed her.

Her phone rang, piercing the silence and shocking her twitchy nerves. She jumped, and then checked the number.

"Sorry to hear about your accident," J.P. said when she answered. "Hope you're following my advice to be careful."

"I am," Lexie lied, since standing on a deserted lakeshore where she'd be an ideal target was the definition of a death wish. She had the urge to hurry back to Nevermore's relative safety, but the trees could very well swallow her signal. J.P. wouldn't have called solely to check on her health. "Did you learn something about Max's murder?"

"Not exactly," J.P. said. "I heard Ben got back with that ex-wife of his, so I looked into her. I was hoping to find something you could use to make her leave Ben alone or at least convince him he was a fool to pick her over you. I lucked out."

"What did you learn?"

"That she's got a couple of problems. One, this past February she had a big investment tank and lost a bundle. And two, in March the SEC started investigating her. Not sure why, but word is she's gonna be facing a major fine. We're talking seven figures, plus mega attorney fees, which her company ain't gonna pick up. So maybe her interest in Ben has a little something to do with his inheritance."

"How do you know this?"

"I might not be the Mafia, but I've got connections. One more thing. The broad showed up at Lakeview for the first time the day Ben was arrested, right?"

"Right. She flew in from New York and came to the jail to pay his bail."

"She didn't fly in from New York. She'd been staying at the Lake Superior Inn in Grand Marais for a couple of days. Less than thirty miles from Lakeview."

"Are you sure?"

"Like I said, I got connections. She hasn't been alone there, either. Day after she got there she had a visitor. Ben's cousin Jeremy."

— — —

"I need to talk to you."

Ben turned from the Ford Focus he'd just finished servicing and looked at Trey. "If you need a rush repair, you've got great timing. I just finished today's last job."

"That's not why I'm here," Trey said.

"What do you need?" Ben asked when Trey didn't elaborate.

Trey hesitated, which was out of character. He always seemed so confident, so sure of what he was doing. "Lexie says I should tell the police about it, and she may be right," he finally said. "About the fight I overheard you have with your grandfather right before Easter. The fight where Max threatened to disinherit you."

Ben slammed the Ford's hood shut. *Damn.* "You're right. We should talk."

CHAPTER 21

She hadn't missed sherry hour, Lexie thought as she stood in the parlor of Nevermore that evening, sipping a glass of white wine and talking to Cecilia. And this one was more annoying than usual. So what if she and Ben had agreed they shouldn't let anyone know they were again working together—let alone sleeping together. He was getting a little carried away pretending to be enthralled with Olivia. Lucky for him, his eyes were on Olivia's face, not her plunging neckline.

Cecilia grabbed Lexie's arm. "Let's go talk to Ben."

Lexie dug in her heels. "I don't think that's a good idea."

"I told him you don't think he's guilty, if that's why you want to avoid him." Cecilia marched across the parlor to Ben and Olivia, dragging Lexie along.

"Cecilia," Ben said, pointedly ignoring Lexie. "How's Peter? I haven't seen him since the street dance."

"He's fine," Cecilia said. "We went out to dinner last night."

"I'd love to meet him, especially if he might be a member of our family soon," Olivia said. She shifted deliberately so that her barely covered left breast rested against Ben's arm.

"I think that's pushing things a little," Cecilia said.

Olivia nodded. "You probably want to take your time before you get married again. Now that you're an heiress, you have to make sure you aren't being married for your fortune."

"I was referring to the fact you're not a member of our family." Cecilia's disdainful look and tone would have made Lexie's mother proud.

Olivia wasn't fazed. "I've always considered myself a member of your family." She brushed her fingertips over Ben's cheek. "I'm hoping to become an official one again very soon."

Ben smiled down at Olivia. "This isn't the place to discuss that."

Lexie pressed her arms against her sides, fighting the urge to slug him. Granted, she and Ben were just having a vacation-type fling, and Barringtons didn't do jealousy—Rule Number 21—but *really*.

"Aren't you going to greet Lexie, Ben?" Cecilia asked.

"It's nice to see you again," he said, barely sparing her a glance.

Olivia fastened both hands around Ben's arm in an obvious show of possession. "I thought you'd have left by now, Lexie."

"The trustee wants me to stick around a while longer."

"Has anyone asked for Grandfather's '67 Corvette yet?" Ben asked, finally meeting Lexie's eyes.

Lexie's fingers tightened so hard around her wineglass stem she was surprised it didn't snap. "That was Max's car?"

"Have you seen it, Lexie?" Cecilia asked. "Isn't it hot?"

"It's definitely hot." As were her cheeks, which were probably also turning the same hue as the car.

"I'd like it as part of my share." Ben smiled, his eyes darkening and still on Lexie's. "It's got some terrific memories."

"Like when you nailed Savannah what's-her-name in it, and Grandfather found out and got so mad he refused to let you drive it anymore?" Cecilia asked.

Ben's lips quirked, and he shifted his attention to Cecilia. "He eventually relented. And she was the only one. Grandfather told me that only a special woman was good enough for that car, and he was right."

"How come you never showed it to me when we were married?" Olivia asked.

"I didn't think it was your style."

"Well, it might be now." She smiled slowly and touched Ben's cheek with her finger. "Maybe it's time you nailed someone else in it."

"Excuse me, but I need to talk to Trey," Lexie said. She went over to where Trey was sipping a drink.

"Did you talk to the police?" she asked.

"Not yet. I wanted to talk to Ben first, and I didn't do that until a couple of hours ago." Trey pursed his lips. "He told me their argument hadn't been a big deal, and that if I felt I should tell the police, then to go ahead. I'm still not sure what to do. It could end up causing Ben problems he doesn't deserve. I told him I'd sleep on it."

"What do you know about Igor?" Lexie asked.

"The current Igor? Not much, other than he works hard and he's willing to be called Igor. Max hired him."

"Max did? Was that unusual?"

"Max always handled hiring employees," Trey said. "He found numbers boring, but he was fascinated by people. I have a feeling he viewed everyone he interviewed as a potential book character. Why are you interested in Igor?"

"Because he arrived only a few months before the first attempt on Max's life," Lexie said. "I'm sure it's a long shot, but I thought I should check whether anything in his history gives him a reason to hate Max."

"That's a good idea," Trey said. "His résumé should be in the files in my office. I'll get you a copy." He set his drink on the high table and left the parlor.

"Cecilia told me that you and Ben had a one-night stand."

Lexie shifted her attention to Olivia, who'd suddenly appeared at her side. "Really." It was currently a two-night stand, but Lexie didn't feel like sharing that information with Olivia.

"I think she was trying to make me jealous, but it didn't work," Olivia said. "I wanted to reassure you that you shouldn't feel uncomfortable about it. I don't hold it against you. I wasn't in the picture then."

"No, you weren't."

"And it's not like you're Ben's type." Olivia gave Lexie her version of a condescending look.

But then she hadn't been trained by the master. "Really," Lexie said again, this time delivering a condescending look of her own that would have made her mother proud.

It was so effective it made Olivia look away.

"Here's your wine, Olivia," Ben said, approaching them with a glass of white wine. "What are you two talking about?" His expression seemed a little leery, but maybe that was Lexie's imagination.

"Girl talk," Olivia said, taking the glass from Ben. She kissed his cheek. "Thanks for the wine."

Muriel clapped her hands, her bracelets and rings clanging. "Your attention, please." She was standing in front of the fireplace, wearing a burgundy silk caftan and matching turban, hot pink lipstick, and an abundance of sparkly jewelry. The drink table and a folding chair were beside her.

"We are gathered here tonight to honor my dear brother." She folded her hands together and pressed them against her heart. "I believe the best way to do that would be to identify his murderer."

Jeremy groaned from across the room. "Not another séance."

"Of course not," Muriel said. "When he appeared to me, Maxwell said he doesn't like séances. I have no reason to think dying has made him any fonder of them." She lowered her hands. "I am going to gaze into my crystal."

Seth appeared at her side like a well-trained magician's assistant. "Aunt Muriel is an expert at crystal reading." He was holding what looked like a basketball covered by a cloth the same burgundy silk as Muriel's outfit.

Muriel's fingertips fluttered. "To be perfectly honest, tea leaves and tarot cards are more my specialty. But this will work better for the task at hand. Please help me clear the drink table, Seth."

"What did I miss?" Trey asked.

"Muriel's going to try to identify Max's murderer by looking into her crystal," Lexie said.

Trey rolled his eyes. "I think I'd better retrieve my drink before she starts." He handed Lexie a sealed envelope. "I think you'll find this interesting."

"Thanks," Lexie said.

"What's that?" Jeremy asked.

"Some information about the trust," Lexie said, sticking the envelope into her purse.

"Please position the crystal for me," Muriel said. She and Seth had moved the wineglasses to the lower shelf of the drink table and the liquor bottles onto the fireplace mantel. Seth picked the covered object off the floor and placed it on the table.

"Dim the lights." Muriel sat down on the folding chair so she was facing the crystal. "And close the drapes."

"This is ridiculous," Jeremy said as Seth complied.

"Look on the bright side," Cecilia said. "Maybe Aunt Muriel will discover you killed Grandfather. If you're in jail, you won't have to sit through more of these kinds of things. Or any more sherry hours."

"Hush," Muriel said.

"Let Muriel work," Olivia said. She and Ben were sitting close together on the love seat.

"Thank you, dear," Muriel said.

"Since I know Ben's innocent, I hope you can find the truth," Olivia added.

"The crystal never lies." Muriel pulled off the cloth and dropped it onto the floor.

"That looks just like the one in *The Wizard of Oz*," Lexie whispered.

"Maybe she swiped it from Grandfather's movie memorabilia collection," Jeremy said, not bothering to lower his voice. "If she starts talking about witches or tornados, I'll be suspicious."

Muriel leaned over the crystal and looked down into it. "I can see a mist, swirling around," she said in a breathy voice.

"That's almost a tornado."

"Be quiet," Muriel told Jeremy. "Someone is trying to come out of the mist."

"Is it Grandfather?" Seth asked from the side. As usual, he was snapping photos.

"It's too foggy to see who it is. It's a person, but I can't even tell if it's a man or woman."

"Is the person at Nevermore?" Seth asked.

"I can't tell that, either. The surroundings are obscured by the mist." Muriel tapped the crystal a couple of times. "That's better. I can see someone else. It must be a woman since she's wearing a skirt."

"Unless the mist is in Scotland and it's a kilt," Jeremy said.

Seth glared at him. "Who is the woman, Aunt Muriel?"

"I can't see her well enough to be able to tell."

"Did she kill Grandfather?"

"I don't know. The first person has disappeared. I can't see anyone besides the woman."

Everyone was quiet, so quiet Lexie could hear the grandfather clock in the living room mark six forty-five with the haunting *Carmina Burana*. She shivered.

"I can see the first person again—at least I think it's the same person I saw before," Muriel said when the clock had finished. "The person is carrying something."

"What? Can you make it out?" Seth asked.

Muriel rested her hands on both sides of the crystal and looked at her audience. "The object is a gun."

"Like the one that killed Grandfather?" Dylan asked.

"It looks the same, but all revolvers look alike to me. The figure is moving toward the woman."

"I thought you were going to find out who killed Max," Olivia said.

"The crystal doesn't always show what you want to know. It sometimes shows what you need to know." Muriel studied the crystal for a moment longer, breathing heavily. Then she raised both hands as well as her voice. "Oh my God! The first person shot the woman." She shook her head, her hands moving spasmodically over the crystal, her bracelets and rings flashing. "She's been shot. She's bleeding and falling to the ground. The person's moving away, letting her fall." Muriel's agitation seemed so genuine that not even Jeremy made a sarcastic remark.

"Who's the shooter?" Seth asked.

"I can't tell, and the shooter has disappeared from the crystal. The mist is breaking up enough that I can see the woman. She isn't on the ground; she's in the water. It could be a lake or the ocean; all I can see is blue water." Muriel's words were coming fast, her voice an octave too high. "The water's turning dark from the woman's blood. She has blood coming from her stomach, and she's sinking into the water. I can see her—"

Muriel broke off, slumping forward, covering her face with her hands. She was statue still, so quiet she didn't appear to be breathing.

Seth immediately ran to his aunt and rested his hand on her shoulder. "Aunt Muriel, are you all right?"

Muriel slowly lifted her head. "I am fine. But I saw something horrible."

"The killer's face?" he prompted.

"Not the killer but the woman, the woman who was shot and is sinking into the water. The woman the crystal felt it important to warn." Muriel's words were low and round, as if she were making a pronouncement. She turned to Lexie and pointed. "The woman was you."

The blood drained from Lexie's head.

Muriel picked the cloth off the floor and covered the crystal. "This has been very upsetting. I need to lie down. Please eat dinner without me."

"I'd think it's a little more upsetting for Lexie," Jeremy said as Muriel hurried out of the room.

"You do look pale," Cecilia said. "Are you okay? You know it doesn't mean anything."

The dramatic announcement coming on the heels of her brake failure had momentarily unsettled Lexie. But this had a logical explanation. "I'm sure Muriel subconsciously chose me as a victim because she's upset I was spying on everyone," she said, firmly enough to convince herself, she hoped. "Or maybe because I was the victim of an accident yesterday."

The dinner gong clanged.

"The end of yet another delightful sherry hour," Jeremy said, offering Lexie his arm. "I hope you'll sit beside me. I promise I'll protect you."

"As tonight's in honor of Grandfather, I think we should toast him before we start eating," Cecilia said when everyone was seated at the dining room table. "You should give the toast, Ben. You're the oldest grandchild."

"Only by two weeks," Jeremy said. "In case you've forgotten, Ben's also been arrested for killing Grandfather."

"I didn't do it," Ben said.

"How do we know that?" Jeremy said. "I think it's inappropriate for you to give the toast." He got to his feet. "I'll do it."

"No way in hell," Ben said, also getting to his feet.

Trey stood, coughed, cleared his throat. "Sit down, both of you. I will give a toast to Max. I've known him longer than either of you."

He waited until Ben and Jeremy were seated to continue. "I knew Max for more than thirty years. He could be annoying, demanding, and opinionated. His ego was second to none—he always assumed he knew what was best for everyone else."

Everyone chuckled at the truth in that.

"Max was also brilliant, loyal, and had a wicked sense of humor. He was kind and generous and one of the best people I ever met. He gave me a job years ago when I needed it, shared his family with me, and gave me emotional support and the will to go on when Maria died. Max was my employer, but he was also my best friend. I miss him every day. The only thing that makes this bearable is that he's finally back with his beloved Jessica."

The tears that had welled up in Lexie's eyes overflowed now, making hot tracks down her cheeks. She didn't bother wiping them away.

Trey raised his wineglass. "Here's to you, Max. I hope you're enjoying yourself as much in death as you always enjoyed life."

Everyone else at the table raised his or her wineglass.

And then Trey fell facedown onto the table, his Baccarat crystal glass shattering, his pinot noir staining the white damask cloth.

CHAPTER 22

Ben was out of his chair and behind Trey in an instant. "Someone call 911. Help me get him onto the floor, Jeremy."

"I'll call," Lexie said, loud enough to be heard over everyone's sliding chairs and agitation. She grabbed her purse, digging out her phone as she hurried into the quiet of the hallway to make the call. When she returned to the dining room, Ben, Jeremy, and Seth had Trey on the ground and were loosening his tie. His immobile features had a waxy, grayish tinge.

"The dispatcher said you should give him an aspirin," Lexie said. "In case it's his heart."

"Cecilia's getting one, since that's probably what it is," Jeremy said.

"He had heart surgery last year," Ben added.

"I've got an aspirin," Cecilia said, running into the dining room with Igor on her heels.

"Give it to me," Ben said.

"Is Trey going to be okay?" Cecilia asked. "He's like family. He can't die, not after Grandfather—" Her voice caught, then faded.

"He won't if we've got anything to say about it," Jeremy said.

Olivia rested her hand on Ben's shoulder. "How can I help?" She'd been lurking behind him.

"Go out front and let the paramedics in," Ben said, his attention still on Trey.

"I can't leave," Olivia said. "Trey's like family to me, too."

"I'll do it," Lexie said. She resisted the urge to point out to Olivia that virtually ignoring someone seemed an unusual way to treat a near-family member she hadn't seen in years.

On the other hand, it was obvious that to everyone else, Trey really was family. The way they'd responded to his collapse and especially the way Ben and Jeremy were actually working together to help him showed how important he was to all of them. Seth had even stopped taking pictures.

Lexie unlocked the front door and stepped out on the porch. It was getting dark, an approaching storm bringing in early clouds and gray fog, making the air heavy. Lightning flashed far away, but she could feel its electricity jolting her already jittery nerves. She strode up and down the stairs, then back and forth along the driveway, trying to work off some of the adrenaline swirling through her body. Trey wasn't going to die. Stress must have triggered his collapse—stress from Max's death and now his concern for Ben. Stress had probably also kept him from eating and drinking enough. He'd be fine once they got an IV in him.

He couldn't die. The family couldn't handle his death, even from heart problems. And she couldn't handle his death. She'd only met Trey recently, but she'd corresponded with him for years. Because of that and because he'd been close to both Max and her aunt, Trey felt like an old friend.

Lexie heard the ambulance a few minutes before it arrived, but didn't stop pacing until it pulled up in front of Nevermore. Three paramedics jumped out, carrying medical gear and a stretcher. She led them to the dining room.

"Is it his heart again?" one paramedic asked as he knelt beside Trey.

"I assume so," Ben said. "He was giving a toast to Grandfather when he collapsed. He never stopped breathing, but his breathing is shallow, and his heart's beating way too fast. We managed to get an aspirin in him."

"We'll take it from here," the paramedic said.

Everyone watched as the paramedic took Trey's vitals. Lexie was no expert, but they didn't sound good. He also hadn't appeared to have moved since his collapse. That couldn't be good, either.

"We'll have someone from the hospital call here as soon as they know anything," the first paramedic said. "You all are as close to family as he's got."

The paramedics secured Trey on a stretcher, then carried him out of Nevermore. Every person in the dining room followed them, waiting silently on the front steps until the ambulance took off, red lights flashing and siren blaring.

"Will you want dinner?" Igor asked when it was quiet enough to be heard.

"I've lost my appetite," Cecilia said.

"Me, too," Dylan said. "Although I could use another drink." He headed into the house.

"I think I'll go back to my motel now," Lexie said. "Call me when you hear anything about Trey, Cecilia."

– – –

Lexie was just getting into bed when Cecilia called with news.

"Trey didn't have a heart attack. He was poisoned."

Lexie's blood chilled. *Someone had poisoned Trey?* "God, no. Is he going to be okay?"

"He's awake and able to talk, and Peter says he should be okay. But that's not the worst part." Cecilia paused, taking a harsh breath. "They've arrested Ben for trying to kill him."

– – –

When Lexie strode through the front door of the police station—surprised she hadn't been ticketed for speeding on the way over—she found Olivia already there, standing in front of an unoccupied gray metal desk.

Olivia whipped around toward her. "Ben's attorney can't get a bail hearing on this latest charge until tomorrow, not that a judge is likely to grant bail anyway. That means even though Ben's innocent, he'll be stuck in jail for least one night and will lose his share of the trust. Even though he isn't guilty." Her voice had the same whiney quality as a dentist's drill, making Lexie long to plug her ears. "That can't be what his grandfather wanted. You've got to make sure that doesn't happen."

"I think it's more important right now to get Ben cleared of the charges," Lexie said.

Olivia planted her hands on her hips and raised her chin and voice. "That's easy for you to say. You aren't the one losing a fortune. But you are the one who drafted the trust, and you should have provided an exception for something like this. If Ben loses out, we will definitely be suing you for malpractice."

Before Lexie could respond, a policeman came into the room.

"I need to see Ben," Lexie told him.

"His wife was here first. I was just getting him set to see her."

"She's his *ex*-wife, and I need to see him because his arrest could have legal ramifications for Max Windsor's trust, which I represent," Lexie said. "I need to hear Ben's side of the story before I can advise the trustee what to do."

The policeman shrugged. "Okay, you can go first since you've got legal business. Come on." He led Lexie to a hallway behind the desk, then to a closed door. "Ben's in here," he said, unlocking and opening the door. Lexie stepped into the gray-and-beige room. The policeman followed.

"Could I please talk to Ben alone? Some of the things I have to discuss with him involve confidential trust matters." She pulled a small notepad and pen out of the side pocket of her purse. "You can take my purse with you and search me. I'm not going to try to help Ben escape, and he's not going to hurt me. You must know him."

"I thought I did, but I never suspected he'd kill his grandfather or poison Trey."

"He hasn't been found guilty of either of those things," Lexie said. "Since you plan on keeping him in jail overnight, he stands to lose a fortune under the terms of his grandfather's trust. If Ben's proven innocent, he could very well sock you with a lawsuit for false arrest, and your department will end up owing him all the money he's lost, which I doubt you can afford. It's in your best interests to let me talk to him so I can figure out a way to avoid that outcome. And as I said, some of that is confidential." Lexie had adopted the tone she used on those occasions when her argument had a few holes that she hoped authoritative decisiveness would make up for.

The tone apparently worked on small-town policemen, or maybe it was the threat of a lawsuit. "You can have ten minutes," the policeman said, and then he left the room, closing the door behind him. He didn't bother to lock the door or take her purse.

"I thought Olivia was coming in," Ben said as Lexie approached the gray metal table where he sat. In the fluorescent light, his skin looked a sickly yellow green, and his left ankle was shackled to the table. At least they hadn't stuck him in an orange jumpsuit. "Thank God it's you instead."

"I convinced the cop outside to let me see you first because I'm concerned about the trust's interests. Fortunately neither the cop nor Olivia knows anything about trust law, since everything I said was pretty much crap."

She sat down on the chair across from him and set the notepad on the table. "Cecilia said the cops found a vial under the dining room table and that it had contained turpentine that had been put into Trey's drink. That's why they're sure Trey was poisoned. But how could they know all that so soon? You don't have a crime lab in Lakeview."

"There were a few drops of liquid in the vial that the cops thought smelled like turpentine, so they used our fire department's hazmat kit to confirm that's what it was. Then they checked Trey's gin and tonic and found more turpentine."

"What a time for them to be efficient," Lexie said.

"They also sent everything to the state crime lab for further verification," Ben said. "I have a feeling they called some other police department for advice since I can't see them thinking of all this on their own."

"Were there any prints on the vial?" Lexie asked.

"Of course not."

"I assume the police think you tried to kill Trey before he told them about Max's threat to disinherit you."

Ben nodded. "Trey was awake enough to mention that, after they pumped his stomach and informed him he'd been poisoned."

"But you told Trey to go ahead and tell the cops, that it wasn't a big deal."

"Right. I was concerned that he was so stressed out about it. We all worry about Trey after his heart attack least year," Ben said. "'Trey told the cops that, but they assume I just said that to make

Trey complacent, and that I planned to kill him before he could do it."

"Why didn't you mention your argument with Max to me?" Lexie asked.

"Because I'd honestly forgotten it," Ben said. "Grandfather lectured me about my current career all the time. I didn't take his threat to disinherit me any more seriously than I'd taken his previous threats to open a competing garage and steal all my business or to never speak to me again."

"If you didn't take Max's threat to disinherit you seriously, why did you drop your plan to expand the garage?" She wanted to believe Ben, but she needed to consider all the facts dispassionately. She couldn't let her personal feelings interfere with her obligations to the trustee and Max.

"How did you know about that?" Ben asked.

"Lakeview gossip."

He smiled wanly. "Figures. I dropped my expansion plans when Grandfather told me about the attempts on his life and asked for my help. I didn't want to be distracted by remodeling until I was sure Grandfather was safe."

With the exception of her ex-husband, Lexie had always been good at detecting lies, and she'd swear Ben was telling the truth. Besides, his reasoning made sense. "Who knew that Trey talked to you about the argument?"

"You think Grandfather's murderer overheard and tried to kill Trey to strengthen suspicions of me?"

"It's possible," Lexie said. "Could you have been overheard?"

"Trey told me at the garage, so I guess so. Both Trudy and Shawn had left for the day. I didn't see anyone, but that doesn't mean someone wasn't lurking around, since I hadn't locked up yet. Or maybe Trey mentioned it to someone else."

"I'll talk to Trey as soon as he's well enough for visitors," Lexie said, putting it on her list.

"Tell Trey that I didn't poison him." Ben shook his head. "It's hard to believe someone would try to kill him just to frame me. Maybe the real motive was that Trey knows something relevant to Max's murder, something he hasn't yet realized is important."

"And framing you was a fringe benefit."

"Yeah," Ben said. "When you talk to Trey, also warn him to be careful. He could still be in danger."

"I will." Lexie glanced at her watch. "I'd better go. My ten minutes are almost up, and I'd hate to annoy the cop. I'm counting on his goodwill and my lawsuit threat to get me in again."

She got to her feet. "Olivia's going to be coming in next. She's very concerned you stand to lose a fortune because you'll be stuck in jail overnight. She doesn't think I'm sufficiently focused on that issue at the moment."

"More evidence her desire to reconcile has a lot to do with my improved financial situation."

"Here I figured it was because you're unbelievable in bed."

He managed a faint smile. "And in a '67 Corvette."

Lexie chewed her bottom lip as she stuffed the notepad and pen back into her purse. "I should have thought to convince Max to include an exception for something like this." Much as she hated to admit it, Olivia had a point. Probably not a malpractice-worthy one, but a point nonetheless. "He obviously didn't intend for you to forfeit your share of the trust because the cops made a mistake. But you could end up with a judge who's a stickler about following the language of the trust, to hell with intent."

"Grandfather would never have let you include anything like that," Ben said firmly. "Since he wasn't really dead, his primary concern was making sure no one could weasel out of staying at

Nevermore. He told me he didn't even want to include that hospitalization exception you suggested, but thought it would seem suspicious if he didn't agree."

The door opened. "Time's up," the policeman said, stepping into the room.

"Thanks for letting me talk to him." Lexie headed for the door.

"I'll bring your wife back now," the policeman told Ben, and then he followed Lexie out of the room. "I think this is yours."

Lexie turned around to see him holding out a manila envelope with "Catherine Barrington" printed on it. "What is it?" she asked, taking it from him.

"A bracelet we found in Ben's room the first time he got arrested. We assumed it must belong to you. I just noticed we still had it."

"I didn't lose a bracelet," Lexie said, managing to keep her tone level although her pulse had accelerated with annoyance and excitement. Annoyance because she couldn't believe they'd ignored something that could be relevant to a murder investigation by assuming it was hers—and excitement because if she were lucky, that something would help clear Ben.

She opened the envelope, hoping it was Olivia's, but was disappointed to recognize it as Cecilia's tennis bracelet, the one with the faulty clasp. The one she claimed was her only good memory of husband number two.

Sadness gathered in Lexie's chest and pricked at her eyelids. When they'd discussed that bracelet, Max had still been alive, even though they hadn't realized it.

"It isn't mine, but I know whose it is," Lexie said. "I'll make sure she gets it." She closed the envelope and stashed it in her purse, then spotted another envelope. The one containing something Trey had assured her she'd find interesting. She couldn't believe she'd forgotten all about it, although between Muriel's crystal reading, Trey's collapse, and Ben's arrest, it had been a heck of a night.

When she got to the car, Lexie flipped on the dome light and ripped open the envelope. It contained a photocopy of a note: "Grandfather, this is the college friend I told you about. He's a great guy, and I know he would be a terrific butler." It was signed "Seth." Attached with a paper clip was a photocopy of a résumé submitted by Jason Stephenson, presumably Igor the Eighth's real name. She skimmed through his credentials—a B.A. from the University of Southern California, several stints as a waiter at restaurants with names she didn't recognize, and three years working as a butler in L.A. She flipped to the end to check his references. Seth's was the only name listed.

So Seth had recommended the current Igor for the job and been his only reference.

As she'd realized before, Igor could easily have poisoned Max and shot out the window, and he could also have poisoned Trey. She now knew he could have been hired by Seth to do it. Or maybe he'd convinced his old friend Seth to recommend him for the butler job because he had some reason of his own to want Max dead.

It was curious that Igor's résumé didn't list as references any restaurant owners or people he'd been a butler for, even though that experience would have been relevant. Maybe Max hadn't wanted to bother checking more references because he trusted Seth's judgment for butlers, if not for directing.

But it also could be that Igor had something to hide.

She needed to check into this Jason Stephenson. She'd start with the University of Southern California. They undoubtedly wouldn't release information on former students, but she knew someone who could hack into almost anything. He lived in Boston, where it was after midnight, but fortunately he was a night owl. She'd call him now.

Because whoever had killed Max was clearly willing to kill again, which meant everyone could be in danger until Max's killer was behind bars.

Especially her.

CHAPTER 23

Trey had one of the nicest rooms in Lakeview Memorial Hospital, according to the woman at the information desk. Which, she added, was only fitting since Trey's late wife had been responsible for raising most of the money for the hospital's new wing.

Lexie took the elevator to the fourth floor, and then walked down the disinfectant-scented hallway until she reached a large single room with a view of Lake Superior. Trey was watching CNN on a flat-screen TV that he muted when Lexie walked in. His face was still pale and pinched, but he at least was sitting up in bed, although propped up by pillows. Several colorful floral arrangements decorated the windowsill and nightstand.

"How do you feel?" Lexie asked, taking a seat on one of the gray tweed chairs beside the bed.

"Incredibly lucky," Trey said. "If the doctor hadn't suspected poison because of what happened to Max, I might not have made it."

"Thanks for agreeing to see me."

"I assume it has something to do with the trust," Trey said. "If I don't know it off the top of my head, it will have to wait. They want to keep me two more days to make sure the poison didn't affect my heart."

"I'm not here about the trust," Lexie said. "First, Ben asked me to tell you that he didn't poison you."

"Do you believe him?" Trey asked.

"Of course. Don't you?"

Trey was silent for a moment, and then let out a long breath, seeming to crumple against the pillows and age at least a decade. "Hell, I don't know what to think. Ben did say it was okay for me to go to the cops. But I told him I'd do it the next morning, if at all, and that night someone tried to kill me."

If even Trey suspected him, Ben was in big trouble. "Maybe someone overheard you at the garage and seized on another opportunity to make him look guilty."

"That's possible," Trey said. "I mentioned it later to Cecilia outside the parlor at Nevermore." He looked sheepish. "Deep down I didn't want to tell the cops. When I ran into Cecilia, I decided to ask her advice, knowing full well she'd tell me not to because Ben was innocent." He straightened again. "Is Ben going to lose his share of the trust even if he had nothing to do with this or Max's death?"

"I'm going to try to find a way around that."

"I hope you can, since it's my fault he ended up in jail last night," Trey said. "When the cops asked if anyone had reason to kill me, I was so woozy that I wasn't thinking straight. I didn't even consider that they'd use what I said to arrest Ben, and it would be too late to go to court to have bail set." He shook his head, sadness coloring his expression and tone. "I was worried telling the police would cause problems for Ben, and it has. Especially if he's innocent."

"You had to tell the police everything," Lexie said. "Did you make your drink yourself?"

He nodded. "Someone must have doctored it after I made it. Since Dylan drank a couple gin and tonics, too, and was fine."

"I saw you set it down when you went to get Igor's résumé for me," Lexie said. "When did you pick it up again?"

Trey shifted against his pillows. "Not until after Muriel finished her performance," he said.

"Did you drink from it right away after you retrieved it?"

"No," he said. "The dinner gong sounded, so I went to the dining room. I decided I'd better take a pit stop before dinner—one of the joys of getting old—so I left my drink at my place on the table and headed for the powder room. The cops think Ben slipped turpentine into it before I got back, since he was sitting beside me." He frowned. "I was so upset about everything that I didn't even notice the taste was off. Thank God I only had time for a couple of sips before I switched to wine for Max's toast."

"I remember everyone was milling around the dining room for several minutes before taking their seats at the table, so everyone had the opportunity to doctor it, not just Ben," Lexie said. Including Igor, who'd been pouring wine and setting out the first course. "Can you think of any reason someone else might have wanted to kill you? Besides the discussions everyone had with Max about money. Something you might have heard or seen but considered insignificant?"

Trey's forehead creased for a moment, then he shook his head.

"If you think of anything, no matter how minor, let me know," Lexie said. "I hate to worry you, but if you know something, you're still in danger." She got to her feet, and then something occurred to her. "One more question. Do you know how Max felt about Olivia?"

"He hated her, which isn't too surprising after the way she treated Ben."

"Did Max hold the affair against Jeremy, too?"

"He didn't approve of Jeremy's conduct, but Jeremy was blood," Trey said. "Olivia wasn't. To be honest, I'm not sure Max liked her much even while she and Ben were married. I guarantee he wouldn't be pleased that she and Ben are thinking of reconciling now. If he were alive, Max would be doing everything he could to stop it from happening."

_ _ _

Lexie's cell phone was ringing when she walked out of Trey's room.

"I heard something I think you'll find interesting, Catherine," Melissa said. "From Linc."

Linc Jackson was Melissa's on-and-off boyfriend.

"He heard from one of his colleagues that there's going to be an auction of a soon-to-be-completed biography of Max Windsor," Melissa went on. Linc worked as a lawyer for a New York City talent agency with a publishing division. "The manuscript's expected to make it into the high six and maybe even seven figures. Linc called me because he knew my firm represented Max and thought I'd be interested."

Catherine's eyes widened. "You're kidding, right? Max would never authorize a biography while he was alive. And it would be hard to get information about him considering how private he was."

"Which is why this is such a big deal, because it's written by someone who had access to him," Melissa said.

"Who's that?"

"Max's grandson, Seth Windsor."

Seth. Suddenly all those questions and photos took on a greater significance. "I assume it was first submitted after Max supposedly died the first time."

"A few days later," Melissa said. "Which makes sense, since with Max dead, it's bound to generate the maximum interest and money. Seth might be scrambling to finish writing it."

"He also wouldn't have dared publish it while Max was alive, since he'd have risked being disinherited," Catherine said, thinking out loud.

"You're thinking Seth might have killed Max so he could publish his book?" Melissa asked. "It seems more likely he'd have killed Max for his share of the trust. From what you've told me, that's way more than he'll get from any book, even if it's a bestseller."

"If he needs money right now, Seth will probably get the advance from his book a lot sooner than he'll get the trust money, especially if it's tied up until Max's murderer is convicted," Catherine said. "Writing the biography will also get Seth's name out there and remind people that he's related to the über-talented Max Windsor. That's bound to help advance his directing career."

Those reasons could have motivated Seth to make the initial unsuccessful attempts on Max's life. But Catherine now knew that Seth had an even stronger motive for having shot his grandfather down by the lake. If Max were alive, Seth lost a lot of book sales and his share of the trust until Max died for real. But even worse, he might have lost his chance of *ever* getting a share of the trust. Because Max would no doubt hear that Seth had tried to sell a biography about him, even if Seth tried to withdraw it. Max might be willing to forgive a couple of tabloid articles, but a biography was a different matter. Knowing Max's hatred of publicity, that biography could very well be the end of Seth's inheritance.

Seth also was working with Igor, whom Catherine's hacker friend had assured her was *not* a college buddy of Seth's.

She probably should talk to Seth, but not until she had more information.

Right now she needed to talk to Igor.

— — —

Lexie had just parked at Nevermore and gotten out of her car when Jeremy came down the front steps.

"I was just thinking that I can't stand eating at Nevermore tonight, and then I run into you," he said. "It's a sign you should go out to dinner with me this evening."

Wrong. It was a sign that it was time to confront Jeremy. Igor could wait. Seth wasn't the only suspect, after all.

"Why have you been lying about your relationship with Olivia?" Lexie asked.

Jeremy's face went blank. "I haven't been. We don't have a relationship anymore."

"You had lunch with her in New York around Easter," Lexie said. "You also called her about Ben's arrest. She was already in Grand Marais, which you know because you visited her there."

"Who told you that?" he asked.

"Someone I consider absolutely reliable." That was pushing it, but Lexie wasn't about to call J.P. a liar, even behind his back. "I plan to tell the police unless you convince me your lies had nothing to do with Max's murder. Knowing the local police, if I do tell them, they're likely to decide that you, Olivia, and Ben are in this together and arrest all of you. You'll probably end up spending a night in jail and have to bring a lawsuit to get your share of the trust, a lawsuit that might not succeed. That's *after* you're tried and found innocent, assuming you actually are innocent and the local judges and juries are more competent than the cops. Are you willing to risk that?"

Jeremy stared at her for a moment, then let out a long breath. "All right. A few months ago Olivia asked me to lunch. She told me she needed my help and couldn't talk over the phone. I was curious, so I went."

"What did she want?"

"She said she'd been a fool to leave Ben and wanted me to help her get him back. I told her I'd do what I could. To be honest, I'd always felt a little guilty about my part in breaking up their marriage."

"Did you help her?"

He shrugged. "There wasn't much I could do. Ben would be more likely to reject Olivia if he thought I was trying to get them together. That's why I lied and told you I hadn't talked to her, so Ben wouldn't find out I was involved. I didn't hear from Olivia again until after we thought Grandfather died the first time. She said she'd called Ben and wanted to come to Nevermore, but he'd told her not to bother. She asked me to keep her apprised of what was going on."

"Did you tell her to come here anyway?"

"Not until you showed up," Jeremy said. "You seemed so different from Ben's usual girlfriends that I had a feeling he might be serious about you. I warned Olivia she'd better try to convince Ben to get back together before it was too late. She decided she'd have better luck if she talked to him in person, so she came to Grand Marais two days before Grandfather really died. I took her to lunch the day after she arrived, but otherwise only talked to her on the phone."

"When did she see Ben?" Lexie asked. He hadn't mentioned meeting with Olivia.

"She was waiting for the perfect time," Jeremy said. "Too many people were around him at work, and she was afraid that if she came to Nevermore and you were there, Ben wouldn't want to put you on the spot and would order her to leave. When the mayor called and Ben had to go into work alone at night, I called and told her it was her chance."

"She talked to him that night?"

Jeremy shook his head. "She said when she got to Lakeview, she realized the garage wasn't a good place for their discussion since their biggest fights had been about Ben wanting to do something other than work in finance. She went back to Grand Marais without seeing him. So now that I've come clean, how about dinner at Cleo's?" He flashed a smile that probably made most women agree to anything he asked.

Unfortunately for him, Neil had the same smile. "Sorry, but I've got things to do," Lexie said. "Thanks for the help, Jeremy."

The night Ben had worked on the mayor's car was the same night Max had been killed. Olivia could have gone to Nevermore to wait for Ben, figuring she'd confront him outside when he got out of his vehicle. She could have seen Max while she was waiting and realized Ben wouldn't inherit after all. So she'd later killed Max using the gun she knew was in Nevermore's basement and that she'd somehow retrieved, or maybe Max had the gun and she'd gotten it away from him. Olivia wouldn't have tried to frame Ben, not when she was counting on his fortune to save her from the SEC. But maybe she'd hidden the gun under the pickup's seat, planning to dispose of it later. Maybe she hadn't even realized the pickup belonged to Ben.

Or maybe she was working with Jeremy after all.

Olivia had just moved up the suspect list. But much as Lexie would like her to be guilty, she couldn't ignore other potential suspects. Taking a deep breath, Lexie walked up Nevermore's front stairs.

She was just about to ring the bell when Muriel stepped out. Today she was wearing a rose cardigan, white blouse, and gray skirt. Her gray hair was in a tight bun, and her lipstick matched her cardigan.

"That's an interesting pin," Lexie said, referring to a silver pin with a unique design that decorated the neck of Muriel's shirt.

"It's actually a Wicca symbol, but hopefully no one at First Baptist will figure that out," Muriel said. "I lost the top button and didn't have time to change blouses."

"Do you know if the rest of the family is around?"

"Dylan is still in bed, Jeremy went boating, and Seth's gone, although I don't know where. But Cecilia's in the living room." She narrowed her eyes behind silver bifocals. "After what I saw last night, I hope you're being careful."

"I'll stay away from water when it's misty," Lexie said.

"Be careful everywhere. The crystal isn't one hundred percent accurate. It showed Maxwell dying in bed, which was wrong, but he's still dead." The wrinkles in Muriel's forehead deepened. "Maybe it was also wrong last night, and the next victim was Trey. You may be fine. Although Trey was poisoned, not shot. And nowhere near water."

"Maybe the water you saw was a metaphor for poison," Lexie suggested. "Since both are liquids."

"Could be," Muriel said. "Although Trey certainly wasn't wearing a skirt." She nodded, her forehead smoothing slightly. "I'll have to consult the crystal again, but not until later. I have Bible Study at First Baptist. After that I thought I'd stop by St. Rose of Lima and say a prayer for Ben and a few rosaries for my brother. Have a nice day."

– – –

Item one on Lexie's To Do list was returning Cecilia's bracelet. Starting with an easily achievable task was always good psychologically. "I think this is yours," Lexie said, crossing the living room to the chair where Cecilia was reading. "The police found it in Ben's room and assumed it was mine."

"I've been looking for that," Cecilia said, taking the bracelet from Lexie. "Thanks. I didn't even think about checking Ben's room. I was only in there for a couple of minutes to use his laptop. I wanted to see whether my divorce is final."

"Is it?"

She nodded. "I'm officially a free woman. Once again."

"Have you talked to Peter about your previous marriages?"

Cecilia worried her lower lip, twisting the bracelet in her fingers. "I've tried to make myself, but I can't bring it up. I'm afraid he'll never want to see me again."

"I bet he'll understand."

"I'm not so sure," Cecilia said. "I heard you saw Ben. Olivia was furious that you got in before she did. How's he doing?"

"He's anxious to get out of jail," Lexie said. "Which is why I'm here. Did you notice anyone around when Trey told you about Ben's argument with Max? Someone who could have overheard and decided to poison Trey to frame Ben?"

Cecilia thought for a moment, and then shook her head. "I didn't see anyone, but we were at the bottom of the stairs, so anyone could have overheard us. Sherry hour didn't start for another fifteen minutes, which is plenty of time to find turpentine. That's what Trey was poisoned with, if you didn't hear."

"I heard," Lexie said. "Did your grandfather have turpentine in the house?"

Cecilia nodded. "He kept a huge can of it along with a bunch of old paint in the basement. On some shelves right next to the shelves where he kept the gun."

Where—as with the gun—anyone could have found it. "Do you know where Igor is?"

"I saw him in the kitchen," she said. "He was polishing silver, which should take him a while. I can't believe how much silver Grandfather owned."

Lexie walked into the kitchen. Igor was standing next to the sink, an enormous chest of silver to the left of him. "I was just looking for you, Igor."

"Why?" He rinsed a fork, and then set it on a rack on his right.

"The trustee currently owns Nevermore and will be running it for a while. I need to talk to all current employees."

"Am I being fired?" Igor asked.

"Actually, just questioned," Lexie said. "Why don't you take a break and sit down."

She waited until Igor was seated to continue. "I know your real name is Jason Stephenson," she said. "I also know you never went to USC, so you obviously weren't a friend of Seth's. What are you really doing here?"

Igor's face never wavered from his normal impassive expression. "I'm working as a butler. Why else would I be polishing silver?"

"I mean why did you want this job? Why did you come here in the first place? Working as a butler in the middle of nowhere isn't the kind of job most people would lie to get without a good reason."

He didn't respond, his face still revealing nothing.

"Look, you could easily have poisoned Max and even Trey. You also could have tried to kill Max by shooting out the window of Nevermore. The issue is whether you were doing it for some reason of your own or because you were working for Seth."

That finally got a reaction from him. His jaw dropped, and his eyes narrowed. "You're crazy. I have nothing to do with any attempts on Max's life. Or Trey's."

"If you don't tell me the truth, I'll have to tell the police you lied to get your job here," Lexie said. "Maybe Seth doesn't know anything about it, doesn't know you used his name to get the job. You have to agree that lying to get your job makes you look suspicious. Especially if you have a criminal record. Do you?"

"I don't want any trouble with the police," Igor said, ignoring the criminal record question. "I'll admit I'm working for Seth, but I had nothing to do with Max's death. Seth is writing a biography of Max."

"I know."

Igor blinked a couple of times, although Lexie didn't know whether it was out of surprise or more contact lens issues. "He apparently decided to do it because Max pissed him off by refusing to help him professionally," Igor said. "If Seth wants to write a book to get back at him, that's his business. It's not illegal."

Lexie nodded.

"Seth apparently talked to his mother and a few other people, claiming he was interested in family history. And he knew a lot on his own, and his mother apparently kept a scrapbook about Max. But he also wanted photos of Nevermore, of things Max had used in his books, and family photos. Things Seth couldn't get without looking suspicious in his short visits here. And he wanted someone to snoop around and listen."

"So he hired you to do it?"

"First he hired the guy who played Igor before me," Igor said. "Alton's an actor and a good friend of Joanna's. They staged this elaborate thing with fake references, using actor friends who Max actually spoke to. That way Max had no idea Alton was connected to Seth. But then Alton started missing California and all his acting opportunities there, so he got a job at Disneyland. He could only give two weeks' notice, and he knew he was putting Seth in a bind, so he convinced me to take his place. I've been trying to break into acting, too, but I've spent most of my time waiting tables, among other things. I decided playing a butler might be about as close to acting as I'm going to get, so I agreed. We didn't have time to work out the references since Max was about to contact an agency. So Seth told his grandfather I was an old friend from college."

"What did you do at Nevermore?"

"Besides being a butler?" Igor asked. "Take photos of the stuff in the basement. Snoop around. I'm the one who told Seth about the shooting through the window. He told me he sold the story to the tabloids and to let him know if anything like that happened again. A few weeks later I also saw a copy of that trust amendment that requires everyone to spend two weeks here. I told Seth about it, but I don't know what he did with the information. I reported on some conversations I overheard between Max and his grandkids and sister when they asked for money. None of that was illegal."

"Did you know that Seth wasn't going to publish the biography until after his grandfather died?"

"He said he wouldn't, out of respect for his grandfather," Igor said.

"So now that Seth's going to publish it, you stand to make a lot of money."

"No, I stand to make less," Igor said. "I was being paid by the hour. I don't get any share of profits from the biography, if that's what you're getting at. That was the same arrangement Alton had with Seth. And now that Max is dead, I'm out of a job."

"Where did Seth get the money to pay you?"

"I don't know. All I cared about was that he paid me on time, and he did."

"As part of your snooping, did you look through Max's bedroom?" Lexie asked.

"No. I've never been in there. Max hasn't left Nevermore since I started working here, so I didn't dare try to break in. But I know Seth searched the room after everyone thought Max died the first time. He made me keep watch once while he searched it, pretend like I was cleaning the second-floor hallway so I could stop anyone from going up to the third floor."

"Did he find anything in Max's room?"

"Not that he told me," Igor said.

"Did he go there any other time?"

"I don't know," Igor said.

"Where did he get a key to the room?"

"I have no idea. Maybe a skeleton key?"

"Did you know that Max was alive?"

"God, no. I thought Seth was kidding when he told me that's why all the police were there."

"Did Seth know Max was alive?"

"If he did, he didn't tell me."

"Do you think Seth killed Max?"

"I have no idea," Igor said. "It's hard for me to imagine anyone killing their grandfather. But neither of mine is leaving me a fortune, so maybe that makes you feel differently. And I don't know whether Seth's the kind of person who could kill, because I honestly don't know him very well."

"Have you seen anything suspicious since the family arrived here? Or someone here who shouldn't have been here the night Max died or the night Trey was poisoned?"

"Nothing when Trey was poisoned, but I did see something unusual the night Max died. Although it's probably nothing."

"Tell me anyway."

"I happened to be looking out my bedroom window at just before one and saw her on the path that leads to the lake."

Bingo. "Ben's ex-wife, right?"

"Not her," Igor said. "Cecilia."

CHAPTER 24

"*Cecilia* was on the path that night?" Maybe Lexie hadn't heard him right.

Igor nodded. "I'd gotten up to take a leak at ten to one and spotted her. I checked the clock because I thought it was kind of late for her to be out. But I never saw her come back."

"Did you mention this to the cops?"

"They only asked whether I saw Ben, and I didn't. I didn't volunteer anything else. I've learned the hard way that's the best thing to do when you're dealing with cops." His tone held touches of belligerence and bitterness that made her suspect she'd been right about him having a record. "I also didn't want them looking too closely at me since I was here under false pretenses."

"You didn't think it was unusual for Cecilia to be out that time of night?"

He shrugged. "I assumed she wasn't going to be out there alone. I figured she'd sneaked out to meet some guy at the boathouse, which is her own business. She's been married three times, after all."

Lexie was having trouble believing this. "You didn't mention seeing her even though Max was murdered at one o'clock by the lake?"

Igor's eyes widened. "I didn't know that's when he was killed. When the coroner got here, it was after ten. He just said Max had been dead a few hours, so I figured the murder happened a lot later than one."

Lexie thought for a moment. The police had withheld the text of the note, saying simply that Ben and Max had planned to meet, which is all the press had reported. She only knew it specified a one o'clock meeting time because Ben had told her. "Was Cecilia carrying anything?"

"A flashlight," Igor said. "I didn't see a gun, if that's what you mean. Although I suppose it's possible she had it in her other hand. Do you think I should tell the cops about this after all?"

"Let me check it out first," Lexie said. "I don't want to cause her any problems if she had an innocent reason for being out."

"I'm sure she did," Igor said. "She seems like too nice a lady to kill anyone."

It was hard for Lexie to imagine, too. But it was also hard to come up with an innocent reason for Cecilia to have been heading to where Max had arranged to meet Ben, at the exact time of their meeting.

– – –

The policeman on duty at the jail that evening had apparently gotten the word to cooperate. He escorted Lexie to the back room, brought Ben in, and then left them alone, all without her even breathing the word "lawsuit."

The room seemed more claustrophobic every time Lexie came into it, as if the cops were moving the walls in a few inches every day. She couldn't even imagine how it seemed to Ben. She didn't bother asking how he was doing—his features were strained, and his pallor wasn't solely attributable to the room's dim fluorescent lighting. "You're not going to be in here much longer," she said with more confidence than she felt. She had a theory, but she didn't have proof.

Her tone was apparently convincing because Ben leaned over the table, color spiking his cheeks. "You found something?"

Lexie looked around the room. She couldn't see a camera, but she didn't want the cops messing this up. "Do they tape everything we say in here?"

"They're not that high-tech," Ben said. "What did you find out?"

"You're not going to like it. Actually, you're going to hate it."

"If it gets me out of here for good, I'll love it. What?"

"I learned that Olivia lied about being in New York the night Max was killed. She was really in Lakeview and might have visited Nevermore. That means she could have known Max was alive and even killed him. I also learned that Seth has been writing a biography of Max that he submitted to publishers right after he thought your grandfather had been killed. He's been snooping around for more material and was in Max's room at least once, so he could have discovered Max was alive. And Seth would have realized that if Max learned about the biography, there was a very good chance he'd be disinherited."

"I'm sorry that my ex or Seth killed Grandfather, but it's a lot better than me being convicted of it," Ben said. "Why would I hate it?"

"Because I don't think either of them killed Max," Lexie said. "I think the person who killed Max and framed you is Cecilia."

His jaw dropped, and he stared at her openmouthed for a moment. "You're crazy."

"Igor saw Cecilia on the path heading toward the lake just before one the night your grandfather was killed," Lexie said. "He didn't see her come back. He didn't mention it to the police because the cops never publicized that Max was murdered at one. He figured she was meeting a boyfriend, and it was none of his business."

"Did you ask Cecilia about it?" Ben asked.

"Not yet. But why else would she have gone there in the middle of the night? And that isn't all I've got." Lexie looked down at the list she'd made after talking to Igor. "The cops found Cecilia's bracelet in your room, although they assumed it was mine. I remember she had it at breakfast the morning before Max was killed, which means she was in your room sometime between then and when the cops searched your room the next morning. Maybe she saw Max's note, freaked out when she realized he was alive, and went to meet him. Or maybe the note wasn't written to you at all. You said the note didn't have anyone's name on it, so maybe Max wrote it to Cecilia after learning she'd made the previous attempts on his life. She killed Max, and then left the gun in your truck and the note in your room. And in the process lost her bracelet."

"I'm sure she had a logical reason for being in my room."

"She said she used your laptop to check whether her divorce was final. But according to the court records, her divorce was final ten days before she came to Nevermore."

"Why the hell would Cecilia kill Grandfather?"

"For the money," Lexie said. "Trey said she showed up a couple of days before Easter and seemed agitated. She had a long conversation with Max in his office, and afterward she was even more agitated. Apparently Max was especially upset about her current divorce. Maybe he didn't just turn down her request for money but also told her he was fed up enough to disinherit her."

"Even if she murdered Grandfather, why kill Trey?" Ben was barking questions like an attorney on cross-examination.

Lexie forced herself to answer calmly, to not be offended by his pummeling. This was hard for her to accept, and she'd only known Cecilia a week. "Maybe she was afraid Trey had overheard your grandfather threaten to disinherit her. Or maybe when Trey told her about your argument with Max, she realized poisoning him would make it appear even more likely that you killed Max. She might not have given Trey a fatal dose."

At that Ben shook his head, then looked away, staring at the photo of the current U.S. president that was the windowless room's only decoration. "I can't believe Cecilia would do that to me." His defeated tone showed he was starting to take Lexie's theory seriously.

"I've got more," Lexie said. "Several days ago Cecilia said she couldn't imagine any family member shooting out Max's window or giving him arsenic. I didn't focus on it then because I didn't consider Cecilia a suspect. But weren't you keeping the specific poison secret? Unless the cops released that—"

"I don't think the cops cared enough to ask. The only people who know it was arsenic are you, me, and Dr. Watson."

"And Max's murderer," Lexie said, although the point gave her no satisfaction. "Also, when Cecilia saw your grandfather's body, she was the only one crying. She claimed the reality of seeing his body upset her, but maybe she wanted everyone to think she was too grief-stricken to possibly be a suspect."

"You're way off base," Ben said. "Cecilia's more like a sister to me than a cousin. She would never kill Grandfather, but if she did, she certainly wouldn't frame me for it."

"Which is why she framed you, because she knew then no one would suspect her." Lexie rested her palms on the table. "Look, I hate this, too. I considered Cecilia a friend, although maybe she stayed close to me even after she found out I was Max's lawyer to keep up on the status of the investigation."

Ben was silent for several minutes as he looked everywhere but at Lexie. Trying to figure out a way to refute what she'd said, no doubt. He closed his eyes for a moment, and then opened them. "This really sucks."

"I agree."

"What are you going to do about it?"

"I obviously need to talk to Cecilia, but I want to search her room first and see if I can find more evidence. The more I have, the more likely I'll get the truth out of her."

"Is it legal for you to search her room without her permission?" Ben asked.

"The trustee currently controls Nevermore, so I've got authority to look wherever I want." That could be true, and Lexie wasn't about to check Minnesota law and risk discovering she was wrong. Barringtons didn't knowingly disobey the law. Of course, Barringtons didn't snoop, either, but this was important. "I'll do it tomorrow morning. I've still got your key to Nevermore, so I can park in back and sneak in again. I assume the master key in the pantry works on her room."

Ben nodded. "I can ask Cecilia to bring me some things tomorrow morning so you'll be sure she's gone."

"Have her come by at ten. That's late enough that everyone but Dylan should be up and hopefully have left Nevermore. Or at least left the second floor."

"I'll give you a call after she leaves me so you'll know to get out of her room," Ben said. "You're going to talk to her afterward?"

"As soon as she gets back to Nevermore."

"Make sure someone else is around," Ben said. "I can't believe she's guilty, but you can't be too careful."

Lexie met his eyes. Their vivid blueness seemed to have faded since he'd been jailed. "I promise I'll be careful."

He took her hand, squeezed it. "When I swore off smart women I was an idiot. Can you imagine if I had to depend on Amber to get me out of here?"

CHAPTER 25

"I'd better go. The cop told me I could only stay for a few minutes," Cecilia told Ben the next morning. He'd asked her to bring his phone charger and the clothes he'd left at Nevermore. "If you need anything else, call me."

"What I need is to find out who killed Grandfather so I can get the hell out of here," Ben said. Mike was in charge again today and had let Ben meet Cecilia alone in the jail's conference room. However, unlike at last night's meeting with Lexie, Ben's leg was cuffed to the table, a tangible reminder that he was in jail accused of something very serious. As if he could forget that for even one second.

Ben's gloom apparently showed on his face, because Cecilia touched his forearm. "You can't lose faith, Ben. Lexie's working on it, and she's really smart. I know she'll find Grandfather's killer."

She sounded confident and encouraging, but then she'd been a cheerleader at Arizona State during a couple of abysmally bad seasons.

And she could very well be responsible for his plight.

"I hope you're right," he said, feeling even gloomier.

"I know I am." Cecilia's tone was still confident, but Ben detected a hint of stiff-upper-lip desperation. "Once she's done that, Lexie will figure out how to get you your money. Grandfather never intended for you to be disinherited because the police arrested the wrong person. If Lexie can't get the provision over-turned, I'll convince everyone to give you your share anyway. It's only fair."

"I doubt Jeremy will be in favor of that. Assuming anyone else will go along with it."

Cecilia waved her hand. "If they won't, I'll give you half of my share. But first we need to get you out of here." She met his eyes. "I'll call Lexie and ask how I can help. I'll do anything I can, Ben. Not only because I know you didn't do it, but because I can't imag-ine how horrible it must feel to be suspected of killing Grandfather when you loved him so much." She got to her feet and started for the door.

She seemed as sincere and caring as when she'd dropped everything, flown to Manhattan, and shown up at his condo right after she'd heard about Olivia and Jeremy. She didn't sound like someone who was framing him.

And suddenly Ben couldn't believe she was, or that she'd killed Grandfather. He'd bet she had logical explanations for everything. If Cecilia was innocent, Lexie was wasting valuable time focusing on her.

Or maybe he was lying to himself because he couldn't stand the possibility she could be guilty. Hopefully he wasn't about to make a horrible mistake.

"Cecilia, did you know Grandfather was alive?"

She paused with her hand on the doorknob.

"I asked if you knew Grandfather was alive," Ben said.

She slowly turned back toward him. Her expression was unreadable, which worried Ben because Cecilia's face was nor-mally a virtual marquee of her emotions. Then she spoke, words that knocked the air out of him. "How did you know?"

— — —

Lexie slipped into Cecilia's room and headed for the closet. After she'd left Ben last night, she'd remembered that Cecilia had been wearing a white sundress the day they'd met. If the button she'd found in Max's bedroom had come from that dress, it would make it even more likely that Cecilia had known Max was alive.

Lexie located the sundress and pushed away the red silk beside it so she could examine the back buttons. She'd remembered right—they were white. But these buttons were pearlized with shanks, not flat with four holes like the one she'd found. She inspected the other dresses, skirts, and blouses hanging in the closet, but nothing had buttons like the one she'd found, missing or otherwise.

She did a quick check of the room, feeling especially guilty when she went through the dresser drawers. All she learned was that Cecilia was extremely neat and a fan of sexy underwear.

Okay, so she'd have to play it by ear when she talked to her. Lexie glanced at her watch as she tiptoed down the stairs. Maybe she'd go for a walk while she waited for Ben's call and Cecilia's return. She was too nervous to sit still.

She'd just started toward the front door when Jeremy stepped out of the dining room. "What are you doing here?" he asked.

"Checking some things for the trust, since Trey won't get out of the hospital until tomorrow," she said, using her planned excuse. "I also wanted to talk to Cecilia, but she doesn't seem to be around."

"She went to see Ben at the jail, but she should be back soon. You can keep me company while you wait."

"I could use another cup of coffee." Talking to Jeremy would distract her as much as a walk would. A little more caffeine couldn't hurt, either. She followed Jeremy into the dining room.

"I'll pour you one," he said. "Black?"

"Yes, thanks," Lexie said, sitting down at the table. A hardcover book was across from her, a bookmark protruding. *Water over the Bridge.* "Are you rereading Max's books?"

Jeremy set a cup of coffee in front of her. "Aunt Muriel left it."

Lexie took a couple sips of coffee. "Ben and I were talking about Max's early books." That conversation seemed months ago, not just days. Lexie took another sip, then set down her cup. "Including this one, where the shark eats the lawyer. Max probably chose that fate as a play on all those lack of professional courtesy jokes. And in—"

She never finished her sentence.

CHAPTER 26

Ben hadn't seen that coming. He paused, breathed, regrouped. Just because Cecilia had known Grandfather was alive didn't mean she'd killed him. "Did you spot him in his bedroom?"

She shook her head. "I've never been in Grandfather's bedroom. He was outside, walking in the woods. I saw him right after I got to Nevermore. I almost fainted."

"Why didn't you say anything?"

"I figured it was one of his practical jokes, and I didn't want to spoil it because I'd taken an early flight and arrived three hours before I was expected. I kept waiting for him to pop up somewhere and say 'Surprise, I'm alive,' but he never did." She chewed her lower lip. "I couldn't believe it when he really ended up dead."

The quiver in her voice did a lot to convince Ben she hadn't killed him, but Lexie had some compelling evidence. He went directly to the big one. "Did you go down to the lake the night Grandfather was murdered?"

Cecilia's eyes widened. "You know that, too?"

"Igor saw you. What were you doing?"

"I was going to sit by the water. I couldn't sleep, and I wanted to think."

"Late at night?"

She shrugged. "I went there all the time when I was a kid and we were visiting, especially when Dad drank too much and fought with Mom. That usually happened at night."

"What did you need to think about this time?"

She frowned, touching her lips with her fisted knuckles. "About how I'm going to tell Peter that I haven't only been divorced once, but three times. Since I'm sure that's going to send him running in the other direction."

"He already knows. Did you see Grandfather or anyone else that night?"

"What do you mean, Peter already knows?"

"I told him before I suggested he ask you out," Ben said. "I also said I thought you were always looking for someone to take care of you because of your mother, but you'd grow out of it if you found the right man."

Cecilia's eyes narrowed. "I can't believe I've wasted all this time agonizing over telling Peter, and he already knows. You could have told me."

The sharpness in her tone surprised Ben. It hadn't occurred to him she'd worry about that, but they needed to focus. He held up a placating hand. "We'll discuss this later. Did you see Grandfather's body when you went down by the water?"

She shook her head. "I didn't see anyone. I'd only gone a few feet in on the path when I heard something. I assumed it was a wild animal, a moose or even a wolf, and it creeped me out." She smiled faintly. "I guess I'm not as brave as when I was a kid. Or as desperate to escape. So I turned around and went back to Nevermore."

She didn't blink or fidget or talk too fast, things she usually did when she was lying and trying to cover. "Question three," Ben said. "Did Grandfather refuse to give you money after this divorce? Or threaten to disinherit you?"

"I didn't ask him for money," Cecilia said. "I was smarter this prenup and got enough to support myself for a while." She made a face. "After two divorces, I'd finally lost my romantic notion that this one will be forever. But I was too embarrassed to admit that to anyone, since I'd still gone through with the marriage and ended up divorced again."

"Why did you come early at Easter if it wasn't to ask for money?" Ben asked.

She came over and sat back down by the table. "Because I wanted him to threaten to disinherit Dylan unless he cleaned up his act. I probably shouldn't have done that, but I was desperate. Although Grandfather refused. He said he'd never disinherit any of us, and he wouldn't use that threat when it was a lie." Her forehead creased. "So why did he threaten to disinherit you?"

"He wanted me to know how upset he was. He knew I'd never take his threat seriously."

"That makes sense," Cecilia said. "He did say he wasn't giving Dylan another cent no matter who he owed money to." She worried her lower lip again. "I probably should have mentioned that to the police or at least to you and Lexie. But I didn't want Dylan suspected of killing Grandfather. He's got issues, but I know he isn't a murderer. I guess I could have told the police I also knew Grandfather was alive, but I didn't think it would help you."

"You're right. Question four: How did you know the poison Grandfather was given was arsenic?"

"Peter told me after Grandfather was shot, and everyone knew he'd been poisoned before. Was it a secret?"

"I guess not." Peter had obviously seen Max's medical records and assumed that since the entire family knew Max had been poisoned, they also knew what had been used. "One final question. What were you really doing in my room when you lost your bracelet? Your divorce had been final for almost two weeks, so I know you weren't checking on it."

Cecilia's cheeks pinkened, and she looked at the bracelet in question, twisting it on her wrist as she spoke. "I was there to use your computer, but not about my divorce. I googled Peter. I always check out guys before I date them, but I didn't want you to know, because Peter's your friend, and I didn't want you to think I didn't trust your judgment." She met his eyes again. "Why are you asking me all this? Do you think I killed Grandfather?"

"If I thought that, I wouldn't have asked you to explain the things that looked suspicious," Ben said.

To be honest, he'd had a smidgen of doubt, not that he'd ever admit it to Cecilia. But that was gone.

Now he needed to get hold of Lexie so she wouldn't waste any more time looking into the wrong person. Unfortunately, they'd lost their best suspect. And they were no closer to identifying the real killer than they'd been back when Grandfather was still alive and the crime had just been attempted murder.

– – –

Lexie's smile faded. "Oh my God. It was *in*, not *is*."

"What are you talking about?" Jeremy asked. "Seth? Or Muriel?"

Lexie shook her head, jumping to her feet. "I just realized I need to check one last thing in the trust accountings. Thanks for the coffee."

As she racewalked out of the room, Lexie's heart was pounding so hard she was surprised it didn't burst through her chest. Max had more faith in her than she'd deserved.

She glanced over her shoulder to make sure no one was

watching, then slipped into the library and headed for the book-shelf. Less than a minute later, she was in Max's secret room. She dug through the pile of magazines and envelopes on the nightstand, pull-ing out the royalty and mutual fund statements she'd noticed earlier.

She returned to the library, and then headed for Trey's office. It was locked, but the master key she'd used on Cecilia's door worked on it, too. She went inside, locking the door behind her. Trey might still be hospitalized, but someone else could come by, and she didn't want to explain what she was looking for. Not until she was sure she wasn't way off base.

Trey had two file cabinets. Lexie first went to the one with drawers labeled "Accountings," "Expenses," and "Miscellaneous." She held her breath as she grabbed the handle of the accountings drawer and pulled, breathing again when it wasn't locked. It con-tained several years' worth of the monthly accountings that Trey prepared for Max showing his income, expenses, and assets. She removed the most recent accounting, which was for the past April. Then she went to the other cabinet, which had drawers labeled "Income," "Investments," and "Taxes." All three of those drawers were locked. Trey's desk was locked, too.

If she was lucky, what she had would be enough.

She started with the May royalty statement, which was accom-panied by a check—no direct deposit, which could be further evi-dence she was on the right track. The statement reported earnings for Max's newest book, which had been released in hardcover in April. Lexie flipped until she found a summary that listed both the advance Max had gotten and the total net royalties he'd earned after repayment of the advance. She deducted the May royalty shown earlier in the statement from the total net royalty to get what must have been his April check amount, since luckily he'd been able to negotiate monthly royalty payments. Then she located the royalty that Trey's accounting showed the book had earned in April.

It was ten thousand dollars too low.

The mutual fund statement she'd found in Max's secret room showed that May investment income had been credited. The only other mutual fund transaction was a ten-thousand-dollar withdrawal identified only as a "Moneyline payment," whatever that was. She checked the April accounting Trey had prepared for a similar transaction, but couldn't find one. However, she did find something else interesting. Her law firm had been paid the last day of April for work done during the first quarter of the year. She remembered the amount because she'd prepared the bill. According to the payment shown on the accounting, she'd billed Max a thousand dollars more than she actually had.

It wasn't much, but it supported what she was convinced Max had been trying to tell her. He'd discovered that Trey had been embezzling from him.

God knows how long it had been going on—she'd need an accountant to figure that out. Max was so rich, unconcerned, and trusting of Trey that he probably hadn't even noticed until boredom had driven him to read all of his mail, including his royalty and financial statements. And he'd discovered what his old friend Trey had been doing.

Max had obviously realized what was going on before he'd appeared to her, but he'd tried to be clever and give her a clue instead of telling her outright. Knowing Max, he'd arranged to confront Trey later that night, assuming Ben would also be there. When Ben hadn't shown, Max had no doubt confronted Trey anyway. And she'd bet anything Trey had killed him.

Lexie still didn't know who'd made the prior attempts on Max's life—back then, Max hadn't been aware of Trey's embezzling, so Trey had no reason to want him dead. At the moment, the only thing that mattered was proving Trey was Max's murderer.

Her next step was to get a locksmith to open the other file cabinet, the one that contained all the original financial statements. After comparing them to the amounts shown on Trey's accountings and hopefully confirming she was right, she'd turn everything over to an accountant. Gathering up the mutual fund and royalty statements and Trey's April accounting, Lexie got to her feet.

A key turned, the office door opened, and Trey walked in.

"I thought you were in the hospital until tomorrow," Lexie said. Her heart was hammering, but thankfully she sounded calm.

Trey closed the door, and then parked himself in front of it. "I hate hospitals. I couldn't stand another day, so I left against medical advice. What are you doing in here?"

"Checking a couple of things for the trust, since I didn't think you'd be back until tomorrow. I'm done now." She stepped around him and reached for the door handle.

Trey grabbed her arm, stopping her. "Are those new statements?" He was looking at the papers Lexie held in her free hand.

"I forgot about those," Lexie said. "I checked Max's secret room to make sure nothing important had been left there. I found these and knew you'd need them to prepare the final accounting for the trustees."

"I see you also have an accounting." Trey was still looking at her papers. "I woke up this morning with the awful feeling I'd forgotten to lock that cabinet after I'd gotten Igor's résumé for you. Apparently I was right. Although as an excuse, I had a lot going on that night."

His voice was level, conversational. But something in his eyes had Lexie's heart hammering harder. "I was trying to get a handle on the money part of the trust, since Max never gave me specifics." The coffee she'd drunk with Jeremy was etching away at her stomach wall, but she managed a faint smile. "He just said it was worth enough that the estate taxes on it would make a big dent in the federal deficit."

Trey shook his head. "Those accountings were the only things Max ever looked at. He just left his royalty and financial statements on the desk unopened for me. But apparently Ben gave him his mail while he was pretending to be dead, and he looked at all of it. He noticed some things that made him suspicious enough that he picked the lock on my desk so he could get the keys to open the file cabinets. Then he compared the accountings I'd prepared to the actual statements." Trey dug a key out of the pocket of his suit coat, then moved to his desk and unlocked it.

She needed to get out of here. Lexie reached for the door handle again. "I'll let you—"

"Stop!" Trey spun around, the gun he'd pulled out of the top desk drawer aimed at her. "I assumed Max had brought all the statements to our meeting, but I should have guessed he'd be sloppy and overlook a couple. And because of that, now you've also discovered my secret. Which means you have to die, too."

Between the gun and Trey's words, Lexie felt as though she'd taken a mid-January dip in Lake Superior. "What secret? I don't know anything." Her words sounded breathy.

"That I was embezzling from Max, and of course you know that. Why else would you have lied about why you were checking the accountings? I sent Stan Sorenson at First Trust an asset list two days after we thought Max had died in that car accident, and he confirmed he'd e-mailed a copy to you. He said you were both shocked by how much Max was worth."

She could keep lying, but Trey wasn't buying it—and unfortunately he'd also just admitted the truth. "Max actually told me when he came into my room and pretended to be a ghost. I realized he didn't say to remember the money *is* the key, but the money *in The Key,* his book where the accountant is embezzling from someone and ends up killing him."

Trey's benign smile was at odds with the gun he still held. "Max wrote that book before he knew me. Who'd have guessed how prophetic it was?"

"I told Ben all about it when I talked to him this morning," Lexie said.

"I very much doubt that," Trey said.

"You can check my cell phone," she said. "It will prove I talked to Ben this morning."

"I'm sure you did," Trey said. "But you couldn't be positive what Max had said or that you understood what he meant. You'd want to check such a tenuous theory out first and make sure you were right before you mentioned it to anyone, even Ben. That's why you were in here."

As if on cue her phone rang. "I'll bet that's Ben," Lexie said, reaching for her purse. "He knows I'm checking into this and will worry if I don't answer."

"Don't touch it," Trey said. The phone rang three more times before switching to voice mail.

"Why did you steal from Max?" Lexie's heart was pummeling her chest, making her voice shaky. "You have so much family money that you refused a bequest."

"I went through what my family left me years ago," Trey said. "It was damn tough to pass up that bequest, let me tell you. Max owed me even more than I'd managed to take, for all those years I put up with him and his ego and being at his beck and call. But if I'd gotten too much when he died, some other beneficiary might have been upset enough that we'd have ended up in court or have the trust audited."

"Why did someone try to kill you?" Lexie asked.

Trey chuckled. "I fooled you all, didn't I? I took the poison myself. I figured that would make Ben look even guiltier of killing Max, and I was right."

Lexie's eyes widened. "You risked your life to frame Ben?"

"It wasn't much of a risk. It's nearly impossible to drink enough turpentine that it kills you. I also knew the doctor who treated me would think of poison since Max had been poisoned, and as added insurance, I put the almost empty vial where I knew the cops would find it."

Her phone rang again.

"Let's go," Trey said, gesturing with his gun. "We'll take my car. Then people will think you're still here."

Lexie reached for her purse, the phone still ringing inside.

"Leave it," Trey said. "Now start walking."

"Where are we going?"

"You're distraught because you just found a note Max left you the night he was killed. He said he'd discovered Ben was trying to kill him, planned to meet with him, and wanted you there, too. I'll leave the note in your purse. When people notice your car and purse are still here but you aren't, someone will find the note. Everyone will assume you went walking around Max's land and either killed yourself or were so distracted you met with an unfortunate accident. Since you'd realized you'd not only let Max down but also slept with his murderer."

"Someone will see me leave with you," Lexie said with more conviction than she felt.

"Nope," Trey said. "I dodged Igor, and the rest of the staff has the day off. I also came around the back way, so no one saw me. Now walk."

Lexie managed to make her legs move, although her entire body felt numb. She couldn't feel anything besides the hard nose of the gun Trey was jabbing into her side. She looked around, frantically searching for someone, anyone, as they walked from his office to Nevermore's back door and then to Trey's Lexus SUV. They didn't see a soul, with the only sounds their footfalls over grass and dirt in an otherwise ominously silent world.

Trey opened the driver's side door of his vehicle, gestured with his gun. "Get in, and slide into the passenger seat. Don't do anything to attract attention. Because if anyone tries to rescue you, you'll die with another death besides Max's on your conscience."

CHAPTER 27

Now he understood what a caged tiger felt like, Ben thought as he paced back and forth between the walls of the prison cell, his eyes on the bars that covered one side. Although tigers weren't pacing because they were too worried to sit still.

He called Lexie's cell phone for the fifth time, once again got her voice mail. No big deal. She probably wasn't answering because she was in the middle of something and assumed he was calling to tell her Cecilia was on her way home. Or maybe Lexie's phone had lost service. That occasionally happened at Nevermore. Nothing was wrong.

But he couldn't sit still, couldn't quiet the worry buzzing under his skin, jazzing his nerves.

Maybe he was being paranoid, but he'd feel better once he talked to Lexie. Ben stopped pacing and called the main phone at Nevermore.

Igor answered and informed him that he hadn't seen Lexie. Ben had him check out back for her car. It was still there, so she must be around, although Igor had no idea where she could be. Cecilia hadn't returned. However, Jeremy was there if Ben wanted to talk to him.

Not his top choice, but he was desperate.

"Have you seen Lexie?" Ben asked when Jeremy came on the line.

"Are you sure you should be talking to her?" Jeremy asked. "It's probably a conflict of interest since you're in jail for killing her client."

The smirk in his voice had Ben swallowing a cutting response. That would only make Jeremy hang up. "Have you seen Lexie?" he repeated, emphasizing each word.

"She's in Trey's office," Jeremy said. "She was having coffee with me when she suddenly remembered something she had to check."

Thank God. Ben's hand loosened on the phone, only to immediately retighten. Why wasn't she answering her phone then? "Will you make sure she's still there?"

"What am I, your servant? Cecilia might be willing to run errands for you, but I've got more important things to do."

"Check whether she's in Trey's office. Please."

Jeremy let out a sound of annoyance. "Okay, but only because I'm bored. I want to ask her to finish up and come back and talk to me."

Ben heard footsteps, a knock on the door, Jeremy's voice calling Lexie's name, a door opening. "She isn't here," Jeremy finally said. "Although she left her purse by the desk, so I doubt she went far. Good morning, Aunt Muriel."

"It's such a beautiful morning," Muriel trilled. "I've just finished an hour of meditation and yoga. You should try it. It's very calming."

"Jeremy, ask Aunt Muriel about Lexie," Ben yelled into the phone, trying to get both Jeremy's and his aunt's attention.

"I think it's Ben who needs calming," Jeremy said.

"We have to make allowances, as he's in jail," Muriel said. "That's bound to be upsetting."

"Ask her, damn it!"

"Why are you so worried about Lexie?" Jeremy asked Ben.

"Because she's looking for Grandfather's killer and doesn't answer her cell phone."

"Maybe she's ignoring you," Jeremy said. "Have you seen Lexie, Aunt Muriel?"

"I think she went somewhere with Trey," Muriel said.

"He's still in the hospital," Ben said.

"Ben said he's still in the hospital," Jeremy told Muriel.

"He must be out, because he was here this morning," Muriel said. "I saw him park his car and come into Nevermore."

"I didn't see him," Jeremy said.

"That's because he came around back, which you can only see from the entertainment room," Muriel said. "I decided to do yoga in there because my knees are a little sore, and I thought the thick carpet would be good for them. As an added bonus, the acoustics make it easy to concentrate on your breathing. I may just have to use that room every day."

"And you saw Trey leave with Lexie," Jeremy said.

"I didn't see Lexie at all, and I didn't see Trey leave," Muriel said. "But his car's gone now, so he must have left after I switched to meditating. If Lexie's no longer here, she may have gone with him."

"Aunt Muriel says Trey's car is gone—"

"I heard," Ben said. Why would Lexie have gone with Trey? "You said she suddenly left to check something. What?"

"I have no idea," Jeremy said.

Jeremy was being his normal uncooperative self. Ben managed to keep the last threads of his temper from fraying. "Did she say *anything*? Aren't you always bragging that you have a nearly photographic memory?"

"Okay, I'll tell you exactly what she said," Jeremy said. "Lexie and I were talking about one of Grandfather's books. *Water over the Bridge*. Aunt Muriel had left a copy on the dining room table."

"I'm not actually reading it," Muriel said. "I have too many other things to do before I die to waste time rereading one of Maxwell's books. But Seth wanted to take a picture of me pretending to read it."

"Lexie said that you two had talked about Grandfather's early books, including this one where the lawyer was killed by a shark. She thought Grandfather had probably chosen that fate as a play on all the jokes about sharks not hurting lawyers out of professional courtesy." Jeremy was talking again. "Then she said, and I quote, 'It was in, not is.' I asked what she was talking about, but she just said she had to check something in the trust accountings and left."

"Thanks," Ben said, hanging up. Lexie had no doubt thought of some issue related to the trust. She'd been in Trey's office checking it out when he'd arrived. She'd wanted to talk to him about it, so they'd gone somewhere they wouldn't be overheard by one of the beneficiaries. She'd left her phone in her purse, which is why she hadn't answered. It made perfect sense. Being caged up was making him paranoid.

He plopped down on the bed. Lexie was fine.

– – –

She had to focus, to figure out some way to convince Trey not to kill her. But Lexie was having trouble focusing on anything other than the gun he was pointing at her with his right hand as he drove away from Nevermore. The cold panic her heart was pumping through her veins had now numbed her brain in addition to her body. This man had killed Max. If she didn't stop him, he was going to do the same to her.

Surely Ben would worry when she didn't answer her phone. Then what? Ben was stuck in jail. He'd also never suspect she was with Trey, let alone in trouble because of it. No one had seen them leave Nevermore together. And she'd never mentioned her suspicions about Trey to anyone.

After a couple of minutes, Trey turned off the road and drove onto the grass, then into the pines and birch trees. He had barely enough room, and branches and needles brushed and scraped the vehicle. After several seconds he stopped and shut off the engine.

"This seems an appropriate place, where we thought Max died. Get out." He gestured with the gun.

"Where are we going?" Lexie asked as she exited. They weren't very far from the road, but the trees were so thick she couldn't see the blacktop.

Which meant no passerby would notice the dull gray SUV, let alone wonder if something was wrong.

"This way." Trey pointed his gun toward more pines and birches. Lexie stepped through them, then onto a leaf- and needle-strewn dirt path. "Stay in front of me. If you try to run, I'll shoot you.

"I'll bet you didn't know this path was even here," he said as they trekked the gradual uphill. "Max had paths cut all over his land so he could walk and cross-country ski everywhere. Overseeing his land like he's some kind of lord of it all. This will be a bit of a hike, but it's worth it. The path goes to a cliff a couple of hundred feet above Forest Lake. It's a gorgeous view, and I'm sure you'll appreciate it. Since it will be the last thing you ever see."

The air was warm and muggy, but Trey's words turned Lexie's chest into a chunk of ice, making it hard to breathe. She was going to die unless she could talk her way out of this. "Why don't you just leave me tied up here? That will give you time to disappear. You don't have to kill me."

"Tie you up with what?" Trey asked.

"With my belt," she said. "And your belt, and—"

"I really don't want to disappear, and with you dead, there's a good chance I won't have to," Trey said. "You know, this is all Max's fault for getting you involved in the first place. And for living so damn long. The rate he was going, he could have made it to a hundred. I wanted to retire, especially after having triple bypass surgery. But I couldn't until Max died."

"Why not?"

"Because my replacement might have needed to check out something from a prior month or year and noticed the accountings I prepared for Max every month don't match the actual financial statements. Or that the income shown on Max's tax returns doesn't match the accountings, since I didn't dare cheat the IRS. Now that Max is dead, I'll prepare a final accounting for the trustee with date-of-death values and the actual post-death transactions. No one will look at past accountings, because the trustee doesn't have to get court approval of them, and no beneficiary is going to check out and second-guess anything Max did while he was in charge. The beneficiaries only care how much they get."

"Why didn't you just disappear with your money?"

"Because Max would have known something was wrong," Trey said. "When he figured out how I'd outsmarted him, he'd have been so furious he'd have spent a fortune tracking me down. I had to kill Max so I could finally enjoy my money and my life. The same reason I had to kill my wife."

Lexie had thought she couldn't feel any colder. She was wrong. "You killed your wife? Everyone says she was so wonderful."

Trey snorted derisively. "She was. You know what it's like living with a saint? She drove me crazy. But if I divorced her, she'd have looked at my finances and maybe discovered my secret accounts. They're right about those tangled webs you have to weave when you deceive. Thank God I'll finally be able to quit lying once you're out of the way."

CHAPTER 28

Ben had been able to sit still only for a minute before he'd gone back to pacing while obsessing over Lexie's strange comment to Jeremy. What the hell had she been talking about? It must be related to the trust agreement—the preposition "in" instead of the verb "is" would make a difference in what a provision meant. Except as far as he knew, the only unusual part of Grandfather's trust was the requirement everyone spend fourteen nights at Nevermore to inherit. He'd read that provision so many times that he knew it by heart, and he couldn't think of a questionable "in" or "is."

She'd made her comment right after talking about those books, so maybe it was related to the night they'd discussed Grandfather's early books. That had been the night they'd checked out the Ferrari and the curve, but Grandfather hadn't really died that way, so that wasn't it. *Water over the Bridge* had a lawyer bad guy, but he couldn't think of anything otherwise significant about it. And the other one they'd discussed had a woman who'd gotten killed in a car lot by an accountant who—

The Key. It was called *The Key.* Not the money is the key, but the money in *The Key.* It was so damn obvious.

Then the ramifications hit him, and the hairs on the back of his neck jumped to alert. "Mike, get in here," Ben yelled. "It's important."

Mike lumbered into the back room. "What? I was in the middle of winning at online poker for once. A free game, of course. I'd never play for money while I'm on duty."

"I think Trey killed Grandfather."

"Trey? No way. He's a good guy. He's been your grandfather's best friend for years."

"You find it easier to believe I did it?" Ben asked. "I think Trey was embezzling from Grandfather, and when Grandfather found out, Trey killed him."

"Why do you think that?"

"I don't have time to get into it. But I think Lexie discovered what he was doing, and he found out. She left Nevermore with him, and I'm afraid he's going to kill her."

"We know that whoever killed Max also poisoned Trey, which means it couldn't be Trey." Mike spoke slowly and overenunciated, as if he were explaining something to a child. "It makes sense Lexie would go with him since they're both working with Max's money."

"Go over to Trey's house and check," Ben said. "If Lexie's fine, make up some reason, like needing to ask some questions about his poisoning."

Mike's eyes flashed, and he folded his bulky arms over his even bulkier chest. "I let you use your phone and talk to your cousin in private, but I can't do this. Trey was your victim, and I'm not going to harass him for you."

Ben could tell Mike wasn't going to budge on this—he was as obstinate as Grandfather once he made up his mind about something. "Go back to your poker."

Now what? Someone had to help Lexie. Aunt Muriel was out, and Cecilia wasn't back yet. But he knew Jeremy was around. He'd never asked Jeremy for help in his life. He hated Jeremy, and the feeling was mutual. Jeremy had stolen his wife, for God's sake. If he were wrong about Trey, Jeremy would make sure everyone knew his suspicions, including Trey.

On the other hand, Jeremy was tough and could take care of himself. Jeremy wouldn't be willing to do him any favors, but he might do it for Lexie. Ben picked up the phone.

– – –

"You think Trey killed Grandfather? Are you nuts?"

Cecilia had just stepped through Nevermore's front door, and Jeremy's statement stopped her cold. "*Trey* killed Grandfather?" she asked, to clarify.

"That's what Ben claims," Jeremy said, waving the phone. "Because Trey's been embezzling from Grandfather and Grandfather found out, all of which Ben figured out based on some cryptic remark Lexie made to me this morning," he explained. "Now Ben's worried she's with Trey and in danger. Jesus, I was having trouble believing Ben was guilty, but he must be—and getting desperate if he's trying to pin it on Trey. Trey would never hurt anyone." Jeremy's voice dripped with more than its usual anti-Ben disdain.

Cecilia chewed her bottom lip. It did sound a little far-fetched. But Ben would never break down and ask Jeremy for help unless he was convinced he was right. "You have to admit it's possible," she said. "I'm not just taking Ben's side. You know that Grandfather never paid much attention to his money."

"If Trey's behind it, why did someone poison him?"

"Maybe he took poison himself as a red herring," Cecilia said. "Like in that Agatha Christie movie about those ten people on the island, and the real murderer fakes his death so no one will suspect him."

"Grandfather's the one who faked his death," Jeremy said.

"You know what I mean. Trey might be guilty. If he's got Lexie—"

"We don't even know for sure she's with Trey," Jeremy said. "Although her purse is in his office, so she probably went somewhere with him on trust business."

"If she left Nevermore willingly, she wouldn't have left her purse," Cecilia said.

"How do you know that?"

"Because I'm a woman."

"Or she's walking around Grandfather's land and didn't feel like lugging her purse with her."

Jeremy had a point, but searching Grandfather's land would take a lot of time. Cecilia was also getting a bad feeling about this. Of course, her instincts had never been that good—she'd been divorced three times, after all.

But Ben obviously felt the same way. What would it hurt? "Look, Jeremy, it's not that big a deal to check if she's with Trey. What if she's really in danger?"

Jeremy let out an exasperated breath, and then returned the phone to his ear. "Okay, Ben. I'll try to find Trey. I'll start with his house. I'm doing it for Lexie, not for you. And because Cecilia's going to nag me until I do."

"I think Ben's right about Trey," Muriel said when Jeremy had hung up. Cecilia hadn't even noticed her aunt standing at the foot of the staircase, although in hot pink yoga clothes and tangerine Crocs she was hard to miss. "I've never trusted him. Something about his aura is off. Wait here." She started up the stairs. "I want to get you something for protection before you leave."

"I don't think—" Jeremy said. But Muriel was clomping too loudly to hear them.

"It's probably a rosary or a St. Christopher medal," Cecilia said. "Or maybe a Wicca spell."

"Just as long as she doesn't insist on reading her crystal," Jeremy said. "I'd like to get this over with."

"I'm going with you, by the way," Cecilia said.

"Damn right you are," Jeremy said. "Since you're the one who got me into this."

"Here." Muriel was back.

She was holding a revolver.

"Where the hell did you get that?" Jeremy asked.

"It's loaded," she said. "Do you know how to use it?"

"I know how to use it," Jeremy said, taking the revolver. "Is it yours, Aunt Muriel?"

"I bought it when Harold died," Muriel said. "It's dangerous for a woman living alone. After Maxwell was shot, I went home and got it to use for protection while I had to stay here. Since there's a murderer running loose."

"That looks like the gun that killed Grandfather," Cecilia said.

"Of course it does," Muriel said. "I know nothing about guns, so I got the same kind Maxwell had in the basement. One of my friends at First Baptist had her son get it for me so I wouldn't have to bother with all the paperwork. He's the nicest boy." She frowned. "Well, he's in prison now for burglary, but—"

"Let's go, Jeremy," Cecilia said, grabbing his arm and directing him to the front door.

"Remember I saw Lexie shot and in the water," Muriel called after them. "Trey lives on Lake Superior. Be careful."

They would definitely be careful. Because faulty instincts or not, Cecilia had a really bad feeling about this.

CHAPTER 29

"Did you make the earlier attempts on Max's life?" Lexie needed to keep Trey talking. Maybe someone would happen by and hear the hint of hysteria in her voice. Or maybe talking would distract Trey enough that he'd trip and she'd be able to get away. Not much of an escape plan, but the best she'd come up with.

"As I said, I got tired of waiting for him to die," Trey said, his voice simmering with anger. "I thought Easter would be an ideal opportunity to kill him. With all the family around, there would be lots of suspects. I never dreamed Max would survive, not with the amount of arsenic I slipped in his drink, but he always was a tough old bastard. And lucky. He just happened to duck when I shot at him through the window. I was thrilled when Ben called to tell me Max had died in a car crash. Then it turned out he'd faked it." The anger was now at full boil.

Lexie changed the subject before strong emotion made Trey's trigger finger twitch. "Why did you decide to frame Ben? I thought you were close to him."

"I am. I hated doing that, but it just kind of happened." Trey's tone had cooled several degrees. "Max sent me an e-mail that afternoon that he pretended was from Ben, asking me to meet him by the dock at one in the morning. That seemed like a strange time for a meeting, and I was worried that Ben might have found out what I'd done. I don't own a gun, but I knew Max had one in the basement, so I got it and brought it to the meeting, just in case. I couldn't believe it when Max stepped out of the bushes. He told me he'd left Ben a note about the meeting, but he must not have gotten it. Then Max confronted me about stealing from him."

"You shot him in cold blood?"

"It wasn't like I planned it," Trey said, a tad defensively. "I was in shock, first that Max was alive, then that he'd found out what I'd been doing. I'd pulled out the gun and shot him before I'd even thought about it. Then I had to get rid of the gun. I could have thrown it in the lake, but I realized that if the cops found the note Max had left for Ben, they might suspect he was Max's killer. I stashed the gun in Ben's truck, hoping it would make him look even guiltier, especially since he'd bought it in the first place. Like I said, I hated to do it, but I didn't want anyone suspecting me."

Lexie risked a glance over her shoulder. Unfortunately the gun was still aimed at her back. "I thought you were Max's best friend."

"How can you be friends with someone larger than life?" Trey asked, his tone dripping with bitterness. "Someone who thought he ruled me and the rest of the world just because he'd been lucky enough to make it big? It's only fitting that his arrogance got him killed, thinking he could face me alone."

"Did you intend to kill me when you tampered with my brakes?" Lexie asked.

"Actually I didn't," Trey said. "I just wanted to make you suspicious of Ben. I like you, and I feel like we've got a bond, having both spent years catering to Max, doing whatever he asked, no matter how unreasonable. I found out what to do on the Internet, but I assumed the brakes would go out in town when you were driving slower." He let out a long sigh. "I hate to have to kill you now, but I don't have a choice."

The combination of regret and resignation in Trey's voice terrified Lexie. "You'll never get away with it," she said, the words spurting out like blood from a sliced artery. "My car's at Nevermore, so they'll search the area when they realize I'm missing. Someone is bound to find my body, even if it ends up in the lake. A bullet hole's going to look suspicious."

"If I have to shoot you, I'll throw the gun into the water with you, and everyone will assume you killed yourself," Trey said. "This is the gun Max kept in his nightstand in his bedroom. The way you've been poking around Nevermore, it makes sense you would have found it. If I can't make the shooting look like suicide, I won't bother writing that note about Ben being guilty. The police will assume one of the other beneficiaries killed you because you discovered who really killed Max. No one will suspect me since no one else knows I have a motive."

That he'd thought this through with accountant-like thoroughness added to Lexie's terror. He was actually going to do it. "What?" she asked, abruptly realizing Trey was still talking.

"I said I should have known you were going to be trouble. You're a lot like your aunt, and she caused me as many problems as you did."

"What do you mean?"

"I mean she finally agreed to marry Max."

Lexie tripped, and she caught a pine branch to steady herself, her sweaty palm barely able to keep hold of the needles. That's what was wrong with the photo in Max's nightstand. Aunt Jessica was wearing a diamond ring on her left hand. Lexie turned back toward Trey. "I never knew that."

"It's true. After all those years, she finally gave in. Too bad for her. If she hadn't, she'd probably still be alive today."

– – –

The trees along the road blurred together as Jeremy drove from Nevermore, the images as muddled as Cecilia's brain. She was having trouble believing that Trey could be guilty and Lexie in trouble. Ben must be overreacting. Although it wasn't any easier to believe anyone else in her family had killed Grandfather.

Ben's theory about *The Key* made sense, too. Grandfather might not have come out and told Lexie that Trey was guilty. He might have decided to first give her a hint, like he sometimes did in his books. He'd always said he should write mysteries because one of his favorite things was doling out just enough clues that the smartest readers could figure out what was about to happen before it did. And if Trey was guilty and Lexie was with him—

Something flashed. "Stop."

"Why?" Jeremy asked, not even slowing.

"Because I saw something in the trees just past the last curve," Cecilia said. "It could have been Trey's headlights."

"Why would he have pulled off there? It's not like Grandfather really died there."

She hadn't realized that's where she'd seen the flash. "If it isn't Trey, who else would it be? Stop the car and back up." Her tone was sharper than she'd intended.

At least it persuaded Jeremy to stop. "Your wish is my command, Queen Cecilia." He backed around the curve, and then pulled off the road onto the narrow shoulder. "I don't see anything."

"It was in the trees." Even squinting, Cecilia couldn't see anything, either, but she swore she had.

"Probably lightning. It certainly couldn't be reflected sunlight in this gloomy weather," Jeremy said.

"We need to check it out." Cecilia grabbed her phone from her purse, and then opened the door.

"No way. I'm not about to get caught outside in a thunderstorm doing a favor for Ben."

"The favor is for Lexie," Cecilia said, getting out of the car. "It isn't stormy, just cloudy." The warm air did seem to have absorbed moisture since they'd left Nevermore, but the sky was more gloomy than menacing. "Lock the door. And bring the gun." She quietly closed the door behind her.

"Yes, your royal highness," Jeremy said, exiting the car. "I never realized you were so bossy."

The opening in the trees led straight down the ravine. Jeremy was right—that's where Grandfather had supposedly crashed his Ferrari. Cecilia couldn't see anything down there now.

But she saw something out of the corner of her eye, a little farther back on the road. "Did you see that flash? And it for sure wasn't lightning—it was too bright to not be followed by thunder."

"I didn't see a damn thing," Jeremy said, coming up beside her. "Are you maybe getting a migraine? Or having some sort of seizure?"

"I feel fine. Come on." She headed for an opening in the trees, just wide enough for a vehicle. The grass was flattened, but that could have happened anytime, and the ground was too hard to show tire tracks. She took several steps, rounded a slight curve, and nearly bumped into a gray SUV.

Her blood chilled. "That's Trey's. The headlights must have flashed. Although I don't know how, since I can't hear anyone."

"Maybe Grandfather flashed them," Jeremy said.

"If he did, it means Lexie's in real trouble."

"I was kidding," Jeremy said. "The headlights probably shorted out."

"Why would they do that?"

"How the hell am I supposed to know? Ask Ben."

"All that matters is that we've found Trey's SUV," Cecilia said. "What's he doing here?"

"He must be checking on something related to when Grandfather faked his death," Jeremy said. "I'll bet that path leads to the bottom of the ravine." He pointed. "We'll follow it until we find Trey and hopefully Lexie. Then you can assure Ben everything's okay, and I can do something more fun."

"There's a path there, too," Cecilia said, pointing at a rough path just beyond the SUV, one that appeared to go up. "Maybe they took it instead."

"Why? The Ferrari went into the ravine. Come on." Jeremy started toward the first path.

Cecilia grabbed his arm, stopping him. "Wait." She dialed her cell phone with her free hand.

"Did you find her?" Ben asked when he answered the phone.

"Not yet," Cecilia said. "We found Trey's SUV, parked off the road in the trees. Where we all thought Grandfather crashed."

"Is Lexie with him?" Ben asked.

"We haven't found Trey, just his SUV. You know this area since you helped Grandfather stage his death here. If Trey plans to hurt Lexie, would they more likely go down the ravine or take the other path? It looks like it goes up."

"Damn."

"Which one, Ben?"

"The path does go up. It leads to a cliff that overlooks Forest Lake. If Trey wants to kill Lexie, he could push her off and into the lake."

"Aunt Muriel saw Lexie shot and in water," Cecilia said.

"I know." Ben's words sounded strangled.

Cecilia shut off her phone. "We're going up," she told Jeremy. "Hurry."

CHAPTER 30

Her brain admittedly wasn't at its sharpest, but Trey's words made no sense. "Agreeing to marry Max caused Aunt Jessica's stroke?" Lexie asked.

"Of course not," Trey said. "Her supposed stroke was caused by an injection of a certain paralytic poison that she gave herself, thinking it was her insulin. It took longer to work since she injected it subcutaneously, but it eventually did the trick."

The blood left Lexie's head and the world seemed to recede, as if she were looking through the wrong end of a pair of binoculars. "You killed Aunt Jessica because she was going to marry Max? For God's sake, why?"

"Walk," he said, gesturing with the gun.

Lexie slowly turned back around. She still felt dizzy, but managed to resume walking.

"Jessica insisted on having a prenup. Faster." Trey poked Lexie's back with the gun. "Jessica was successful, but nowhere near Max's league, and she didn't want anyone thinking she'd married him for his money or his family hating her for it. She insisted on an agreement that she wouldn't get a cent from him if they divorced or he died. Max had given her attorney some accountings I'd prepared, but the attorney wanted copies of Max's income tax returns and financial statements as part of that damn full-disclosure requirement before he'd let Jessica sign anything. By then I'd been stealing from Max for a few years, so the accountings her attorney already had wouldn't jibe with the financial statements or tax returns. I realized I had to get rid of Jessica so there'd be no need for a prenup."

Lexie was having trouble breathing. "No one suspected? Even though it happened right after Max asked you for the documents?" Her voice sounded strained and an octave too high.

"Why would they?" Trey asked. "Max trusted me, and no one knew what I was doing. Jessica had also suffered a small stroke a month earlier. I think that's why she finally agreed to marry Max. And Max was so broken up by Jessica's death that he convinced your mother to refuse to allow an autopsy. He didn't want anyone cutting up Jessica's body, which is ironic considering all the bodies Max has eviscerated in his books. Not that they could have detected the poison I used anyway."

Trey's words and self-satisfied tone flicked a switch inside Lexie. She was no longer scared, she was angry. Angry for Jessica's sake, that she'd been murdered when she still had so much to live for. Angry for Max's sake, that he'd never achieved his dream of marrying Jessica and had lost so many years with her.

And Lexie was angry for herself, not only because she'd loved and missed her aunt, but because her aunt had encouraged her to stand up to her mother and live her own life. Who knows how different things would have been if her aunt had lived—for one thing, Lexie probably wouldn't have given in to her mother's pressure to marry Neil.

She whirled around. *"You bastard! How could you kill my aunt?"*

– – –

"Did you hear that?" Cecilia asked, quickening her pace. "It sounded like a woman."

"She said 'you bastard,' but I couldn't make out the rest," Jeremy said.

"Neither could I, but it must have been Lexie. Who else would be out here? She's in trouble." Cecilia started walking as fast as she could over the rough path. The voice had sounded too far away for comfort.

Jeremy pushed by her. He'd been holding the gun loosely at his side but now had it raised. "Let me go first."

– – –

Trey grabbed Lexie's arm and squeezed it painfully. "Shut up!"

Anger gave her the strength to disregard the pain and jerk away from him. Ignoring the gun, she took off running.

Lexie immediately regretted her impulsiveness since she was guaranteed to end up dead. But it was too late to back down. Not that the adrenaline surging through her veins would have let her stop. She kept running, bracing herself for a shot in the back.

It never came.

Suddenly she was out of the trees—and standing less than twenty feet from the edge of a cliff overlooking Forest Lake. With nowhere to run.

"I apologize for the fog," Trey said, stepping out of the trees. "It must have drifted in from Superior. I guess you won't be able to enjoy your final view after all."

Lexie's heart was hammering from adrenaline, exertion, and fear as she analyzed her options. Even from here she could tell that the cliff went straight down probably two hundred feet to the lake. Jumping was a definite last resort.

She needed to get Trey talking again. Talking would hope-fully distract him enough that she could rush him and grab the gun, now that they were in the open. She should certainly be able to take down a sixty-something man who'd just gotten out of the hospital. If she tried now, he'd shoot her before she reached him. If she waited, let him get closer—

"You know how this is going to end," Trey said as he approached her. "Why don't you make it easy on yourself and jump?"

"Easy on you, you mean."

"I'm actually thinking of you." Trey gestured with the gun. "Why incur a painful gunshot wound if you don't have to?"

"You don't need to kill me," Lexie said. "You can take me somewhere and make sure it will be hours, if not days, before someone rescues me. I'm sure you've planned to make a quick getaway."

"Why would you think that?"

"Because you're too smart not to have, especially once you killed Max. You've got a plan to leave the country, and I'm sure your money isn't in U.S. accounts."

"You're right on both counts. My money's in a country that couldn't care less how I got it. I've also had an escape plan in place for years."

"You claim you don't want to disappear, but I'll bet you never planned to stick around Minnesota once you retired anyway," Lexie said. "The winters are almost six months long. Six cold and snowy months."

"True. But if I kill you, I can leave on my own schedule. What's one more death on my conscience?"

Trey stopped a couple of feet in front of her. He hadn't lost a bit of his focus, his grip on the gun still sure.

"You've gotten away with the earlier murders, but you can't be sure you'll get away with killing me," Lexie said. "Someone might have seen us leave Nevermore together. You were worried about Max pursuing you if he discovered your embezzling. My father's really rich, too, and he'll spend whatever it takes to find my killer. Don't think that you'll be safe even if you're in a country that won't extradite you back here. My dad's friends aren't all law-abiding."

"You're right that someone could have seen us together in the house," Trey said, although he didn't sound concerned. "I'll have to tell the police that I saw you in my office. You seemed upset, although you wouldn't tell me why, just that you had some thinking to do and were going for a walk. You walked with me as far as my car, and then I left. No one will suspect I'd ever kill you, not the police, not your father. I don't have a motive for doing that or for killing Max. And Max's murderer supposedly tried to kill me."

She didn't even see him lunge toward her. She dug in her heels, fought him as hard as she could, struggled to keep her footing on the cliff. She'd be damned if she'd let this monster who'd killed both Aunt Jessica and Max kill her.

For someone who'd just gotten out of the hospital, he was surprisingly strong. He muscled her over grass made slippery by the fog until Lexie was at the edge of the cliff.

She pushed him with as much strength as she could muster. Trey lost his footing and fell to the ground. The gun slipped from his hand onto the grass.

Lexie grabbed for it, but he beat her to it. He picked up the gun and got to his feet. "If you're not going to cooperate, we'll have to do this the hard way."

Lexie looked behind her. She couldn't make out the water through fog that had thickened in the last few minutes, but she knew it was down there. Her only hope now was to jump. Maybe she'd be able to swim to shore.

Trey raised the gun, pointed it at her.

She needed to jump. But she couldn't make herself step back and off the cliff. She could just as well miss the water and hit the shore. Even if she made it to the water, the impact would probably kill her. She closed her eyes, braced herself. At least if he shot her, he'd have a better chance of getting caught.

The gun exploded, reverberating in her ears. But no pain. She opened her eyes.

Trey wasn't pointing the gun at her; he was pointing it at the sky. "No, Max—"

Then a hand shoved Trey off the cliff.

Lexie's knees gave out, and she collapsed on the damp ground.

"Lexie. Are you okay?" Jeremy was there, a gun in his hand.

She was hyperventilating, could barely force out words. "Trey was trying to kill me," she puffed out. She focused on slowing her breathing.

"Because he was embezzling from Grandfather." Lexie recognized Cecilia's voice before she could see her through the fog. "Ben said you figured it out."

"How did he know?" Lexie asked.

"From what Jeremy told him about your conversation," Cecilia said. "That's why Ben sent us after you."

"You saved my life, Jeremy," Lexie said.

"What do you mean?" he asked.

"You pushed Trey. Thanking you for that seems a little inadequate."

"But I didn't," Jeremy said. "Trey was falling off the cliff when I got here. I assumed you shoved him, which is why his shot missed and he fell."

"I didn't do anything besides shut my eyes and wait for him to shoot me," Lexie said. "When he missed, he said something about Max, then somebody shoved him. I saw a hand."

"It wasn't me," Cecilia said. "I was behind Jeremy."

"No one else is here," Jeremy said. "Trey must have slipped.

Although I can certainly understand why you're confused after what you've just gone through. And the fog is damn thick. No wonder you thought you saw someone."

"I swear—" Then Lexie broke off. They wouldn't believe her, not what she was beginning to think had happened. She wouldn't have believed it if she hadn't been there.

Or maybe she *was* confused. "You're right," she said. "He must have slipped."

"Let's get you back to the car so we can head over to the jail," Cecilia said. "Ben's going crazy worrying about you."

Jeremy chuckled. "For the first time in his life, I think Ben's going to be happy to see me."

CHAPTER 31

"Do you really believe that Jeremy was trying to help Olivia get back together with me because he felt guilty?" Ben asked.

Lexie moved from beneath Ben's arm and rolled over to face him. She'd spent several hours helping get him released, then they'd come back to his house—a Victorian-era place he was remodeling—and made love with an intensity that made her appreciate that truism about soldiers and danger and lust.

She lightly slugged his bare shoulder. "You make love to me, and your first thought is getting back with your ex-wife?"

"You know that's never happening. I was talking about Jeremy."

"I think he meant it when he said he was sorry he broke up your marriage," Lexie said.

Ben rose up on his side, resting his head on his bent arm. "You don't think it's more likely that he knew about Olivia's problems with the SEC and wanted to stick me with them?"

"No, I don't. Can't you accept that Jeremy did something nice for you? Even after he risked his life to save me because you asked him to? I think you should make peace with him."

Ben rolled his eyes. "Next you'll be trying to get me to make peace with my father."

"You do have two half brothers you've never met," Lexie said, treading carefully. "I know it's none of my business, but I nearly died today. It makes you realize that life's too short to hold grudges."

"So you're going to make nice with your mother?"

Touché. Lexie had called her dad—whose friends were all law-abiding, to the best of her knowledge—and told him what had happened, asking him to relay the information to the rest of her family. She didn't think her mother deserved to learn about it from the news or, worse yet, Bitsy Davenport, but Lexie hadn't wanted to talk to her herself. After escaping death, she was feeling so glad to be alive that she loved the world. Talking to her mother might ruin that.

"I'll probably call her in a few days." By then real life was bound to have killed her post–near-death euphoria. "I guarantee she won't have forgiven, let alone forgotten, the way I told her off the last time we spoke. Holding grudges is her specialty, not mine."

Ben reached out and twirled Lexie's hair around his finger. "Maybe the fact you nearly died will have changed her attitude, too."

"Maybe," Lexie said, then shifted to a topic that wasn't such a buzz kill. "You know, I never found out who lost that button. I guess it really doesn't matter, but it still bugs me."

Ben released her hair, his forehead furrowing. "What button?"

"The one I found under Max's bed when I searched his room. The one I was positive was a clue to who knew he was still alive," Lexie added when Ben still looked confused. "I thought I mentioned it to you."

"You didn't. Was it a white shirt button?"

"How did you know?"

He smiled faintly. "Because I assume it's mine. One night when I was changing out of my dress clothes after sherry hour and dinner, I noticed I'd lost a button. I didn't bother looking for it since the shirt had spares. But I'd just done my after-dinner check of Grandfather's room for messages, so I'll bet that's where it fell off. It must have rolled under the bed."

Lexie shook her head, feeling like an idiot. "I can't believe I agonized over that button but forgot to ask you about it. Some Nancy Drew I turned out to be."

"You did figure out the important thing, who killed Grandfather," Ben said. "I can't believe Trey had us fooled all these years. It's a good thing Grandfather never found out that he killed Jessica. He'd definitely have killed Trey as painfully as possible. And Grandfather had quite an imagination for brutal deaths."

Lexie stared at the stained glass window over Ben's dresser, thinking. She probably shouldn't bother mentioning it since Ben wouldn't believe it anyway. On the other hand, he might help her figure out a logical explanation for what had happened.

Lexie turned from the window to Ben and plunged. "I think Max got his chance after all."

"What do you mean?"

"You'll probably think I'm losing it," she said. "But Trey was aiming the gun directly at me. I shut my eyes and prepared to die. Only he ended up shooting into the air. When I opened my eyes, I swear I saw someone's hand shove him off the cliff. I'll admit it was foggy, and I've never believed in ghosts before, but I think it must have been Max. Trey even said Max's name before he fell."

She expected Ben to agree she was losing it or at least laugh. Instead he looked thoughtful. "So Walt was right," he said. "Since Grandfather got you into this, he sure as hell wasn't going to let you die, especially not on his property. Just like when he made sure you weren't hurt when your brakes went out."

Lexie had rejected Walt's theory before, but now she smiled faintly. "I guess if anyone could figure out how to come back as a ghost, it would be Max." Then her smile faded, replaced by a hollowness in her chest. Max had saved her, but she'd let him down twice, not only by failing to prevent his murder but also by screwing up the trust. "If it was Max, it's too bad he didn't stick around long enough to get rid of the requirement that you spend every night in Nevermore to inherit," she said. "I'll do my best to find a way around it."

"I wouldn't work too hard on it."

"Why? You're opposed to inheriting a fortune?"

"No, but I happen to know Grandfather drafted an amendment that eliminates that requirement completely if and when his murderer is identified," Ben said.

Lexie rolled back up onto her side, her eyes wide, her temper flaring. "You didn't tell me about it? Even though you knew I was worried to death about it?"

Ben held up one hand. "I didn't know until this afternoon. He had a lawyer in New York draft it and told him to let me know about it only when the condition had been satisfied."

"I can't believe Max did that," Lexie said, shaking her head. "Knowing him, I'd have assumed he'd be positive he'd identify his potential murderer and still be around to amend the trust afterward."

"Actually, the provision was my idea, although Grandfather claimed it was unnecessary, and I had no idea he'd done it," Ben said. "I pointed out to him that unthinkable things sometimes happen, and he must have realized he was in no position to disagree. Look at his books."

Max's trust would be distributed the way he'd wanted. In addition, even though he was dead, he was finally reunited with Jessica, and Ben agreed that he'd gotten his revenge against the man who'd killed both of them. And she'd been the one who'd identified Max's killer—and she hadn't ended up another victim.

Lexie had felt good before, but now she felt terrific.

Until Ben ruined everything. "With that resolved, I assume this is where you say your work here is done and head back to Philadelphia."

"I guess it is, since my work here is done." Her words came out slowly, forced out, even though she knew this had been coming. "I've got a huge backlog of work waiting for me."

"What does that mean for us?"

The hollowness that had previously filled Lexie's chest had been replaced by a vise that was squeezing her heart. But this is the way it had to be. "We agreed this was only a vacation fling. Vacation is over."

"It doesn't have to be." Ben's eyes were fixed on hers. "We could do a long-distance relationship."

Lexie refused to let herself even consider that. "A long-distance relationship is the same as a fling when there's no way the people will ever end up living in the same place. We won't, since you're happy being a Lakeview mechanic, and I'm happy being a Philadelphia attorney."

"Are you really?" Ben asked. "You seemed to enjoy being Lexie."

"It was fun for a little while. Being here has also made me realize I need to stand up to my mother and live life on my own terms, not according to her rules. But I can't change who I am. It's time for me to go back to being Catherine." She got out of bed and pulled on her clothes, needing to get out of there before she started crying. Although she knew it was for the best, this was harder than she'd anticipated.

Which forced her to acknowledge something she'd tried hard not to. Despite her best intentions and that she knew it would never work, she'd fallen in love with Ben, fallen for his brains, his perceptiveness, his sense of humor, his basic decency. Shallow though it was, she'd fallen for the handsome, sexy *GQ* Ben and the equally handsome, sexy NASCAR version, had fallen for the way he made her feel when they made love. She even loved him for his damn decision to leave a high-paying career for a life that was more fulfilling in small-town Minnesota, the very thing that guaranteed they'd never have more than a fling.

Her red tank top, skirt, and underwear were scattered on the maple floor beside the bed. She didn't look at Ben as she threw on her clothes, and then sat down on the bed to fasten her red sandals.

She got to her feet, took a deep breath, and finally faced Ben. He was lying on top of the sheet, his hair in sweaty spikes, looking so hot Lexie had the urge to hop back into bed again and put off leaving until tomorrow. But that was just more of that post-danger lust. She'd miss him, but things had to end, and there was no point in dragging it out. She'd always been a rip-off-the-Band-Aid kind of girl anyway. "I'd better go," she said, delighted her voice was level. "If I drive to Duluth tonight, I can get a flight out first thing tomorrow morning. Good luck with expanding the garage."

"Thanks." Ben's face was expressionless, probably because this wasn't a big deal for him. He had a lot more experience ending things than she did. Like he'd said, he enjoyed variety when it came to women. He was no doubt looking forward to replacing her with a younger, sexier model. "If you ever want another vacation fling, I'll be here," he said.

Maybe he meant it; maybe he was just being polite, like when he'd suggested a long-distance affair, knowing full well she'd never agree. It didn't matter. "I don't think that's a good idea. Rule 149, you know."

He raised an eyebrow. "I thought you were done following your mother's rules."

"That's one of mine." Lexie swallowed hard. "Catherine doesn't do flings."

Because they hurt so damn much when they ended.

She turned and walked out of the room.

CHAPTER 32

Six weeks later

Catherine glared at her office phone. She couldn't ignore it, even though the call had a better than fifty-fifty chance of making her headache worse. At least she knew it wasn't her mother, since her mother currently wasn't speaking to her.

She picked up the phone.

"Sorry, but I couldn't get your secretary," the receptionist said. "There's a man in the lobby who wants to hire you. I told him you're not taking new clients, but he's insisting on seeing you anyway."

The throbbing in her forehead intensified. Catherine massaged it with her free hand. She'd figured it was probably a client either wanting something yesterday or completely changing what he or she had wanted yesterday, but this was worse. A former client who wouldn't work with anyone else, and one she'd end up handling a new project for because her firm would ask her to, even if she didn't have time. "Who?"

"I don't know. He won't give his name. He says he was referred by Max Windsor, which is really weird since he's dead."

Catherine moved her hand from her forehead and instead pressed it to her stomach, which had begun twisting and whirling. Her heart was drumming double time against her chest. "Send him back."

In three minutes Ben Gallagher was standing in the doorway of her office. He was wearing a perfectly tailored suit and a tie that matched his vivid blue eyes, the same thing he'd worn that first night at Nevermore, back when she'd realized how attractive he was.

He looked even better now. And she was so glad to see him.

He strode into her office with his usual confidence, closed the door behind him, and sat down on one of the leather chairs in front of her desk. "I need some estate-planning work done," he said. "I've recently come into a little money."

"A *little* money?" Catherine asked.

A corner of his mouth quirked. "Okay, enough money to support a small country, which is why I'm also thinking of using a good chunk of it to set up a charitable foundation. I know you'll be able to help me with all of that. Max Windsor told me you're one of the smartest people he ever met."

"Even though I've got a stick up my ass."

Ben grinned outright. "He was wrong about that part."

"I can't do your work myself, but I can refer you to someone else."

His grin faded. "You won't do it?"

"As I said, I can't do it. I'm leaving the firm in a couple of weeks."

He'd seemed completely at ease, but now his body tensed. "You're leaving? Why?" His voice sounded strained, like his vocal cords were tense, too.

Catherine got up and rounded her desk. "I need a change. I considered being a cocktail waitress or maybe an exotic dancer, but my relationship with my mother is too tenuous for me to try that." She sat down in the chair next to Ben's. "Aunt Jessica left me money to use to follow my bliss, as she phrased it in her will. I've never touched it, because I didn't think practicing law was her idea of bliss. I think she'd approve if I used it to support myself while I write."

"You're quitting law to write?" He sounded a little less tense.

"Don't tell me you disapprove, too. My mother had a fit. But she'll get over it easier than she would exotic dancing. At least I hope she will. If she doesn't, that's her problem. Dad thinks it's great."

"Actually, I agree with your dad," Ben said. "Coincidentally I'm also going to be starting a new career. I'm selling the garage to Shawn."

Catherine blinked. "Selling it? I thought you'd be expanding it."

"It didn't seem appropriate to use Grandfather's money to do that." He shrugged. "To be honest, I've gotten bored with being a mechanic. Being around a smart professional woman made me realize Grandfather was right. I miss using my brain the way I did in my old career. I'm going to start a financial consulting business. Although I'll only take clients I want to work with, since I certainly don't need the money."

"In Lakeview?" Catherine asked.

"Most of my clients so far are on the East Coast. I can do most of my work online and over the phone, although I will have to travel a little. That means I can live almost anywhere."

"I thought you were going to buy Nevermore." When the trustee had mentioned that Ben had asked about purchasing it, the news had stabbed the pieces of her already broken heart. He clearly didn't care enough about her to ever contemplate leaving Lakeview, conclusive evidence things were over between them forever.

"I considered buying it," Ben said. "Grandfather would have liked it kept in the family, and no one else wants it. Maybe he'll even decide to haunt it, which could be interesting. But I can't, because I have this problem."

"What's that?"

He reached out and took her hand. "I'm in love with a woman who's got a rule against flings. Not that I'd be satisfied with a fling with her. I'd actually like a relationship, maybe even a permanent one. She puts long-distance relationships in the same category as flings, though, so we need to be in the same city. That city is Philadelphia."

Catherine's stomach untwisted, replaced by a bubbling warmth that filled her body. "And here I've realized I'm tired of Philadelphia and the lifestyle I can't escape if I live here. I also have a feeling my mother and I will get along a lot better if we aren't in the same city."

"Where are you planning on going?"

She met his eyes. "I'd consider Lakeview," she said. "I'm not crazy about the possibility of snow in June, but the nice people who live there more than make up for it. Aunt Jessica said she did some of her best writing at Nevermore, and it obviously worked for Max."

"Who turned out to be a hell of a matchmaker, much as I hate to admit it." Ben got out of his chair and pulled Catherine to her feet. "I love you, Catherine." He kissed her thoroughly.

"I love you, too," Catherine said. "So much that if you'd waited until I'd finished my job, I'd have shown up in Lakeview." Even knowing he'd planned to buy Nevermore and there was an excellent chance he'd reject her, she'd realized she had to risk it. She owed it to herself. And she owed it to Aunt Jessica, since she had a feeling Ben might be even more her bliss than writing was. "With my fingers crossed that you hadn't gotten back with Amber," she added.

"No way." He kissed her again, even more thoroughly. "Would you really be willing to move to Nevermore?"

"On one condition."

"You want me to promise I'll never make you ride a motorcycle." Ben held up his hand. "I swear it."

She narrowed her eyes at him. "Are you kidding? If I'm going to be living out there, I want my own motorcycle, and you're going to teach me how to operate it."

He chuckled. "I knew you were just pretending to hate it. What do you want? Besides a motorcycle."

"I want you to promise that you'll never call me Catherine again," she said. "From now on, my name is Lexie."

ABOUT THE AUTHOR

Photo by Steve Rouch, 2008

Award-winning author Diana Miller has wanted to be Nancy Drew ever since she started looking for hidden staircases as an eight-year-old girl (though she's never found a single cryptic clue for all her trouble). Since then, she has worked happily as a lawyer, a soda jerk, a stay-at-home mother, a hospital admitting clerk, and a conference host. Still, she itched for a way to inject some suspense into her otherwise satisfying life, until she realized fiction was the key. Her debut novel, *Dangerous Affairs*, won a Golden Heart Award from the Romance Writers of America, and has been nominated for a Booksellers Best Award and an Aspen Gold Readers Choice Award. She has received five Golden Heart nominations, including one for *Fatal Trust*. She lives in the Twin Cities with her family.